Previous titles in

MW01130660

OVID
GERMANICUS
THE LYDIAN BAKER
SEJANUS
OLD BONES
LAST RITES
WHITE MURDER
A VOTE FOR MURDER
PARTHIAN SHOT
FOOD FOR THE FISHES
IN AT THE DEATH
ILLEGALLY DEAD
BODIES POLITIC
NO CAUSE FOR CONCERN (novella)
SOLID CITIZENS
FINISHED BUSINESS
TRADE SECRETS
FOREIGN BODIES
FAMILY COMMITMENTS

Other Roman titles

I, VIRGIL
NERO
THE HORSE COIN

GOING BACK

David Wishart

DRAMATIS PERSONAE

(Only the names of characters who appear or are referred to in more than one part of the book are given. The story is set in August/September AD44).

Albus, Lucius Cornelius: a local historian, now dead. Cornelia's father
Bathyllus: Corvinus's major-domo
Cestius, Decimus: the victim. His sons are **Publius** and **Quintus**
Chilo, Cornelius: Albus's former major-domo
Claudius Caesar: the current emperor
Cornelia Alba ('Elissa'): Albus's daughter
Cycnus, Laenius: Justus's partner
Eulalia: a kitchen slave in the Cestius household
Galba, Servius Sulpicius: the provincial governor
Gratius, Sextus: the Cestius family's factor
Justus, Titus Appius: a visiting slave-dealer
Lautia: one of the guests at Galba's dinner party
Lepida, Domitia: Claudius's mother-in-law (Messalina's mother), and an old friend of Verania's
Maenius, Titus: former owner of a bakery
Marilla: Corvinus and Perilla's adopted daughter, married to **Clarus**
Medar: leader of a group of itinerant harvesters. His son, now dead, was **Adon**
Meton: Corvinus's chef
Perilla, Rufia: Corvinus's wife
Pettius, Gaius: a trainer of gladiators
Quirinius, Sextus: Galba's aide
Scarus, Gaius Cluvius: a professional sword-fighter
Spadix: a slave in the Cestius household
Syrus, Aponius: a property agent
Verania: Cestius's widow
Vettius Rufus: the father of Publius Cestius's fiancée Vettia
Virria: Marcus Virrius's sister

Virrius, Marcus: the young man accused of raping Cornelia. His father is also Marcus

1.

It's not often that you get an invitation to dinner at the palace; me, I'd only ever had the one, and the result had been a tad too memorable for comfort. That, of course, had been when Gaius had had the top job, and although on the whole I'd got on pretty well with our ex-lord and master there's no denying that the bastard was mad, bad and dangerous to know, and that he deserved everything he got. Claudius was a different kettle of fish altogether; at least you could be certain that when you turned up in your glad-rags with your party slippers under your arm he wouldn't be got up like a brothel tart or Jupiter God Almighty complete with gold-wire beard and matching toy thunderbolt; our Gaius had had style, sure, no argument, but you can take that sort of thing too far. With Claudius, the worst you could expect was a lecture on Etruscan marriage customs and a detailed explanation of why the alphabet could really, *really* do with a few extra letters. Bad enough in its own way, admitted, but nothing compared with what I'd had to put up with over the years at dinners with my mother and stepfather. Besides, palace invites being what they are the chances of us being within even shouting range of the top table were well inside of the flying pigs category.

So anyway there we were, Perilla and me, dolled up to the nines and being ushered into one of the smaller dining rooms by an impeccably-dressed flunkey. Which was the first big surprise of the evening. These affairs are usually choreographed to a nicety, and the preliminary stage involves being shown into a reception room to fraternise with your few dozen or so fellow-guests, get as much wine down you as you can for the purpose of anaesthesia, and check the seating plan to see who you'll be stuck with – and who'll be stuck with you – for the next two or three hours...

Only this time it wasn't like that at all. Forget the 'few dozen'; we didn't even make up the obligatory quorum of nine. There were just us two and the lad himself plus his wife Valeria Messalina, who was lying next to him and grinning at me like the cat that got the tame sparrow.

Bugger. I stopped.

'Ah, C-Corvinus, you've arrived!' Claudius beamed at me. 'And Perilla, my dear! Don't stand on ceremony, please! Come in, lie down, make yourself at home.' He turned to the hovering major-domo. 'Trupho, a cup of wine for Valerius Corvinus. Juice for you, Perilla? It's pomegranate, Messalina's favourite, but we can change that if you like.'

'Pomegranate is fine, Caesar.' Perilla smiled at him and stretched out on the couch next to me. 'How are you?'

'Fair to middling. Busy as always, you know how it is. No time for writing, I'm afraid.' He held out his own cup for a refill. 'I'm delighted you could come, and Messalina has really been looking forward to it. Haven't you, love?'

That got me the cat's grin again. A shiver went down my spine.

'Oh, yes,' she said. 'Corvinus and I are old friends. Aren't we, Marcus?'

Not exactly how I would've put it, but she knew that damn well already. Still, the niceties had to be observed.

'Yeah,' I said. I took the cup that the slave handed me and sipped. Imperial Caecuban, no less. At least the evening would have some high spots. 'Yeah, we are.'

'You look surprised, my dear fellow.' Claudius took a hefty swallow from his refilled cup: from the looks of him, I'd reckon he was at least half a jug ahead of the game already, but then our latest emperor always had been the drinker's drinker. 'Don't be. I t-told you the last time we met that I'd have the two of you round for dinner *en famille* when you got back from Gaul; I'm just sorry it's t-taken so long. And Messalina insisted that we make it a surprise. Didn't you, darling?' He kissed her unresponsive cheek. 'The little schemer.' Well, where that bitch was concerned I couldn't quarrel with the nomenclature. Although I wouldn't've added the 'little', myself. 'Mind you, I'm afraid I have to confess that I do have an ulterior motive.'

Hell's teeth. This didn't sound good; not good at all.

'And what would that be, sir?' I said cautiously.

'Oh, tush, tush! Don't be so formal. There are just the f-four of us here. "Caesar" will be quite sufficient. And there's no hurry, the thing can wait its turn. We'll discuss it over the dessert.' He turned back to the major-domo. 'Tell the chef we're ready to eat now, will you? There's a good lad.'

Uh-huh; me, given the track record of our relationship up to now, I could make a fairly good guess as to what the 'thing' involved, at least in general terms. All the same, you didn't twist the arm of the most powerful man in the world west of the Parthian border. I just hoped that this time round whatever he had in mind would involve somewhere closer to home than bloody Transalpine Gaul.

However, we'd just have to possess ourselves with patience, and keep our fingers crossed.

He did us proud as far as the meal was concerned, at any rate. Oh, sure, having Meton for our chef makes us pretty choosy eaters, but the standard of the dinner would've drawn a grunt of approval from even that surly, egotistical bugger, and that doesn't happen all that often. The wine was top notch as well, naturally: imperial Caecuban is the best of the best, there was plenty on offer, and if I was going to be stuck with doing another little investigative favour for the bastard then I didn't feel too guilty about making a sizeable hole in his current stock. Which I duly did. By the time the table was cleared and re-laid with the fruit and nuts, plus a good dozen more recherché dessert items, I was well on the way to being pleasantly stewed.

'Now, Corvinus.' Claudius reached over for a stuffed date. 'This little private favour I wanted to ask of you. Ever hear of a chap by the name of Decimus Cestius?'

Here it came. I braced myself. 'He's been murdered, right?' I said. 'Or at least died in suspicious circumstances.'

Claudius blinked. 'Yes, as a matter of fact he has,' he said. 'How on earth did you know that?'

'An educated guess, Caesar.' Oh, bugger. Bugger, bugger, bugger! Still, I couldn't say it came as much of a surprise. I caught a faint snigger from Messalina. 'So who was he?'

'One of the city judges fifteen or so years back, in my Uncle Tiberius's time.' A praetor, eh? Not quite the top of the political tree, then: his next step would've been the consulship, and if he hadn't made it that far, or at least bagged a suffect consulship, in the last fifteen years then he must've been pretty much a political lightweight. Odd.

'He was a personal friend of yours?' I said.

'No, I can't say I ever met the man. But then fifteen years ago I wasn't much involved with politics myself.'

True; until his sudden elevation after Gaius got his in the underpass Claudius had been pretty much kept under wraps by the imperial family. Still, it made his interest in the guy's death that much the odder.

'Then I don't see why–'

'His wife is a close friend of my mother-in-law's. She happened to mention it in her last letter, and Lepida asked me as a favour if I could look into things.' Beside him Messalina shifted irritably and he turned to her. 'Yes, dear, I *know* that for some reason the two of you don't get on so well these days, but your mother is family after all. She has the right to ask, and I have a duty to do what I can for her.'

Uh-huh. 'Don't get on' was putting it mildly; the two ladies hated each other's guts. Oh, sure, the reason was more or less an open secret, known to everyone but Claudius, but I wasn't going to take the top off of that particular can of worms, no way. Or even allude to it. Besides, it was none of my business.

'Also, Cestius's elder son is recently betrothed to one of Vettius Rufus's girls. You know Rufus, Corvinus? The consular?'

'Uh-uh. Pass.'

'No, I don't suppose you would, come to think of it. It doesn't matter. But Rufus will want the business investigated too, and he's quite a f-force in the senate.' He smiled. 'Politics again, I'm afraid. Still, that's the job I'm in nowadays.'

'So when did this happen? The murder, I mean.'

'About a month ago.'

'A *month?*'

'About that, yes.' He cleared his throat. 'So Lepida tells me, at any rate.'

I was beginning to get a nasty feeling about this. 'Uh...and this happened in Rome, did it? Or at least close by?'

'Not exactly.' He cleared his throat again. 'My dear fellow, your wine cup's empty.' He signalled to the major-domo. 'Trupho? More wine for Valerius Corvinus, please.'

'No, that's okay, I'm fine for the present.' I held my hand over the cup, and Trupho backed off. Oh, shit, here we went again! The nasty feeling was there in spades. 'You care to tell me where, then?'

8

'Carthage.'

'*What?*'

'Cestius decided to retire there. Directly after his praetorship. I'm afraid he and my uncle – or at least my uncle's representative in Rome at the time – didn't see eye to eye about things.' Well, fair enough; that'd been Aelius Sejanus, of course. We hadn't been exactly bosom buddies ourselves, Sejanus and me, so I sympathised: Rome fifteen years before hadn't been a very healthy place for senators. 'Then, naturally, there was my predecessor with all his little idiosyncrasies, and–' he shrugged. 'Well, Cestius hasn't been back since.'

Gods almighty! 'You want me to go to *Carthage?*' I remembered myself and who I was talking to just in time. 'Uh...that is–'

'If it isn't too much t-trouble, yes. As my personal representative, of course, as you were on the last occasion. An imperial procurator.' He held out his hand. Trupho took a folded document from his belt and gave it to him. 'Fully accredited. I've, ah, taken the liberty of preparing your authorisation in advance.'

He passed it over.

So. That was that, then, all done and dusted. Hell's teeth. I didn't even dare look at Perilla. Mind you, she'd seen the whole thing for herself so she couldn't blame me for getting involved this time around.

'It's an interesting place, or so I'm told at least.' Claudius lifted his own cup for the refill; now the terrible truth was out, he was obviously beginning to relax. Well, at least he'd had the decency to feel embarrassed; emperor or not, Claudius was a decent old stick at base. 'Not that there's anything left of the original city, of course – Scipio Aemilianus made damn sure of that – but it's made great strides since the Divine Augustus's day, and it's quite prosperous. You'll like it.'

'I'm sure I will, Caesar,' I said, through only slightly-gritted teeth. I'd have to, wouldn't I, because it seemed that I didn't have much fucking choice in the matter.

'Excellent. Good egg. That's the spirit.' He turned to Perilla, 'You'll want to tag along as well, my dear, like last time, yes? At least, I assumed you would. Unless you have other plans, of course.'

'No, Caesar, no other plans.' She smiled and helped herself to one of the cinnamon and honey pastries. 'Actually, I'd love to go.'

I breathed again. Yeah, well, she sounded sincere, at least, which was a good sign. You never knew with that lady, particularly where shoving your nose into inconvenient murders was concerned. Perilla could get quite intense on that score.

'Jolly good, that's settled, then. Don't worry, I'll make all the arrangements, let the governor know you're coming and all that. Galba will see you're properly taken care of when you get there, I'm sure.'

Oh, shit. 'Uh...Galba?' I said. '*Sulpicius* Galba?'

'That's the man. You know him?'

'We've met, yes. Quite a while ago, now.' Eleven years, to be exact. Galba had been consul when one of the Vestals had been found dead at his house the morning after the rites of the Good Goddess and the chief Vestal had given me the job of finding out why. To say we hadn't exactly hit it off was putting it mildly.

I doubted if he would've forgotten me, either. Bugger.

'Marvellous. You'll have a lot of catching up to do, then. Meanwhile, I'm afraid as far as poor Cestius's death goes I've told you all I know myself, but if you talk to Lepida I'm sure she'll be able to fill in a bit more of the background. Now' – he smiled – 'you'll be glad to know that that's the business part of the evening concluded, and I must say I'm considerably relieved to get it over with. Between ourselves, my dear fellow, Domitia Lepida is *not* someone I'd care to disappoint. I'll be glad to get the bloody woman off my back.'

Yeah, right. Mind you, I'd've been happier if the selfish bastard had managed it without involving me. But then that's imperials for you. We were just lucky that this time around we had one in charge that could feel a smidgeon of guilt in the process.

2.

We'd just finished breakfast next morning when one of the palace slaves came round with details of our travel arrangements. Suspiciously fast work, sure, but then Claudius had never been one to let the grass grow under his feet where making arrangements was concerned, and in any case I'd've risked a fairly hefty bet that the sneaky bastard had done all the preliminary organisation well before he'd slipped me the glad news over the nuts-and-sundries. Which was fair enough, I suppose: like I say, as emperors go – and I've had personal experience of three of the buggers so far – he might be unusually conscientious in complying with the niceties where asking favours was concerned, but he also knew damn well that the chances of being turned down were as close to zilch as made no odds.

Not that, having got his own way, he was doing things on the cheap: as on the last occasion we were booked on one of the imperial yachts, and at this time of year – we were three-quarters through August, well inside the sailing season – I reckoned we could do the run inside of three days; plus the fact that we'd be leaving from Ostia, which would save a good few days of being shaken up in the carriage-crawl to Puteoli. Added to which, this time around, at least we were bound for somewhere civilised and that had a bloody harbour.

So all in all the business could've been a lot worse. I gave things another couple of hours – when you go visiting a lady it's best not to turn up on the doorstep too early –, left Perilla to supervise the packing in association with our major-domo Bathyllus, and went over to the Palatine for my chat with Domitia Lepida.

Not something I was looking forward to, by any means: Lepida and her daughter were two of a kind, which probably went a long way towards explaining why they'd always got on together like cats in a bag. A situation further complicated by the fact that, a couple of years previously, after the guy had refused to sleep with her Messalina had conned Claudius into having her mother's then husband Junius Silanus chopped on a trumped-up treason charge.

Little things like that do tend to spoil mother-daughter relations just a tad.

Anyway, I gave my name to the door slave and twiddled my thumbs in the entrance hall for a good ten minutes while he checked whether the lady was At Home and Receiving: not one who believed in putting visitors at their ease, our Domitia Lepida, even though I was a relation by erstwhile marriage.

Finally, the guy reappeared and led me through to the atrium, where Lepida was artistically draped on a couch having clearly just had her morning primp and make-up session. Her maid finished packing up the bibs and bobs, gave a quick curtsey – ignored – and scuttled out.

'Valerius Corvinus!' Lepida must've been my age, mid-forties at least, but she looked a good fifteen years younger, and even without her morning beauty treatment she would've been a stunner: with a wife like that to come home to I wasn't really surprised that Silanus had sent the daughter packing. Besides, given the lady's notorious temper, he'd have known that if he had succumbed to temptation she'd've had him pegged out for the crows. Probably literally. 'What a pleasure! It's been far too long. How is Pandora?'

'Perilla. She's fine.'

'Of course. Perilla.' Not a beautiful mascara'd eyelash did she bat. 'Now, pull up a stool. Make yourself comfortable.' I did. 'I suppose my son-in-law sent you, about this Carthage business.'

My son-in-law. Not *Claudius Caesar.* Lepida was always careful to stress her status, particularly since she'd know how shaky it actually was these days. I almost felt sorry for her. Almost.

'That's right,' I said. 'He said you'd be able to fill me in a bit on the background before I left.'

'Not to any great degree; about the actual circumstances, that is. I only know what Verania told me in her letter.'

'Fine. Anything you can give me would help. Anything at all.'

'Well, then.' She settled back. 'The man's name was Cestius. Decimus Cestius. But you probably know that much at least already. *Not* one of Rome's high flyers, I'm afraid; he only managed as far as a praetorship before he took poor Verania off to the back of beyond about fifteen years ago, and frankly, Corvinus, she was completely wasted on him. I told her so in my letters, many times, to absolutely no avail. Why she hadn't got shot of the man ages since was a mystery to me.'

'You don't think they might just have been fond of each other?'

That got me a pitying look. 'Don't be silly. They were married. Oh, to give Verania her due it was an open marriage, she made sure of that. But for some arcane reason she didn't seem to want a divorce.' She sniffed. 'Or perhaps the reason wasn't too arcane, come to think of it. Believe me – and I speak from experience, both personal and at extensive second hand – to a married woman a truly complaisant husband is more precious than rubies, and so not to be given up lightly. Besides, Verania has always had, shall we say, a penchant for men below her station, and without the husband's compliance, or indeed ignorance, that can cause no end of problems.' She smiled. 'But I'm embarrassing you.'

'Uh...no. No, not at all.'

'Nonsense, darling. Your ears have gone red. Anyway, that was the situation, as far as I know. Of course, Cestius was extremely wealthy, which was bound to have some bearing on the matter.'

'Is that so?'

'Absolutely dripping with the stuff. Well, he'd been out there for fifteen years, hadn't he? What else is there to do in the provinces other than make money? Compared with Italy land is dirt cheap, if you'll forgive the pun, as is the bought labour, and if you can stand being away from Rome for that length of time, the gods help us, you can do extremely well financially. I don't know exactly how many square miles of the African hinterland the man owned, but it was a considerable number.' She sniffed again. 'Not that there would be much that was worth Verania's spending the money on out there, mark you.'

Yeah, well, I certainly took the point about the land side of things. Together with Egypt and to a lesser extent Sicily the African coast is the bread-basket of the empire, and in a good year you're looking at three harvests, easy. Bumper ones, at that, and with demand being what it was no problems about selling the crop. If Cestius was the kind of major landowner that Lepida said he was he'd be loaded and no mistake. Would've been loaded. Whatever. Which reminded me...

'What about his heirs?' I said. 'He have any sons?'

'Oh, yes. Two boys, Publius and Quintus. Although when I say boys they're no such thing; Publius must be in his mid-twenties now, and Quintus is only three years younger. I did intend to ask Claudius if he'd put the elder's name down for quaestor next year, but of course with the man's death everything's up in the air at present.'

Right; I supposed that made sense, particularly if – as Claudius had told me – the lad was scheduled to marry into a consular family. The post of city finance officer is the first real step in a political career, and in his parents' absence as young Publius's de facto patroness in Rome getting him it would've been Lepida's job.

'He'll be coming back to Rome, then?' I said. 'The son, I mean.'

'Yes, indeed. In fact, the whole family are, or at least they were before this happened. Not before time, as I say, as far as Verania is concerned, but better late than never.'

'So it was a sudden decision?'

'Oh, no, not at all. Cestius had been planning the move for years, ever since...well, to tell you the truth ever since he got the news that Gaius was dead and my son-in-law was emperor. They never really hit it off, you know, he and Gaius, and he didn't think a move back to Rome – or even to Italy – would be practicable. Let alone safe. But everything was quite settled; he bought a rather nice property a year ago on the Quirinal, and he was negotiating for an estate near Veii. I'm not sure what stage that's at, of course. Presumably with his death there'll be some hiatus over probating the will, or whatever the expression is, so everything, as I mentioned, is probably in abeyance for the present.'

'Okay. So what can you tell me about that, exactly? The death, I mean.'

'I said: nothing much, only what Verania told me in her letter, which was not a lot. It happened about a month ago. Seemingly Cestius had ridden over in the morning to part of his estate to check on how the grain harvest was going. He failed to return by nightfall, and the next day the slaves sent out as a search party found first of all his horse and then his body. He'd been stabbed through the heart.' She shrugged. 'That's all, really.'

Short and concise, and delivered with about as much feeling as if she'd been reciting a laundry list. Well, to be fair she'd no close links with the man, or at least I assumed she hadn't, and from what she'd already told me not much sympathy with or liking for him to begin with. What interested me, though, was if that was really all she'd got from Verania's letter – and I'd bet it had been a fair and honest summary – then it didn't show much feeling on the part of the poor bugger's widow, either. Still, to give her her due, Lepida had signalled that one as well: just because the pair had been married it didn't presuppose that they'd liked, let alone loved, each other.

We'd just have to shelve looking into that aspect of things, along with everything else, until we got to Carthage.

'Uh...just one more question before I go,' I said.

'Of course. Anything you like.'

'Nothing to do with the actual murder. Or not really. But I was just wondering. Why should you bother, yourself?'

'Why should I bother to do what?'

'To take the trouble to go to Claudius and ask him to look into this guy's death. I mean, by your own showing you'd no time for him and you'd been trying to split him and his wife up for years. Me, I'd imagine that you'd be happy just to let things slide, especially if your friend Verania didn't seem to be all that upset on her own account. I mean, if she'd asked you to take things to the emperor that'd be different, but I don't imagine she did. Or am I wrong?'

'No, Corvinus, you're not wrong. In fact, you're absolutely correct. Verania would never have wished her husband dead, of course she wouldn't; as I say, they'd been together for, what, thirty-odd years. All the same–' She stopped and frowned. 'How can I put this? Pets. Did you ever have a pet, when you were younger? One that died, and that you'd been fond of? If it's any help, think of Decimus Cestius as a favourite pet.'

Jupiter Best and Greatest! I just didn't believe this, not even from Lepida! A pet, right? The guy had been this Verania's husband for half a lifetime and she still thought of him as a fucking *pet?*

I just stared at her, which only got me another shrug. 'I knew you wouldn't understand,' she said. 'But believe me it's a perfectly fair analogy. Quite an apt one, too, so whatever your personal feelings on the matter are I'd ask you to bear it in mind.'

'Okay,' I said. 'Still, that doesn't answer the original question.'

'Why I should use up a valuable favour by going to Claudius? But Corvinus, I'd no choice. Not only was Cestius the husband of one of my oldest and closest friends, he was also an ex-praetor. And you do *not* allow some provincial hobbledehoy to murder an ex-praetor without doing something about it. Of course I had to go to the emperor! What on earth else would you expect me to do?'

It was a genuine question, I could see that, and backed by genuine puzzlement. And put by the woman who'd just compared a husband of thirty years' standing to a domestic pet.

15

Gods! I'll never understand how people like Domitia Lepida's minds work! Scratch even the most louche, world-weary upper-class Roman and the likelihood is you'll find that whether they normally practise them or not they believe absolutely in the old code of values. They can't help it; it's bred in the bone.

I stood up. 'Fair enough. Thanks for your help, Domitia Lepida.'

'Don't mention it, darling. Have a safe journey. And do give my very best regards to Verania when you see her.'

'I will. Thanks again.'

I left.

When I got home Perilla was stretched out on her usual couch in the atrium with an open book roll in her hands.

'Ah, Marcus, so you're back. And in one piece, too,' she said. 'Congratulations. How was Lepida?'

'Amazingly enough, she was fine. Quite affable, really.' I kissed her cheek and lifted the title tag on the roll. 'Claudius's *Carthaginian History*, eh? You smarmer.'

'Nothing of the kind. He sent it over himself as a gift, all eight volumes. Some light reading for the journey.'

'Is that so, now?' Me, I can never be sure, when the lady comes out with a statement like that, whether she's being sarcastic or straight. Probably the latter; compared to some of the stuff Perilla classifies as 'light reading' Aeschylus's *Oresteia* is a bodice-ripper. I settled down on the other couch, just as Bathyllus came in with the wine. 'Packing going okay, little guy?'

He handed me the cup. 'Of course, sir.' He hesitated. 'By the way, you, ah, are really intending to take Meton with us this time, are you?'

'You have a problem with that?'

'Not if you're absolutely certain that it's a good idea.' If Bathyllus's teeth had been gritted any further you'd've had to prise them apart with a crowbar. 'I was just wondering, that's all.'

I grinned to myself. Oh, sure, I knew where our control-freak major-domo was coming from: potentially Meton was the human (if you stretch the term) equivalent of a *kef*-stoned, migraine-suffering rhino let loose in a glassworks. Still, he'd lost out on the jaunt when we'd gone on our trip to Gaul two years before, and the resulting sulk when we got back had affected our dinner menu for a month. This time the situation was different. Oh, sure, travelling again as I would be as an accredited imperial rep I'd no doubt that any accommodation arranged for us would be five-star, which meant it'd come fully equipped staff-wise, chef included; but the package would also include a resident major-domo, and we were definitely taking Bathyllus with us. So leaving Meton behind for a second time just wouldn't be fair. Besides, with only a three-day cheek-by-jowl journey involved rather than the month-long trek we'd had to get to where we were going last time around we wouldn't be stuck with the bugger's direct company for all that long.

'Bathyllus, read my lips,' I said. 'Meton is coming with us, and there's an end of it. You'll just have to rub along together as best you can.'

'Very well, sir.' A sniff. 'On your own head be it. I only hope you won't live to regret it, that's all.'

'Bugger off, sunshine.'

'As you wish.' Bathyllus buggered off, his whole body language radiating terminal disapproval and pure concentrated miffedness.

'So, dear.' Perilla set the book roll aside. 'What did Lepida have to say?'

I gave her the gist, including the bit about the domestic pet.

'Hmm.' She frowned. 'It doesn't sound too happy a household, does it?'

'Lepida could be wrong in her assessment. We only have her word for things.'

'I doubt it, Marcus. Or not far wrong, anyway. After all, by her own showing she's known this Verania for years. And they are close friends; that argues a certain similarity of nature.'

'Yeah, I suppose it does.' I took a swallow of the wine. 'All the same, it's far too early to make value judgments. Me, I'll wait until I've actually met the woman. What's our timetable, by the way? Any updates?'

'Not really.' We were the only passengers this time around, and Claudius's message had said that the ship would be waiting for us at Ostia whenever we were ready to sail. 'The packing's practically all done, barring a few bits and pieces, and I've sent word to Marilla and Clarus that we'll be away for the foreseeable future in case they were thinking of coming through.' Marilla and Clarus were our adopted daughter and her

17

husband down in Castrimoenium. 'So we can more or less start whenever you like.'

'Fine,' I said. 'Call it three days' time.' Ah, the carefree joys of travelling as an imperial rep! I could get used to this. And, *pace* Domitia Lepida, at least this time we weren't heading off into the sticks altogether. It might be quite fun.

There was still the little matter of solving the murder, of course.

3.

We left with Lysias the coach driver for Ostia an hour before dawn three days before the Kalends, the 'we' being Perilla, me, and Perilla's maid Phryne: I'd sent Bathyllus and Meton on ahead with the slow-as-paint-drying luggage cart the day before, with Alexis the gardener driving it and under strict instructions to keep the two stroppy buggers in order.

The ship, it transpired when we got to the quay and de-carriaged, was the 'Leucothea', the same as had taken us to Massilia and back two years before. Sure enough, Bathyllus and Alexis were waiting for us on deck, together with the captain, but there was no sign of Meton. Ominous. I just hoped Bathyllus hadn't taken the opportunity to sandbag the bugger during the hours of darkness and pitched him over the side; another murder this early in the game I could do without.

'Have a good trip, sunshine?' I said to Bathyllus. 'Everything safely loaded?'

'Yes, sir.' We might still be tied securely to the quay, but Bathyllus was looking pale already; he's no sailor, Bathyllus, even worse a one than I am, which is saying something. 'There's only what you've brought with you, and Alexis will help Lysias to bring that aboard now.'

'That's great. Thanks, Alexis.' Alexis gave me a nod and went back over the gangplank, with a shy glance at Phryne in passing: our gardener might not exactly be a callow youngster any longer, but he was still more comfortable with plants than women, particularly if they were little stunners like Phryne. 'Uh...where's Meton, by the way?'

'I really couldn't say, sir.' Bathyllus sniffed. *And frankly,* his tone suggested, *I couldn't give a monkey's.*

I grinned; yeah, par for the course on both sides, although on a ship the size of the 'Leucothea' anyone's exact whereabouts couldn't be all that much of a mystery for long. Still, if the pair of them had reached a *modus vivendi* that would last for the duration of the voyage involving mutual ignorance, selective blindness, and scrupulous avoidance then that was absolutely fine by me.

'He's aft, sir, in your cabin, looking after the food basket.' The captain glanced sideways at Bathyllus. 'Your other slave suggested it. He, ah, thought it wise, under the circumstances.' Uh-huh. Alexis, of course, had always had his head screwed on tight, and the captain was evidently no fool either; no doubt, being the sea-faring man that he was, he could spot a potential squall developing and take action before it scuppered us. 'A pleasure to see you again, Valerius Corvinus. And the Lady Rufia, of course.'

'Likewise,' I said. 'All ready to roll, are we? To coin a phrase.'

He stifled a wince, which was reasonable under the circumstances: ship's captains aren't particularly known for their humour, especially where allusions to their ships are concerned. 'Whenever you like,' he said. 'We've a good wind. And the going should be quite smooth at this time of year.'

Thank Neptune for that, at least; like I say, I'm not at my best away from land – no true Roman is – and although judging by past experience the *Leucothea* was about as stable a ship as anyone could expect I'd no desire to spend the next few days crouched over a bowl throwing my guts up. 'Fair enough, captain,' I said. 'In your own time, then.'

We left him hoisting the marline-spike and clewing the hawsers, or whatever nautical men do to get things moving, and went aft to settle in. That's another good thing about travelling imperial class. Book yourself as supercargo on a merchantman and you're lucky not to have to bed down in the open under a canopy, but those little beauties are built for comfort as well as speed, and we had that anomalous luxury, a cabin to ourselves. Not exactly all the comforts of home, but the next thing to it.

Meton, sure enough, was in temporary residence, sitting on one of the two couch-beds clutching his best set of knives and watching over his food basket like a particularly evil goblin with his chest of gold. Which, in Meton's terms, at least where the last phrase was concerned, summed things up pretty nicely: they may have most of the comforts of home, sure, but even imperial yachts don't run to fully-equipped kitchens, and like usually happens on sea trips we'd brought our food with us. Good stuff, too, albeit of necessity to be served cold: thrawn, evil-minded sod our chef might be in other ways, but when it came to the comestibles he was a true professional.

When we came in, he grunted and stood up, although in the confines of the tiny cabin and Meton being Meton, 'loomed' would be a better term.

'So you got here, then,' he said.

'Yeah,' I said. 'So it would seem.'

20

'Fine. In that case I'll shove off and leave you to it.' He shambled past us to the door. 'Oh...you want to look after that for me?' He nodded back at the food basket. 'And my knives. I don't trust them light-fingered naval bastards further than I could effing throw them.'

'Right. Right. No problem.' Mind you, I reckoned any of the crew who tried to liberate so much as a stuffed date would find themselves swimming home. 'Ah...by the way, sunshine. Just a small word of advice.'

He stopped and wiped his nose with the back of his hand. 'What's that, now?'

'You know what *port* and *starboard* are?'

'Sod that. I'm an effing chef, not an effing–'

'Got you. Even so. Port's on the left side of the boat facing front, starboard's on the right. With me so far?' He just scowled, which for Meton indicated a yes. 'Great. Okay. So here's the idea. The port side's your territory, the starboard's Bathyllus's. You both keep to that rule for as long as it takes us to get to Carthage. Understand? I'll clear it with Bathyllus myself.'

He shrugged. 'Fine by me. So what's the actual advice, like? I mean–'

'The advice, pal, is that both you and Bathyllus stick to the arrangement like glue, because otherwise when we do get to Carthage I'll trade you both in the first chance I get. Clear?'

A snuffle; possibly the nearest the bugger came to laughing, or maybe it was just excess mucus. 'Been there, done that already,' he said. 'Alexis's suggestion, and it's okay by me and the bald-head. No problem. Was there anything else?'

'Uh, no. No, I think that about wraps it up.'

'Good. Let me know when you want to eat an' I'll come back in and see to it. That little bald-headed bastard won't know what's served with what and when, and I'm not having him messing up my effing menus.'

He left. Oh, the joys of communing with staff.

There was a flask of wine and a couple of cups on the small table between the bunks. I picked the flask up, uncorked it, and sniffed. Imperial Caecuban, no less: Claudius had come up trumps again.

'You want to change for dinner, lady, or shall we slum it?' I said.

'I think the latter, Marcus. Just this once.' There was a lurch, and the cabin developed a definite tilt; I grabbed the wine flask just in time. 'Ah, good. We seem to be off.'

The crossing was uneventful. Me, I settled down on deck with the Caecuban and watched the dolphins; Perilla read through all eight rolls of Claudius's *History*; Bathyllus, predictably, had made a dash for the rail as soon as we were clear of the harbour and spent the entire time thereafter alternately throwing up over the side and groaning on his straw pallet in the thwarts. Meton was Meton, throughout. Phryne was trying to persuade the captain every chance she got of a long-standing and deep-seated interest in all things nautical.

Time passed; more slowly than usual, which is par for a sea journey unless things suddenly get more exciting than you'd like.

We made Carthage just shy of noon on the third day.

Oh, sure, I know that the place hasn't been the arch-enemy for almost two hundred years, that its territory has been our property ever since, that there is absolutely zilch left, top to bottom, of the original city, and that what we'd got was going to prove a duplicate for any of a dozen other provincial towns in the empire, but I'm willing to bet that no Roman can cross the harbour bar at Carthage without at least the vestige of a shiver. Because of Hannibal and his army things came within a whisker of being the other way about, with Rome stamped flat, Italy a Carthaginian fief, and all of us speaking Punic. Even today, the guy's name is used by nursemaids to frighten naughty children: be good, or Hannibal will come and gobble you up. I remember having nightmares about him myself.

Some memories take more than just time to kill.

Not that Perilla seemed all that overawed, mind, and she'd obviously slipped into excited-sightseer mode already.

'Oh, look! That must be the Byrsa over there.' She pointed to a hill straight ahead of us, more or less in the centre of the town. 'The original citadel. According to the legend when Queen Elissa asked the local ruler for land to found a city he granted her as much as an ox-hide would cover. So she cut it into strips and surrounded the whole area from the far side of the hill down to the sea.'

I grinned. 'Did she indeed? It must've been one hell of a big ox, then. Besides, if she spoke Punic then why use the Greek word for it?'

'Marcus, I'm sorry, but you really do not have the slightest shred of poetry in your soul, do you? Personally, true or not, as a story I think it's lovely.'

'Suit yourself, lady.' We'd slowed to a crawl now and were nosing our way under oars up the length of the inner harbour. Judging by the number of merchant ships moored to the quays either side, including two or three of the big grain barges, the place was fairly prosperous. At least, *pace* Lepida, we weren't out in the sticks altogether. Which reminded me. 'You think we'll be staying at the residence with Galba?'

'Almost certainly. He is the governor, after all, and you are the emperor's personal representative.'

'Bugger.'

'Yes, well, we'll just have to take things as they come, won't we? In any case, he's probably forgotten all about you. After all, it was quite a while ago, and you only met the man once.'

'Once was enough.'

'Don't grouse, dear. I'm sure he'll be perfectly charming, if only diplomatically so. And he'll have his own duties to attend to, so we probably won't see much of him.'

'Even so.'

We passed through the entrance to the inner harbour, heading towards the prime mooring site at its far end, and got our first sight of the city proper. Like I say, from the buildings – warehouses and storage yards, mostly, much as you'd expect near the port – we could've been anywhere in the empire, if it hadn't been for the palm trees. And the heat. Rome gets pretty hot in late summer, sure, but we were a lot further south now, the sun was higher in the sky, and despite the cooling sea breeze it seemed to be burning a lot hotter than it did at home. Me, I'm fine with that, but Perilla had taken to wearing a sun bonnet while she was on deck.

'Well, from the looks of things we're expected, anyway,' she said.

Sure enough, on the quay beside the empty berth we were aiming for were a couple of litters, a mule-cart, and what was obviously a small official reception party. Par, again, for the course, given the five-star accreditation tucked in my belt-pouch. Hell; maybe I should've changed out of the lounging-tunic I'd been wearing for the past three days into a proper mantle. Or at least had a shave. But there again no doubt the local Powers that Be would prefer to have the visiting imperial rep turn up without his throat accidentally slit or part of an ear missing, and formal mantles are stifling at any time of year. Perilla, now, would look cool and groomed despite the heat whatever she was wearing, and in any case the lady is definitely the mantle type.

We docked, the gangplank was set in place, and we stepped ashore to where a young guy in military undress uniform was waiting for us.

'Valerius Corvinus. And Lady Rufia. I'm delighted to meet you both.' He held out a hand. 'Sextus Quirinius, Governor Galba's factotum and general dogsbody. I'll be looking after you while you're here. You had a pleasant trip?'

'Not bad,' I said. We shook, and he smiled; nice lad, fresh-faced, early twenties, broad-striper-family accent and diplomatic-corps manner, again all par for the course where a provincial governor's aide was concerned. 'Pretty good, really.'

'That's excellent. The governor sends his regards.'

'Good of him. He'll, uh, be putting us up, will he?'

Quirinius hesitated. 'Actually, sir, the residence is a bit too small for entertaining, and Governor Galba thought you might be more comfortable in a place of your own. If you've no objections, of course. I'm to take you there now.'

Glory and trumpets! Well, that was a load off my mind, anyway, and clearly, wrap it up in what diplomatic-speak you will, the bastard was just as loth to rub shoulders with me for the duration of our stay as I was with him.

'Absolutely no problem,' I said. 'In fact, we'd prefer it. Wouldn't we, Perilla?'

'Of course we would.' She gave me a bright smile.

'Marvellous! I'm relieved.' He looked it, too; I reckoned, whatever Galba's comments to his aide had been regarding our previous acquaintance when he'd got the glad news who Claudius was sending, they hadn't been complimentary. Forgotten me, my foot. Still, it was an ill wind. 'It's really a very nice house, in a quiet residential area, with a full complement of staff. Much better than staying in the centre of town, believe me. And naturally the governor would be delighted to have you over for dinner tonight, if you're not too tired. I'm sure you have a lot to talk about.'

'Yeah. I'm sure of that, too.' Was I hell; bugger! Still, there were the diplomatic niceties to be observed. And it would give Bathyllus and Meton a chance to settle in. 'I'm looking forward to it.'

'Then we'll be on our way. If you'd like to take the litters and go on ahead I'll arrange for your slaves and the luggage to follow and meet you there.'

'Actually, pal,' I said, 'I'd prefer to walk, if it's all the same to you. After three days on a ship I need the exercise.'

He blinked. 'Really? That's very–'

'Really. Trust me on this. In any case, I've never been one for litters. The lady will take one, though.'

'Well, if you're sure.' He looked at me doubtfully. 'In that case, sir, I'll accompany you myself.'

'Perfect.' If nothing else, it'd give me a chance to get my bearings. 'Whenever you're ready, then. I'll see you there, Perilla.'

I waved her off, and while Quirinius went to liaise with Bathyllus about the baggage I nipped back aboard to say goodbye and thank you to the captain. Dislike of litters aside, mind, I hadn't been kidding about needing the exercise; three days at sea had left my land-legs feeling pretty wonky, and besides I could get the low-down from Quirinius on the background to the case, as far as he knew it. Plus, and more important, his recommendations for the best local wineshops. Where foreign travel's concerned you need to get your priorities straight right from day one.

4.

The house, it transpired, was in what Quirinius called the Astarte District, west of the centre and about half a mile from where we were. Finding my way around would be easy-peasie: like most provincial towns and cities built from scratch – and Carthage had been effectively that, because the original city had been literally flattened and the debris used for the foundations of the new roads and buildings – the military engineers had laid it out in the standard provincial grid plan, with the two main streets, Boundary Marker and the Hinge, running due east-west and north-south respectively and crossing at Market Square. Or rather, in Carthage's case, just south of it, because the new market square was on Perilla's Byrsa Hill. It was a nice place, all told, when we'd got beyond the harbour area, much quieter, cleaner and more open than Rome, none of which would be all that difficult, with a definite feel of newness to it; fair enough, because as a colony – according to Quirinius – it had only been around for about sixty-odd years, and there was still a lot of new building going on. Then there were the palm trees, which of course you don't see in Rome barring the occasional exception in one of the public or private gardens. The locals obviously went in for palm trees in a big way, and it gave the place a gloss of foreign-ness that otherwise it wouldn't've had.

As far as wineshops were concerned...

'You can try Cladus's to start with, Corvinus,' Quirinius said as we walked down a side street past the blank walls of the upper-class local residences; fortunately, at my insistence, we'd got beyond the 'sir' stage pretty early on in the proceedings. 'In Aesculapius, just east of the Byrsa. It's a nice place with a small garden, and although the wine's local it's not all that bad, as long as you don't expect Falernian.'

'Fair enough.'

'A word of warning, though. Steer clear of the date variety. Regional speciality or not, it's absolutely foul. Even compared with German beer.'

'Is that so, now?' I said. Mind you, it didn't sound the sort of stuff I'd be exactly desperate to try in any case. Where food and drink is concerned – at least the non-alcoholic version of the latter – Perilla's the adventurous one of the partnership. 'Have you ever actually *tasted* German beer, pal?'

'Indeed I have. My father commanded one of the Rhine legions for a while. He brought back a keg of it when he came home, just for a joke, and trust me, date wine is a dozen times worse. If you don't believe me then please do go ahead and try it for yourself. Ah.' He stopped outside the property at the street's corner. 'Here we are.' The door-slave, who'd been sitting on the step, stood up. 'Has the Lady Rufia arrived yet, Flavillus?'

'Yes, sir, just a few minutes ago.' The slave opened the door and stepped back, as did Quirinius.

'You go first, Corvinus,' he said. 'It's your house, after all, at least for the time being.'

I went inside and through the entrance lobby to the atrium, where Perilla was ensconced on one of the couches by the ornamental pool with a drink in her hand. She'd taken off her sun-hat, but it was lying on the table beside her.

'Oh, good, Marcus. You've arrived,' she said. 'Nice, isn't it?'

I looked around. Nice the place certainly was, at least on first showing. The atrium was as big as our one at home, easy, with a good mosaic on the floor (Dionysus in a vine arbour, with the ubiquitous date palms behind it) and some first-rate murals on the walls. There were even a couple of very passable bronzes. I had to admit that Sulpicius Galba, beefcake gladiator fancier and women's shoes fetishist though he might be, had done us more than proud.

'Yeah,' I said. 'It's great.'

'I'm glad you both like it.' Quirinius had come in behind me. 'As I said, it is fully staffed, but since you've brought your own major-domo and chef with you I'm sure Cornelia Alba won't mind if the present incumbents go elsewhere for the time being. In any case, it might be for the best if you want to avoid, ah, friction.'

I grinned. 'You're telling me something I don't know, pal?' I said. 'That's fine with me, absolutely fine. Who's Cornelia Alba?'

'Oh, of course. I didn't tell you.' He pulled up a stool, while I sat on the second couch. 'She's your...I suppose you could call her your hostess, although she doesn't live here now herself.'

'No? Why's that?'

'It was her father's house. The old fellow had an accident a month or so ago, a fatal one, and him being a widower and her an only child she's gone to stay with her aunt and uncle in their house near the centre. The place

28

will probably be sold eventually, but for the moment the uncle's happy to keep it on as is.' He smiled. 'Fortunately, under the circumstances, for us.'

'What kind of accident?'

'He took a tumble down the stairs and broke his neck. No surprises there, he was getting on a bit and he'd been shaky on his feet for some time, but we were all very upset when it happened all the same. Albus was a pillar of the scholarly community here; in fact, he'd written several–' He stopped and stood up as a girl – young woman, rather – with a small monkey on her shoulder came through from the lobby.

Now there was something you didn't see every day, not in Rome at least. Pet sparrows, cats and small lapdogs, sure, but not shoulder-balancing monkeys. Still, for all I knew maybe it was normal for Carthage. At any rate, Quirinius didn't seem too surprised.

'Elissa, we were just talking about you,' he said. 'This is Valerius Corvinus and his wife Rufia Perilla.'

I'd stood up as well. 'I'm pleased to meet you, Cornelia Alba,' I said. Then, to Quirinius: 'Uh...'Elissa'?'

'That was my girl-name,' she said before he could answer. She was a looker, certainly, late teens or early twenties, but there was something odd about her eyes, and the set of her mouth: most people would've added a smile to the words; this girl didn't, not a trace of one. I got the distinct impression that smiling was something she didn't do very often, if at all. 'It was my father's choice, originally, and people still call me that, but I think I prefer Cornelia now. If that's agreeable to you, Quirinius.'

Ouch: cold as a Riphaean winter, and barbed as a fish-hook.

'But he's lovely!' Perilla said. 'Your pet monkey, I mean. What's his name?'

Interesting; the lady's tone was one she'd've normally used with a much younger girl. So she'd noticed something odd about her as well.

'Ptolemy.' Perilla reached out a hand towards him. He screeched at her, and she drew the hand back quickly. 'I wouldn't touch him, if I were you. He isn't good with strangers, and he bites.'

'I was just telling Valerius Corvinus that you're quite happy to have him provide his own major-domo and chef,' Quirinius said. 'That's right, isn't it?'

She shrugged. 'Of course. You can do as you please, Valerius Corvinus. And you're very welcome here, both of you. I only came to say that. I'll leave you to settle in now.'

As she turned to go, the monkey jumped from her shoulder onto the table, grabbed Perilla's sun-hat, and made for the door. The girl turned, her face expressionless as ever. No reaction. None.

'Oh, I'm terribly sorry,' she said. 'He really is quite the little thief, Ptolemy, especially with hats. He won't damage it, though, I promise you, and I'll give you it back later.'

Perilla smiled. 'That's perfectly all right, my dear,' she said. 'No harm done. And don't worry, I can easily find a replacement.'

'I'll give you it back later.' The same words as before, repeated, in exactly the same tone. The effect was quite eerie. 'I have to go now. It was a pleasure meeting you both. Enjoy your stay.'

And she left, without another word. Perilla and I just looked at each other.

Quirinius cleared his throat. 'You, ah, must excuse Elissa,' he said. 'Cornelia, I should say. She...well, I'm afraid she takes a little getting used to, and she's uncomfortable with strangers herself. Also, with her father's death being so recent–' He stopped.

'That's perfectly okay,' I said. 'Don't give it another thought.'

'Good.' He took a deep breath. 'Now, unless there's anything else I can do for you I'm afraid I must go too. As I said, the governor is expecting you for dinner this evening unless you're too tired after your journey, in which case–.'

'No,' I said. 'We're fine.' Best to get it over with. Besides, it gave us an excuse not to make a night of it.

'Excellent. By the way, the house does have its own small bath suite, and I gave instructions for the furnace to be lit. You'll want to bathe, naturally. And I'll send a carriage for you an hour before sunset, if that's all right.'

'Perfectly.' Perilla smiled at him.

'Don't be too particular about dress, it won't be a formal meal. I'll be there myself, of course, so I'll see you then.'

'Thanks again, Quirinius,' I said. 'We'll see you at dinner.'

We watched him go.

'Well,' Perilla said. 'Now *that* was certainly unusual. The girl, I mean.'

'Yeah.' There was a jug of wine and a couple of wine cups on the table. I poured myself a cupful and stretched out on the couch. 'Yes, it was.'

'Did you notice her eyes? She didn't look at us directly once.'

'Uh-huh.' I was frowning. 'Still, it's none of our business, is it?'

'No, it isn't. Even so–'

Bathyllus shimmered in. Or at least with as much of a shimmer as Bathyllus could manage after three days of unremitting seasickness.

'Is everything in order, sir?' he said.

'Actually, we should ask you that, little guy,' I said. 'You got here, then?'

'Just this minute arrived, sir. And Phryne will be in shortly, with the mistress's bags. She'll take them up to your room and unpack.'

'What about Meton?'

'In the kitchen having a word with the kitchen staff and checking the existing stores.' He sniffed. 'I understand that once he's done that he intends to go straight down to the market.'

I grinned. Right; par for the course. We didn't take Meton along with us – Meton being Meton – very often, but it was a safe bet, my month's income to a used corn plaster, that the first thing he'd do on arrival was check out the range and quality of the local produce. I felt sorry, mind, for the stallholders, who'd still be in blissful ignorance of what was about to hit them. And for the kitchen skivvies, because when Meton had a word with the staff, I knew, it consisted largely of terrifying the wollocks off the poor buggers. Still, I had to admit it got results, and Bathyllus for his part would be no different where the rest of the household was concerned. Worse, in his quiet, control-freak way.

'That's fine,' I said. 'He knows we'll be eating out tonight, doesn't he? With the governor, at the residence?'

'Yes, sir. He told me to say that that would be perfectly acceptable under the circumstances.'

'Good of him. Oh. Quirinius said there's a bath suite and that the furnace was on. You want to make sure of that?'

'Certainly, sir. I'll check on it now.'

'Great.' Well, that was all the boxes ticked for the present. 'Off you go, then.'

He went.

'So,' Perilla said. 'What did Quirinius have to say about the murder?'

31

'Actually, he didn't know much more about it than we do already. I got a couple of names and addresses – the widow's, of course, and the guy's factor's – but that was about all.' I frowned and took a sip of the wine: it wasn't one I recognised, which probably meant that it was local. If so, then Quirinius's assessment was bang-on: not Falernian, sure, not by a long chalk, but on its home ground, at least, not at all bad. 'Strange thing is, what I did get was the impression that no one was busting a gut to trace the killer.'

'But that's ridiculous!'

'Yeah, I know. Oh, sure, Lepida did imply that his wife wouldn't be exactly devastated, but still, there are the two sons, at the very least, and you'd think they'd want some answers. Nevertheless, on Quirinius's showing for whatever reason as far as the immediate family's concerned the general feeling seems to be that any investigation would be a waste of time. And I doubt if Galba could give a toss. Weird, yes, but there you are. Me, I suspect that if Lepida hadn't gone to Claudius the whole thing would've been quietly shelved.' I took another swallow of the wine, emptying the cup. 'Ah, hell, leave it for now. If the baths are hot we'll have a long relaxing steam, make a tour of the property, and then get changed into our glad-rags for the governor's dinner. Fair enough?'

Perilla smiled. 'Perfectly fair.'

I reached for the wine jug and refilled my cup. If I was going to live through a dinner with Sulpicius Bloody Galba later, however short and informal it turned out to be, then I needed serious anaesthetising first.

5.

The dinner turned out to be as bloody as I'd thought it would be. Worse. And forget Quirinius's 'informal': I was relieved we'd chosen to go in best bib and tucker after all, because Galba and the other guests were dressed to the nines. Galba was puffier and more jowly in the face than he had been when we'd last met, but otherwise he hadn't changed all that much: still the pasty white, unhealthy-looking skin, the bulbous nose, and the mouth that wouldn't've disgraced a hungry pike. Plus a manner that embodied all the sensitivity of an aristocratic piledriver. The other guests...

Apart from Quirinius, who was there *ex officio*, as it were, the other five were co-diners from hell. There was Lutatius the banker with the cleft palate and his wife Quadratilla, sixty if she was a day, dressed, coiffeured and made up like a thirty year old, who had a laugh like a marble-saw; Rupilius, owner of the biggest undertaker's business in the city, who looked the part and whose hobby was undertaking, plus his thin-as-a-streak-of-piss, acid-toned harpy of a wife Lautia, whose hobby seemed to be slagging friends, acquaintances, and total strangers off at every opportunity; and finally a guy I can't remember the name of who sat through the whole meal without saying a word to anyone.

Fun, fun, fun. Me, I'm convinced the bastard had chosen them deliberately, partly out of sheer bloody-mindedness and partly to make sure we'd wade through molten lava rather than tout for another invite during our stay. If so, then he needn't've bothered troubling himself, because I'd've done that in any case.

Quirinius had been right about the residence, though, which was small, pokey, over-decorated, and – despite the climate – miserable as an Aventine attic in winter.

So not exactly a joyful occasion, and as far as gleaning information went a complete bummer. With one noticeable exception. Not, as far as I knew, that it had anything to do with the Cestius affair, but still.

'You're staying in old Cornelius Albus's house, so I understand, Valerius Corvinus?' Rupilius was disembowelling a stuffed sardine with all the care he'd probably have put into preparing a body for mummification.

'Yeah, that's right,' I said. 'We–'

'I had the burying of him, you know, after the accident. He made a lovely corpse. Very distinguished. People at the viewing remarked on it.'

'Is that so, now?'

'Also about how well he was looking. Under the circumstances, of course.'

'It was his poor daughter I felt sorry for,' Lautia put in. 'One thing on top of another. And she's never been quite right since...well, since *it* happened, if you understand me.'

'"It"?' Perilla said.

Lautia dropped her voice. 'She was interfered with, poor child,' she said. 'By a man. Two or three years ago, now, but that's something you never get over. And of course since then her chances of making a good marriage have been–' She stopped. 'Well, my dear, I needn't explain the situation to you, need I?'

'You mean she was raped?'

That got the lady a look that would've skewered a rhino. 'If you want to put it that crudely,' Lautia said carefully, 'then yes. Although I wouldn't use the term myself.'

'Do they know who by?'

'Oh, there was no mystery about that. The young blackguard was a Marcus Virrius. A terrible disgrace for his parents, naturally, they're very respectable people. Virrius Senior is in the textile trade and his wife was the daughter of a local senator.' She sniffed. 'Of course if rumour is to be believed there *is* bad blood in the family, on both sides. Virrius's grandfather was involved in some *very* suspect business dealings and his wife's uncle was a notorious womaniser. So perhaps we shouldn't have been too surprised when the son went to the bad.'

'What happened to him?'

'Oh, he fled the city before any charges could be brought. Disappeared completely and hasn't been heard of since. Mind you, he'd already been disinherited by his father, so he'd nothing to lose by running away.' She sniffed again. 'Naturally, though, as I said poor Cornelia is now damaged goods. It's unfortunate, she's a nice enough girl in herself if you make the necessary allowances, but there you are.'

I glanced at Perilla. Her eyes were on the plate in front of her, and she was pushing the remains of her jellied prawns around with her spoon in short, sharp jerks.

Uh-oh. *Not* a good sign.

'Yes, well, Lautia,' she said quietly. 'I can agree with you as far as the word "damaged" goes, but I'm afraid we differ completely in how we interpret the term.'

'Really?' Lautia dabbed at her lips with her napkin. 'You surprise me. But then I suppose moral standards in Rome are so much laxer than ours. What happened may not have been altogether the girl's fault, but there's no smoke without fire. She must have encouraged him, at the very least.'

Perilla's eyes came up. '*That*,' she began, 'is the most–'

–at which point I knocked over my full wine cup. Quadratilla, who was directly opposite me and was reaching for a pickled sea-urchin at the time, got some of the contents on the sleeve of her mantle and squealed like a stuck piglet. She drew her hand back sharply and caught her own cup with her elbow, knocking it over and drenching the mantle's other sleeve. She squealed again, louder and at a higher pitch. Mayhem, briefly, ensued as slaves with napkins converged on the two spreading pools.

'Uh...I'm sorry about that,' I said. 'Misjudged the distance.'

Lautia glared at me. 'Perhaps, Valerius Corvinus,' she said, 'if your spatial co-ordination is becoming so erratic you should consider sticking to water for the rest of the evening.'

'Now just one fucking minute, lady–!'

'*Marcus!*'

'Don't you dare use language like that to my wife, you Roman bastard!'

'Really, Valerius Corvinus, it is too much! This mantle was brand new, ordered specially from Alexandria! Do you *know* how difficult it is to get a wine stain out of silk?'

'Mwaa, mwaa, mwaa!'

Galba held up his hand, beamed, waited for silence, then looked round the stricken table. 'I think we'll move on to the dessert, shall we?' he said. 'Any objections? No? Carried *nem. con.*, then. Jolly good.'

'Honestly, Marcus,' Perilla said when we were safely in the carriage and rattling towards home, 'I could've slapped that stupid woman. I nearly did, too.'

'Yeah,' I said. 'So I noticed. You owe me one, lady.'

'Not that there was any excuse for your little display.'

'Maybe not. Ah, well. I suppose we can consider ourselves crossed off Galba's suitable-dinner-guests list for the foreseeable future.'

'Yes, I suppose we can. What a shame.' She frowned. 'I have to admit that it did liven the evening up considerably, though.'

'Mmm.'

'But that poor girl! It explains a lot, really.'

'Yeah. Not everything, mind.'

She gave me a sideways glance. 'How do you mean?'

I shrugged. 'I don't know. Just a feeling. But six gets you ten things are more complicated than we think they are.'

'Perhaps so, but it's none of our business. You said that yourself.'

'True.' I turned and stared through the carriage window for a while. There was a full moon, and although only a few of the houses we passed had torches burning in the cressets beside their doors there was still something to see outside besides the darkness. 'Problem is, I keep thinking of Marilla. When we first found her.'

Perilla drew her breath in sharply. 'Oh, Marcus, no! Surely not!'

'I never said it was logical. In fact, it's quite the reverse, I've not a single fact to hang the idea on. How could I? We only saw the girl for two minutes.'

'So what prompted the thought, then?'

'The gods know. It was just the look in the eyes, and something in her voice when she used the word "father". There was something there, sure, I'd bet you anything you like on that score, but that doesn't mean to say–' I stopped and shook my head. 'Forget it, it's only the wine talking. Anyway, I reckon our brains've done their whack for one day. Pull down the shutters, call it a wrap. Fair enough?'

'All right. So what are your plans for tomorrow?'

'Have a talk with the grieving widow. See what she has to say and take things from there.'

'Marcus, do you *have* to jump straight into things the moment we arrive? After all, we are abroad in a city we've never seen before. Why not take a day or so to acclimatise, see the sights? I'm sure Claudius wouldn't object, and things aren't exactly urgent, are they?'

I grinned. 'Look, you do things your way, I'll do things mine, okay? Trust me, by the time we leave I'll have seen more of Carthage than you will.'

'Yes, but not necessarily the interesting parts.'

'Define "interesting".'

'All right, please yourself, dear. In any case, I'm too tired to argue.'

'Good.'

'Even so–'

'Bugger off.'

We rattled on in silence.

Well, at least we'd be sleeping in a proper bed tonight. Tomorrow could look after itself.

6.

There was no point in being on the go too early the next day – from what I'd gleaned about her from Lepida I doubted if Verania would be an early riser – so I had a leisurely breakfast with Perilla at her preferred time of surfacing, which is half way through the morning, in the palm-tree-shaded garden at the back of the house and set out an hour before noon.

The Cestius family property, according to Quirinius, was on the coast to the north of the city; not too far away if I cut diagonally across town. It was a pleasant-enough walk. Being laid out from scratch to a definite plan, the streets were straight and regular, easily wide enough to take both pedestrian and other traffic without the frustrating bottle-necks you'd get if you tried the same thing in Rome that time of day, or – unless you were pretty certain of your route – the danger of getting lost in the maze of side streets and narrow alleyways. No tenements, either, which was a definite plus: like I said, the temperature might be higher than it would've been back home, but while in seriously-built-up, closed-in areas like the Subura or the Aventine it felt like walking through an oven the breeze here made things feel a bit cooler.

The villa was on the high ground overlooking the sea. 'Villa' was an understatement: Cestius must've been rolling right enough, because the place was built of coloured marble, took up most of the headland, and was set amid a series of terraced gardens that had been landscaped, topiary-hedged and statued within an inch of their lives. From one of them came the eerie wail of a peacock.

The slave on duty at the main gate took my name inside and reappeared with the news that the lady was At Home.

Verania was sitting under a parasol beside an ornamental pool in one of the gardens. With two grown-up sons she'd have to be in her mid-forties, at least, but she looked ten years younger. From a distance, anyway; when I came closer I could see that a lot of the effect was due to hair-styling and clever make-up. Discount that, and what you'd got was a slightly-too-plump middle-aged woman with over-sharp features, moneylender's eyes, and a mouth like a spoilt child's.

Forget the widow's weeds; if she'd ever bothered with them they'd been replaced by a blue gossamer-light shot-silk mantle that must've cost an arm and a leg.

'Sulpicius Galba told me you'd be coming, Valerius Corvinus,' she said. 'I'm pleased to meet you.' She looked over my shoulder at the slave who'd brought me through. 'Bring a chair for the gentleman. And some wine. Quickly, now!' The slave bowed and left.

'Domitia Lepida sends her regards,' I said.

'Ah, yes.' Cool as an ice bath. 'I understand she's responsible for your presence here. How is Lepida? Well, I hope?'

'Yes. At least she was eight days ago.'

'That's good. She has *such* a problem with that daughter of hers, poor dear. Girls are always a trial. It's something I'm spared, fortunately. I only have sons.' She straightened the hem of her mantle. 'You're married yourself?'

'Yeah. I brought my wife out with me.'

Her eyes widened. 'Did you really? How very unusual! You have children?'

'One daughter. Adopted.'

'You haven't brought her too, I hope. That would be stretching family commitments just a little too far.'

'No. She's married to a doctor. They've a place in the Alban Hills.'

'A *doctor*?' She frowned. 'That is...most progressive.'

'They seem happy enough.' I was beginning to take a severe dislike to this lady.

'Hmm.' The slave came back with the chair, plus another couple of lads carrying a small table and a wine cup. She ignored them as they set the things down. I gave the chair-carrier a nod of thanks, and sat. 'Now. How can I help you?'

'With the details of your husband's death, if you will. My condolences, by the way. It must've been a great shock to you.'

'Thank you. Yes, yes it was.' If ever a line was delivered offhand, that was the one. *Family pet.* 'Terrible.'

'It happened just under two months ago, I understand.'

'More or less. I can't recall the exact date.'

'He was, ah, found on part of your property.'

'That's right. Not here; most of our land, the part under commercial cultivation, at least, is to the west of the city. Seemingly he'd ridden over to check on how the grain harvest was progressing. I'm not sure exactly where; Gratius can tell you that, if you're interested.'

'Gratius?' Oh, right, Quirinius had told me about him. 'Your husband's factor, yes?'

'Indeed. And has been for the past fifteen years. Decimus brought him with us when we came out from Rome.'

'And, uh, "seemingly"?'

She looked blank. 'I'm sorry. I'm not quite with you.'

'You said "*seemingly* he'd ridden over". You don't know for sure?'

'Ah, I see. No, that was definitely his intention, as far as I'm aware, at least from what the slaves told me. But Decimus and I didn't really see much of each other, had not done for several years. We lived our separate lives, for the most part. Quite amicably, I assure you; this is a big house, and such a thing is easily possible.'

Well, I'd be having a talk with Sextus Gratius soon, anyway; in fact, he was the next contact on my list. And Lepida had said the two lived apart, practically speaking. But gods! Just the offhand way she referred to her relationship with her husband, or lack of one, rather, sent a chill down my spine.

'Fair enough,' I said. Now we got to the tricky part. I lifted the wine cup and took a preliminary sip, then a bigger mouthful. Not bad; not bad, at all. If it was local – and it well might be – then we were almost talking Alban standard here. Maybe we weren't as far out in the sticks, wine-wise, as I'd thought we'd be. I set the cup down. 'Did he have any enemies at all, that you know of? Anyone who might've wanted him dead?'

'Decimus? Good heavens, no!' Too fast, and too glib; she must've been expecting the question, sure, because it was the obvious one to ask, but there was still that tell-tale blink that suggested she was being economical with the truth. Or at least that there was something she thought it was better I shouldn't know. 'He was a highly-respected member of the community, and universally liked. If you want my honest opinion he was set upon.'

'"Set upon"?'

'By brigands. We do have them, especially in the inland regions. And of course at that time of year – the main grain harvest – there are a lot of itinerant workers. Foreigners, you know, from beyond the province's boundaries. They shouldn't be allowed in, but they are because there is simply too much work, over too short a season, for our own field slaves to cope with, and then when the harvest is over they simply go back to wherever they came from. Believe me, Corvinus, and I'm dreadfully sorry to say this, but I very much doubt you've had a wasted journey, and my husband's killer will never be found.'

Uh-huh. Well, I supposed she could be right. I didn't know enough about local conditions to comment on her facts, but the way she'd put things certainly seemed reasonable. I'd have to bring the subject up when I talked to Gratius. No doubt he'd know how likely it was.

'Okay, I said. 'Moving on. Domitia Lepida told me you were planning to return to Rome shortly. That true?'

'Yes, it is. I can't see, though, why it should have any bearing on my husband's death.'

'Nor do I. Still, for all I know it might. I'm only collecting information at the moment, whether it seems relevant or not.'

'Very well.' She gave her mantle another twitch. 'Yes, as I said, it's perfectly true, in fact the arrangements are almost complete. Decimus bought a property on the Quirinal last year through his agent back home, and in his last letter the man said that he and the owner had agreed on a price for a villa and country estate near Veii. Then of course our elder son Publius is engaged to an ex-consul's daughter, and he has every hope of a political career. We had intended to return later this year, before the sea lanes close for the winter, but naturally now that will have to wait until the matter of the will and the legal transfer of Decimus's assets is settled.' She frowned. 'It's most annoying, but there you are, what can you do?'

'Your elder son inherits, yes?'

Her lips formed a straight line. 'Valerius Corvinus,' she said, 'I do realise that thanks to Domitia Lepida's intervention, well-meaning although it undoubtedly was, you have both the right and the duty to ask me questions. However, I cannot see why this should entitle you to pry into our family's personal affairs. What on *earth* could my husband's testamentary details possibly have to do with his death?'

Well, if she couldn't make an intelligent guess on that score I wasn't going to enlighten her. Still–

'My apologies,' I said. 'But like I told you I'm just at the information gathering stage at present. If you feel it's too much of an imposition, then–'

'No. No, I suppose not.' Grudging as hell. 'Even so, an imposition it certainly is. Of course he inherits. As the principal heir, at least. But I and my other son Quintus are very comfortably provided for. We've certainly no complaints.'

'So what happens to your property here when you move?'

That got me another icy glare, and a meaningful delay before she answered. 'The larger part – this house and the bulk of Decimus's land holdings – will be sold, naturally. Decimus had already put out feelers to that effect, and although nothing has been formalised as yet it's all well in train. As for the remainder – grain land, mostly, with the slave force to work it – my husband thought it best to keep it on as an overseas investment. But again if you should need, for some reason which I cannot begin to fathom, any detailed information on that subject then Gratius can provide it far more readily than I can.'

'Your two sons live here in the villa with you?'

'Yes. Yes, they do. They have their own private suites. Why do you ask?'

'I thought I might have a word with them, if they're around.'

She drew herself up. 'Valerius Corvinus, this borders on impertinence! Neither of my sons was at all involved in this business in any way, and so they cannot have any information concerning it that you do not already possess. Now I think this interview is at an end.'

I sighed, mentally. Okay; maybe I had been pushing things just a tad. Even so, there was something there that shouldn't be, if everything was as much on the level as the lady claimed it was, that I would bet on. I stood up.

'Thank you for your help, Verania,' I said formally. 'Believe me, I'm very grateful. And again, my condolences on your loss.'

This time she didn't bother to answer. Well, I'd done my best, and if the lady's nose was out of joint that was just too bad. I left.

Next port of call, Sextus Gratius. Which meant, this time, a serious hike: the address Quirinius had given me was on the edge of the harbour district in the south part of town, about a mile and a half away, in other words. Still, there was a fair slice of the day left, and I could fit a talk with him in reasonably easily before heading back home for a sunset dinner. Besides, it'd give me a chance to see more of the city; I could even, since it was on my way, check out Quirinius's wineshop recommendation.

Cladus's wineshop looked promising: big, as those places go, with a walled garden with palm-tree-shaded benches to the side. Even so, it was pretty well full up, but that's always a good sign. I sussed out the garden – benches all taken, unfortunately – then eased my way through the press to the counter and squeezed into the only available space.

The barman came over.

'Yes, sir,' he said. 'What can I get you?'

I looked at the board; none of the names were familiar, so presumably the wines on offer were all local.

'No idea,' I said. 'But nothing that's made out of dates, OK?' He grinned. 'What would you recommend?'

'The Carpian's good. That's the one I'd choose myself.'

'Fair enough, make it the Carpian. Just a cup'll do.' He poured it, I paid, and sipped: more than fair, a bit on the light side and not up to the standard of the wine I'd had at Verania's, but then I hadn't expected it would be. And I certainly couldn't fault the flavour. I turned round, put my elbows on the counter and leaned back to take in the atmosphere.

The door opened, and a big guy came in. I expected him to go straight to the counter, but he looked around for a bit and then made for the table next to me, where two or three punters were chatting over their wine. They glanced up at him without showing much interest and went on talking. The guy put his hand on the nearest punter's shoulder and pulled him round.

The bar went quiet. I straightened, and like everyone else in the place watched developments with interest.

'Your name Syrus?' the guy said. 'The property dealer?'

The three punters were on their feet now. The other two made a move towards the big guy, but his target – he was pretty sizeable himself – held up a hand and stopped them.

'That's me,' he said quietly. 'Aponius Syrus. What's your problem?'

'It's not me who has the fucking problem, pal, it's you. You swindled my father.'

'Is that so?' The man still hadn't raised his voice. 'Tell you what, friend, you let go of my shoulder or I'll break your arm. Then if you want to talk we'll take it from there.' The big guy hesitated, then lowered his hand. 'Good. Now. I haven't swindled no one, to my certain knowledge. What's this about?'

'Two months back you bought the bakery belonging to my father. Titus Maenius. Right?'

'I did. And paid for it at the price we agreed on. Legal sale, duly witnessed, all fair and above board. So?'

'Fair, my arse! What you paid was half what the place was worth, and you know it!'

'The place was falling apart, and as far as being a bakery goes it hadn't turned out a loaf in years. The price was fair, better than fair, and your father was happy with it. So get off my back.'

'What about the land? City centre, prime site. You saying that didn't count?'

'I'm not saying nothing at all, friend. You're the one doing the shouting. Your father was the legal owner, I did the deal with him, and that's the end of it. Now push off before I lose my temper.'

The big guy just stood there, arms by his side, fists working. Then without another word he turned and left. The three punters sat down and got on with their wine like nothing had happened.

Show, it would seem, over; short and sweet. Yeah, well, it'd been good while it lasted. General conversation resumed. I finished my wine and set the empty cup down on the counter.

'Another one, sir?' the barman said.

'No, that'll do me for the present, thanks,' I said. 'You get that sort of thing often around here?'

'Not often.' He reached under the counter and briefly brought out a hefty stick: the usual wineshop pacifier that no doubt was a feature of every bar-room in the empire. 'And if it does get out of hand then we're ready for it. I was watching him. Chummie was okay, just letting off steam.'

'Uh-huh. Thanks again. See you another time.'

I left.

Well, at least it seemed whatever else it was Carthage wasn't going to be boring.

7.

So. Onwards and upwards, or in this case downwards, to the port area where Cestius's factor Gratius hung out.

His house-cum-office, when I found it, was within shouting distance of the outer harbour's eastern quay, fifty yards off the main drag and half way along a neatly-kept alleyway that joined two of the side roads: a two-storey brick building with the office part below and the living quarters above it.

I went in, and the copy-slave at the desk immediately to the right of the door looked up and put down his pen.

'Afternoon, pal,' I said. 'Is your boss around? Sextus Gratius?'

'That would be me, sir.' An oldish guy – sixty if he was a day – wearing a freedman's cap was sitting at another, bigger desk in the far corner by the document-cubbies. 'You'll be the gentleman from Rome, yes? Looking into the master's death?'

'Yeah, that's right.' I closed the door behind me. 'Valerius Corvinus. You mind if I have a word with you? If you're not too busy.'

'No, not at all.' He stood up; not that that affected his height by all that much, because he was about the same size as Bathyllus. Just as bald, too, from what I could see of his pate beneath the cap. 'The mistress said you'd be round at some stage. Welcome to Carthage. You've just arrived?'

'Second day here. And I've already talked to the Lady Verania.' For what that was worth. 'Earlier this morning, in fact.'

'Excellent.' He turned to the copy-slave: 'You can take a break for half an hour, Quadrus. Will that be enough time for you, sir?'

'Sure. Ample.' The man got up, nodded to me and left.

'Now, pull up a stool, sit down and ask away.' He smiled. 'I'll stand, if you don't mind; I do too much sitting in my job as it is. I'm afraid I've nothing to offer at present in the way of refreshment, but if you'd care to wait I can get it from upstairs.'

'No, I'm fine,' I said. I perched myself on the edge of the copy-slave's desk. 'And I don't know enough yet to be specific over questions. Let's assume I'm starting from nothing and we'll take it from there.'

Not so much as the bat of an eyelid, which considering I'd been careful to mention that I'd already talked with the grieving widow was interesting. Evidently he was no fool, Gratius. Not that I'd expected he would be: if

Cestius's estates were as large as I'd been told they were then as the family's business manager he'd have to be well on top of his game.

'As you wish,' he said. 'It happened just under two months ago, exactly on the Ides of July, during the grain harvest. You know that the master died at quite a distance from home, on another part of the estate?'

'Yeah, that much I had got. He was found in one of his grain fields, right?'

'Broadly, yes, although "field" is not the best word, because the area involved is quite extensive.' He smiled again. 'Perhaps I should explain, if you'll bear with me. It'll give you an idea of conditions here, and it may be relevant to your investigation.'

'Fine. Go ahead.'

'Our agricultural land is north and west of the city. There is a great deal of it, several square miles, in fact, but it's made up of a number of large, independent stretches separated by land belonging to other owners. In some cases, quite widely separated; we're talking miles, you understand. It's not an ideal arrangement, of course, and it wasn't deliberate; over the years the master simply bought up suitable land as it became available, wherever it happened to be. Which means that at harvest time the various work gangs, both our own slaves and the extra contracted labour, have to be split into smaller autonomous groups over a very wide area. Causing, as you can imagine, certain potential problems.' Yeah; I was no country boy myself, but even I could see the obvious one. Leave a crowd of agricultural skivvies to their own devices and human nature being what it is the first thing they'll do is bunk off and take things as easy as they dare. Not that I blame them, mind; they're bought help, with no vested interest in a job well done, so why should they flog their guts out? 'As a result, on most days Master Cestius was in the habit of riding over himself to one or other of the stretches to check that all was as it should be.'

'And if it wasn't?' I said. 'Just out of interest.'

'Then pity help the work gang boss and his crew. I had a lot of respect for the master, but he was a bad man to cross, and no one did it twice. Still, it did ensure that we had all our grain in safely in the shortest possible time.'

'Uh-huh. He follow any sort of regular pattern? In choosing where to go on any particular day, I mean?'

'No. He chose the stretches completely at random. Quite deliberately so, of course.'

'So no one would've known on that particular morning where he was headed?'

'Oh, he wasn't as devious as all that, sir. He wouldn't have made a secret of it, particularly where his family and household were concerned. After all, why should he?'

'The place where he was found. Where was it, exactly?'

'On our most northerly stretch, about six miles from town. I can arrange for you to be taken there, if you need to see the exact spot.'

'Yeah, that would be useful.' Not that there'd be anything to see, of course, especially after this long a time. But it wouldn't do any harm, and it might spark off a few ideas. 'So. Is there anything special about that particular stretch? Anything that makes it stand out from the rest?'

He hesitated. 'No. Apart, as I said, from its being the furthest away.'

He was fudging, and it showed. 'Come on, pal,' I said. 'If there was I need to know. It might be important.'

'No, honestly. There's nothing unusual at all. Or not about the place itself, at least.'

'What, then?

'Can we come back to that, sir, if you don't mind? Believe me, I have absolutely no wish to appear mysterious, and I promise you I've no intention of hiding anything. But there are reasons, and I will explain later, before you go.'

'Fair enough.' I frowned. 'Moving on. Cestius was stabbed, yes?'

'He was. Twice, in the chest and throat.' Verania had only mentioned the first, but I couldn't in all honesty blame her, in this instance, for not being more exact. 'He must have died at once.'

'And no one saw the murder? That seems a bit odd, doesn't it, when there must've been a harvesting crew at work.'

'Not odd at all. That particular stretch is quite extensive, as I said, and that section of it had already been done. The harvesters were a good quarter of a mile away.'

'So what was Cestius doing there in the first place?'

'It's practically the only bit of shade for miles, a grove of trees with a pool. I'd imagine the master went there to eat his lunch, as he usually did when he was out in that part of the estate.'

49

'There was no sign of a struggle?'

'That I can't tell you, sir.'

'Would there be anyone who could?'

'I very much doubt it. When his slaves found the body next day they brought it straight back. And I don't think anyone has been out that way since.'

'What about motive? The Lady Verania mentioned bandits.'

'That's always possible – the mistress is right, there's no denying we do have them in the outlying districts – but I wouldn't say it was likely, myself. Not on an open stretch of grain land, and especially not at harvest time when there are plenty of people around. Besides, they'd have been after money. The master might well have had some with him, of course, but no more than you'd expect under the circumstances. It wouldn't've been worth the risk of killing him for, particularly considering his rank. And he was still wearing his belt-pouch when he was found.'

Uh-huh; something, when the lady had promulgated her theory, that she'd omitted to mention. Yeah, well, a pack of marauding brigands hadn't exactly been top of my suspect list to begin with, so I wasn't crying.

'Fair enough,' I said. 'So scratch the bandits. If not them then who? You have any ideas?' He was hesitating again, but this time I was having none of it. 'Look, this bit's important, right? I'm not asking for an accusation, but if I don't know I can't check. So give.'

'The man's name is Medar.'

'He's a foreigner?'

'Far from it; the name's local. Old Carthaginian. But he isn't a citizen in any sense of the word. In fact I don't think he belongs anywhere as such.'

'How do you mean?'

'I mentioned the contracted labour force, the work gangs we bring in to help with the harvest. Not just us, of course, all the big local landowners. They're nomads, extended family groups who live together and move from place to place, depending where the work is. Medar heads one of them.'

'And he and his group were involved in harvesting the stretch where Cestius was found, yes?'

'Yes. Yes, they were.'

'Uh-huh. So apart from the opportunity side of things what makes you think this Medar might've done it? He have some sort of grudge against the man?'

'Oh, yes. The master was responsible for the death of his son. At least, in Medar's view.'

I sat back. 'Is that so, now? You care to explain?'

'Cestius wasn't to blame, not at root. It happened about two years ago. Medar's son – Adon, his name was – was convicted of theft. The master was the local city judge that year, and he sentenced him to a flogging. Nothing too drastic, but half way through the boy collapsed and died. Medar's neither forgotten nor forgiven.'

Well, that would do it, right enough; we had one prime suspect, at any rate. 'You know where I'd find this Medar?'

'Not exactly. As I said, the gangs move around, and they tend to set up camp close to wherever they're working. But there's still a lot of harvesting going on, of one kind or another, and the chances are they're somewhere in the area. Leave it with me, sir. I'll make enquiries, and if I find him I'll let you know.'

'That'd be great. We're staying at Cornelia Alba's house in the Astarte district, by the way. You know it?'

'I do indeed. Very well, and at first hand. Cornelius Albus was a particular friend of mine, a sound scholar and one of the most knowledgeable men in the city. You'll be very comfortable there, I'm sure.'

'You, ah, know his daughter, then?'

Another hesitation, but having met the girl myself and knowing something of her history from queen-bitch-slagmistress Lautia I'd been half-expecting it. 'Elissa? Yes, of course. Charming girl.'

'They got on well, did they? She and her father?'

He looked puzzled. 'Of course they did. And that, if you don't mind my saying so, sir, is a very odd question.'

'Fair enough. Forget I asked it. So.' I had to go careful with the next bit, but it might be the best chance I'd get and the opportunity was too good to let slip. 'You been with the Cestius family for long?'

'Practically all my life. I was a slave in the master's uncle's household in Rome until he died some eighteen years ago, latterly in charge of the old man's accounts. Then, when he freed me in his will, Master Cestius took

51

me on and brought me out here with him as his factor. I've managed the family estates ever since.'

'You know them all well, then? The family as a whole, I mean.'

'Naturally.' He was frowning slightly now. 'How not?'

'Indeed. Look, Gratius, I'm levelling with you here. I've just arrived, my knowledge of the background to this business and the people involved in it is practically zero, and the only way I'm going to improve on that this side of ten years from now is to ask questions. Sometimes embarrassing, interfering questions that under normal circumstances would quite rightly have me sent packing with a flea in my ear. Yes?'

'I suppose so.' He was guarded.

'Fine. So tell me, if you will, about your late master's surviving kin. Anything you like, that you think might be relevant and that I should know, with the assurance that it won't go any further. I don't sit in judgment, either. Can you do that?'

The frown deepened. 'I'm sorry, sir,' he said. 'You'll forgive me, I hope. I appreciate your reasons for asking, and your right to do so under the circumstances, but I'm afraid I can't comply. Not if, as I assume, you expect me to betray confidences or tell you things that may be to their disadvantage.'

Bugger; I'd hit the Old Retainer problem head on. And judging by the tone of finality in his voice he wasn't going to shift all that easily. Still, from the defensive attitude he'd taken straight off I could make certain assumptions of my own, and after my interview with Widow Verania, not to mention what Domitia Lepida had told me before I'd come out, I was pretty sure that all hadn't exactly been sweetness and light where the domestic side of Cestius's life was concerned. Besides, like I said, the guy was probably the best source I was likely to get for the back-stairs stuff. I couldn't just let the opportunity slip only for the asking.

'I appreciate that,' I said carefully. 'Even so, I'd be grateful for anything you can give me in the way of background. Anything at all.' Start on safe ground. Or what I hoped was safe ground. 'Cestius had two grown-up sons, right?'

I felt him relax; good choice. 'Yes. Publius and Quintus, Publius being the elder. Master Publius is twenty-five, his brother is three years younger.'

'They live at home?'

He smiled. 'Valerius Corvinus, if you've talked to the mistress you'll have seen the Cestius villa. It's extremely large, the biggest property for miles around, easily big enough for each member of the family to have their own very private suite and live their own lives, completely separate from the rest.' Including the married pair, naturally, but I wasn't going to risk touching on that side of things yet awhile. 'So yes, they do. Of course, Publius is engaged to be married shortly, in Rome, so whatever happens that arrangement will change.'

'Right. Verania mentioned that. In fact, she said the whole family were planning to move back to Italy permanently.'

'Yes, indeed. The master had already bought a house in the city and was negotiating for a country estate near Veii. That, I think, is practically settled now. The master's death will delay things, of course, but we should be home by next summer at the latest.'

'"We"? You're going as well?'

'Naturally I am, unless Publius as the master's heir decides otherwise. The intention at present is to sell up almost completely here and use the money to buy land in Italy adjoining the Veian estate, which I will manage. Quite sensible, in my view. The master was very much a hands-on owner. He always took a great personal interest in the business side of things, and he would not have been at all happy to return home leaving the estates in their present form under the absolute control of a factor, even a long-standing one such as myself.'

'And what about Publius? You think he'll want to do things any differently?'

'He might, but I very much doubt it. There's nothing to keep him here, and if he's aiming at a career in politics – as I think he is – then he will want a firm Italian base.'

'You happy about this yourself? Going back to Italy, I mean, after being here for so long?'

'It's only been fifteen years, sir, and at my age in retrospect that doesn't seem such a terribly long time. Yes, I'll have some regrets, but Carthage has never really been my home as such. And I was born near Veii. My father had a small farm outside Crustumerium, so I'll be on home ground, as it were.'

'You weren't born a slave?' I said.

53

'Oh, no. I told you, I've been with the master's family almost all my life, but I was born free. My father got into debt, I was the youngest of five sons, and so he had to sell me. I must have been, let me see, five or six at the time.'

Shit. With his age, his shortness and above all his lack of hair the guy was almost a Bathyllus lookalike. And now it turned out that their histories meshed to a degree as well. 'So what's he like, Publius? As a person in his own right, I mean?'

Gratius hesitated. Bugger, we were back to the pussyfooting around. Which, I suppose, was informative in itself, but still. 'Much like any other rich young man of his age,' he said. 'Here or elsewhere.'

'Girls, booze, gambling and hunting, right?' I said. 'Not necessarily in that order. No problem, pal. Been there, done that myself.' Well, I had to admit that, as far as my personal past went, the last one hadn't really figured apart from its tie-up with the first, but that more or less covered the predictable spectrum for the lad-about-town of whatever generation.

Gratius smiled. 'Yes, sir. Marriage and a career to work at will settle him, I'm sure – at least that's what his father hoped – but that's young Master Publius to a T. He has no real bad in him, though, of that I can assure you.'

No doubt time and further enquiry would show. But reading between the lines – and particularly in the light of that unsolicited assurance – Cestius's son and heir was no moral paragon. Interesting. 'What about his brother?' I said. 'Quintus, was it?'

'Yes, that's right.' The smile was definitely there now, in fact the old man was almost beaming; we'd obviously moved on to his favourite family member. 'A completely different kettle of fish, young Master Quintus. He was always a very quiet, serious boy. Sensitive. Oh, don't get me wrong, sir, I mean that in a very positive way. There's nothing soft or effeminate about Quintus, he's simply his own man, as strong-minded in his way as his father was, and always has been from a child. He's a great one for books, especially history, and as that happens to be my own particular field of interest I tend to empathise with him. He's quite a scholar in that area, too, not just a dilettante. In fact, he was the closest thing my friend Albus had to a protégé.'

'Cornelius Albus was a historian?'

'Didn't I tell you that? No, possibly I didn't, as such. But yes, that was the main reason for our own friendship. He was particularly interested in local history – the clash with Rome, in its latter stages – from the Carthaginian point of view. Fascinating, and I'm afraid not altogether showing our political ancestors to their best advantage, morally speaking.'

Yeah, I'd believe that, although about all I knew on the subject was that our poker-rectum'ed arch-statesman *par excellence* at the time, Marcus Porcius Cato, had finished all his speeches in the Senate, on whatever subject, with the words: 'And my further opinion, gentlemen, is that we ought to destroy Carthage'. Ah, well, you don't get to be masters of the world by being nice.

'Fair enough,' I said. Then, keeping my voice carefully neutral: 'So. Moving on to the Lady Verania. What can you tell me about her?'

His face shut. 'You've met the mistress yourself, sir,' he said. 'Surely you can make your own assessment, if you think it's necessary.'

'For about fifteen minutes in total.' I was equable. 'No time at all, compared with your own fifteen years. And yes, I do think I need to know something of her as a person. She was Cestius's wife, after all.'

'Eighteen years, sir. I spent three years as the master's business manager in Italy before he moved here.'

'Eighteen, then.' I waited. Nothing. 'Come on, pal, I'm no prude. I told you, I have a job to do here, an official job, so help me do it, okay? All I'm interested in is building up a background to the case; I don't judge, and I don't tattle.' Still nothing; he might just as well have frozen. 'Fine. I'll start with what I do know, then, or think I know, and we'll take it from there. According to her friend Domitia Lepida in Rome, and from what I gleaned when I talked to the lady herself, she and her husband were estranged long term. Amicably so, but still. That right?' He didn't answer, but his lips tightened. 'I also know, from Lepida, that she...well, let's say she's in the habit of making her own amusements with certain gentlemen below her status. Or have I got that wrong?'

He was quiet for a long time. Then he said softly: 'Valerius Corvinus, if it's dunghill gossip you want then I really am not willing to provide it. No doubt you can find the answers to all your questions on that subject elsewhere. Now I'm sorry, but I've told you all I know for the present. As I said, I'll do my best to locate the man Medar for you and send word if and when I'm successful, but I think otherwise we should end this interview here.'

Hell. I stood up. 'Okay,' I said. 'Believe me, I'm grateful for your help. If there's anything else you can think of, anything at all, then–'

'Then I'll be in touch. Of course I will.'

As dismissals went, they didn't get any more definite.

'Fine,' I said. 'Thanks again.'

I left.

8.

There wasn't really anything I could do further at present, or at least nothing I could think of, so I set off home, taking it slow to get more of an idea of the place.

Like I say, it was much more open and a hell of a lot tidier than Rome, which made sense considering it'd been laid out mathematically as opposed to thrown together any old how over the centuries by guys who thought formal town planning was for Greeks and cissies, and wouldn't've recognised a *groma* if they'd found one in their breakfast porridge. You could actually walk in a straight line, more or less, from one side of it to the other without the topography throwing you a googly every five minutes and see the sky above you as more than a narrow slit between the buildings.

It didn't smell, either, which – particularly in summer when the Tiber's low – is one of Rome's most striking and less amiable features.

All the same, give me Rome any day. Carthage felt just too *new*, a nice, squeaky-clean, modern city with all the mod cons present and correct, and no sense of history. Even the people looked nice, which is something you could never say about your average Suburan: he might not be capable of hurting a fly, and be a doting father to his curly-headed, apple-cheeked kids, but he still looks as if he'd happily murder his grandmother and sell her on for cats'- meat.

Not that I was complaining, mind. Nice I can take, in small doses, and as far as places go I've been in far worse.

When I got to the house Perilla was in the study, examining the book-cubbies, of which there were more than you could comfortably shake a stick at.

'Oh, hello, Marcus, you're back,' she said. 'Did you have a successful day?'

'Yeah, well, yes and no.' I set the cup of wine that Bathyllus had had waiting for me when I came in on the side-table and lay down on the reading couch. 'A bit of a mixture, really.' I told her about the interviews with Verania and Gratius. 'I suspect getting information out of the locals is going to be about as easy as pulling teeth.'

'Is that so? Personally I haven't had any difficulties so far.'

I frowned. Shit; she was looking smug as the cat that not only got the cream but legal rights of ownership to the dairy into the bargain. Always a bad sign. 'How do you mean?' I said.

'Only that I spent a large part of the morning with Lautia.'

'You did *what?*'

'Oh, yes. We've become quite chums, actually. Her word, not mine.'

'Perilla, you can't stand the woman, and judging by events yesterday evening it's absolutely mutual. Why the hell should you–?'

'You're always telling me the best place to pick up local gossip is the local wineshop, dear. That may be true if you're a man, but trust me an all-girls-together chat over a cup of honey wine has the average wineshop beaten hands down. Particularly if your confidante is a five-star cat like Lautia. I had to grovel, of course, initially at any rate, and paint you in very unflattering colours, but it was well worth it in the end.'

'Why should she even let you past the door, lady?'

'Oh, there's no mystery there, not where the Lautias of this world are concerned. You are an imperial procurator, after all, sent here at the personal request of the emperor. That makes you – or me, rather, as your wife – the social catch of the season. She was hardly likely to tell her door-slave to spit in my eye, now, was she?'

'I suppose not.' I grinned. 'As long as you don't expect us to take up any dinner invitations. So. What did you get?'

'First of all – and most important – your Verania's current romantic interest is a gladiator by the name of Gaius Cluvius Scarus.'

'Three names? He's a freedman?'

'No. Actually he's free born, and from a respectable local family. According to Lautia – who, I grant you, is not your most charitable informant – he's a thoroughly bad lot who got himself into debt several years ago. Not for the first time, by any means, or simply that, so the result was that his family washed their hands of him.'

Yeah; it happens. And one of the ways out – drastic, sure, but it suits the wilder spirits – is to contract yourself for a given number of years to a gladiatorial school, which in exchange pays your debts for you. That's assuming, of course, that you're professional sword-fighter material in the first place: no school is going to fork out good money just to see their new boy cut down in his first bout, and from the rookie's point of view he needs to be pretty confident that he can come out at the other end of the deal with all his bits intact before he signs on the dotted line.

'He must be pretty good,' I said. 'As a gladiator, that is.'

'Oh, yes, he is, very; the local school's star attraction, in fact. He has quite a following.'

Uh-huh; that made sense, too, particularly where women were concerned. Successful gladiators are a magnet for a certain kind of high-class lady out for a bit of extramarital excitement. And if the guy was freeborn, from a good family, the liaison wouldn't involve the same degree of social stigma that it would've done had he been a slave, which is usually the case. At least, so long as the affair was managed discreetly. In public, Verania's high-class women friends – who would not, of course, include Perilla's new chum – would turn a blind eye; in private, they were more likely to envy her than turn their noses up.

'Second?' I said.

'Mm? Oh, yes. Not quite as scandalous, this one, but interesting none the less. Cestius's elder son, Publius, is a bit of a black sheep too. Girls and gambling, mostly, the girls being mainly of the gold-digging variety and the gambling very much on the debit side. It caused a bit of tension between him and his father.'

'A *bit* of tension?'

'Yes. No more than that, I think. If there had been – for example, the possibility of disinheritance – then I'm sure Lautia would have been very happy to tell me. Besides, he's contracted now to make a good marriage into a rich consular family and likely to move fairly rapidly up the political ladder. That would be reason enough to forgive a few minor peccadilloes, surely.'

'Yeah, I'm sure it would. Mind you, according to Gratius the guy's all of twenty-five. Most youngsters of his class go through the wild oats sowing in their mid to late teens. If it's not an ingrained trait by his age I'd've expected him to have come out the other end.'

'Perhaps he has. After all, as I say, he's engaged to be married and start off on a career. And don't forget Lautia will always put the blackest interpretation on things.'

'Uhuh. Fair point. Still, we'll add it to the bag. Well done.' I took a swallow of the wine. It wasn't familiar, but not bad at all; I'd have to ask

Bathyllus where he'd got it from, and what it was called. 'Did she say anything more about Cornelia, by the way? Or about how her father died?'

'No, of course not. And I didn't ask. Why should I? It's not relevant to your investigation, is it?'

I shrugged. 'Not that I know of. Even so, I've always been suspicious of coincidental deaths.'

'This one wasn't coincidental, dear. Or not in the sense you mean. There's no reason whatsoever to think it was anything other than an accident.'

'True.' I was frowning. 'Even so, his name's cropped up pretty regularly so far.'

'But of course it has. We're staying in his house and he was a well-known local figure. Anyone you talk to who knows that is bound to mention him. Actually, though, I've just been browsing through his library. Did you know he was a historian? Judging by his collection – and it's a very impressive one – interested primarily in Carthage's final period. The fifty or so years from Zama to the final destruction, I mean.'

'Yeah, Gratius said. They were good friends, seemingly. And according to him Cestius's younger son Quintus was a protégé.'

'Was he, indeed?' She smiled. 'A different person from his brother, then.'

'So it would appear.'

'So. What now? Where the case is concerned.'

'We've got this Medar character, certainly. From what Gratius told me about him he's a clear front runner at present, and I'll talk to him as soon as Gratius finds him for me. Your Cluvius Scarus sounds interesting, too. I can go on over to the gladiatorial school, look him up, see whether he might fit the frame.'

'You think he's a possibility?'

'Pass. It's far too early yet to be thinking in terms of definite suspects, apart from Gratius's Medar, of course, who's so obvious it's embarrassing. Still, if Scarus is Verania's current lover then he's definitely in the game. Her son Publius will inherit the bulk of the estate, sure, but there'll be a fair amount of collateral, and if the guy is freeborn and from a good family there's no reason why he shouldn't've had his eye on marrying a rich widow and engineered things accordingly. We'll just have to see how he

60

shapes up in the flesh. How about you? You got any plans for how to spend your time?'

'Actually, I have. I thought of getting in touch with Cornelia and asking her if she'd show me the sights. It might discourage Lautia from getting too friendly, and besides I suspect the child needs taking out of herself.'

Uh-huh. From the too-bright tone in her voice I suspected there was a bit of rationalisation going on here, maybe even a tad of self-deception. Her use of the word 'child' was a giveaway: Cornelia wasn't all that old – I'd guessed late teens, early twenties – but she wasn't a child. Not in years, anyway, and that was the point. And I hadn't seen many signs, during our short acquaintance, that she needed taking out of herself, either; if anything, barring the strangeness, she'd been perfectly at ease and in command of the situation throughout. What we'd got here were the lady's maternal instincts kicking in. I hadn't been alone in mentally comparing the girl to our own Marilla when we first found her, although I hoped I was wrong and that was where the comparison ended. Still, striking up a friendship with her couldn't do any harm. Quite the reverse.

'That sounds great,' I said. 'You could–'

There was a discreet knock at the door and Bathyllus came in.

'Meton was wondering if you'd care to eat early, sir,' he said.

'Sure. Any time.' It suddenly occurred to me that I hadn't had anything since breakfast, and I was starving. 'He say what's on offer?'

'Fish, I understand. He was most impressed with the local fish market this morning and came back with a selection.'

'Marvellous,' I said, and meant it: what Meton could do with really fresh, really good fish was the subject of poetry. It was part of what made the perpetual strain of putting up with the evil-minded sod worthwhile.

The case could wait until tomorrow.

9.

I'd just finished breakfast on the terrace the next morning – no sign of Perilla, of course; she wouldn't be stirring for another hour – and I was wondering where to make a start when Bathyllus came through with a stranger in tow; from his dress and general appearance, a slave, and not a household one, at that.

'This is Spadix, sir,' he said. 'Sextus Gratius sent him, with his compliments.'

'That so?' I bunched up my napkin and laid it on the table. 'He give you a reason, Spadix?'

The guy nodded. 'I'm to take you to where we found the master's body, sir,' he said.

'Fair enough.' Quick work, on Gratius's part, but then he'd struck me from the first as the efficient type. Well, that was my day sorted for me, or at least some of it.

'Brought a horse for you, 'case you didn't have none of your own handy. That be okay?'

'Sure. It's quite a distance, I understand.'

'That it is, sir, better'n six miles. 'S a good time to go though, 'fore the sun gets up proper. Coming back'll be on the warm side, mind.'

'Uh-huh.' Bugger; I wasn't looking forward to this. I'm no horseman, and twelve or more miles there and back in the heat I could do without. Still, it had to be done, if only for the sake of completeness. 'Right, pal. I'm done here now. Let's get started.'

'I've packed some wine and a water-skin in the saddlebags, sir,' Bathyllus said. 'Also some bread, cheese and olives in case you want them.'

Well, I might fry but I wouldn't starve. That, at least, was nice to know.

The frying part was right on the button: early in the day or not, once we'd left the city with its cooling sea breeze and were out in flat, open country it got hot as a baker's oven, and I was glad of the broad-brimmed straw sun-hat that Bathyllus had added to the supplies. Spadix, plodding along on his mule beside me, was bareheaded, and although like me he was sweating buckets the guy didn't look too unhappy; no doubt the fact that, from what I could see of it, his skin had the colour and consistency of boot-leather had a lot to do with it. The local flies, who seemed to have decided *nem. con.* that we were the best source of moisture currently on offer and were making the most of the opportunity, didn't seem to worry him unduly either. Evidently they bred their outdoor slaves heat-proof in Carthage.

I was impressed with the countryside, mark you. Like I said, the African coast has some of the most fertile ground in the empire, and together with Egypt and Sicily it supplies Rome with most of her corn. That particular crop had been harvested for the time being, sure, but there were gangs of slaves with oxen ploughing up the stubble ready for the next sowing, and other fields filled with lines of fruit trees, trellised vines and vegetables.

The sun was well up in the sky when Spadix pointed ahead of us.

'There's the place now, sir,' he said.

I could see what Gratius had meant when he said it was the only real shade for miles: a grove of date-palms surrounded by what I've always thought of as 'general bosk'. Cestius wouldn't't've chosen anywhere else for his lunch break, or whatever he was doing. And the implication was, of course, that anyone who knew he'd come out that day in this direction would know that, too. Given that he had murder in mind from the start, our chummie – whoever he was – wouldn't have to worry about stalking his victim, looking for his best opportunity; the stage was already set, and all he'd've had to do was turn up.

We rode into the cover of the trees and dismounted. Again like Gratius had said, there was a pool in the centre of the grove, quite a big one and from the look of it pretty deep, so probably fed from an underground spring. The beasts moved over to it straight off and got their heads down to suck up the water.

'Found him over there, sir.' Spadix nodded towards one of the trees set a bit back from the pool.

'You found him yourself?' I said.

'Yeah. Me and a couple of mates.'

I went to look. No signs of the killing, obviously; there wouldn't be, of course, not after all this time, but I had to go through the motions here, if only for my own satisfaction. The base of the tree was screened either side by bushes and in front by the bulk of the grove itself, so anyone sitting there would have no view of the surrounding countryside. Given that

Cestius had no suspicion that he was in any kind of danger – which seemed a reasonable assumption – then taking him by surprise would've been easy-peasie.

'And he'd been stabbed, right?' I said.

'That's right, sir. Blood everywhere, there was, all over the place. My mate Simo, he boaked his guts out when he saw.'

Thank you, thank you for that valuable additional snippet. 'He'd been eating?' I said. Then, when Spadix frowned and opened his mouth to answer, I added hastily: 'Your master, I mean.'

'Oh. Him. Yeah. Yeah, he had. There was a few bits and pieces lying around, bread and cheese and such. Bit of wine, an' all.' He looked slightly uncomfortable; I suspected that he and his mates, once they'd got over their shock and nausea, had shared out what was left of the master's picnic amongst themselves. Ah, well, slaves – the outdoor variety, especially – need to grab whatever chance of a free meal comes their way, whatever the circumstances. And the wine would've been first rate, far better than the watered-down vinegary stuff that they'd be used to.

Well, that was more or less all I could expect to get; not much, I grant you, in exchange for a very uncomfortable couple of hours in the saddle and the prospect of an even more unpleasant ride back, but it couldn't be helped; at least that box was ticked and I could move on. 'Right,' I said. 'Let's see what we've got in the way of a picnic and then we'll start on back.'

'That's okay, sir.' Spadix went over to the mule, who'd had his fill of water and was chewing on one of the bushes, and unhitched the saddle-bag. 'Your man give me some bread and cheese of my own. Wine, too.'

'Fine.' I unhitched my own lunch and we settled down next to the pool to eat. 'What was he like to work for, by the way? Your Master Cestius?'

'He was okay, sir.' Spadix took a clasp-knife from his belt-pouch, opened it and cut a slice from a lump of cheese. 'Din't have much to do with him myself, mind. General gardening duties, that's me. He liked to get his own way, mark you, an' he was the very devil if you got the wrong side of him. Even to family, if what I've heard's true. Still, we've all got our faults, haven't we?'

'Yeah, I suppose we do at that.' So; quite the homespun philosopher at bottom, our Spadix. And I hadn't missed that bit about family, either. 'How about the mistress?'

He chuckled. 'Oh, she's a proper tartar, that one. You don't cross Mistress Verania, neither, not if you want to keep the skin on your back. Even the master kept well clear of her, an' I din't blame him.'

'They lived completely separately?'

'Now that I couldn't say for sure, not being part of the household proper. But they had their own quarters ever since I can remember, an' far as I know they kept to them. Tell you the truth, why they stayed together at all was a mystery to me, but there you are, nobs live by their own rules. Saving your presence, sir.'

'Uh-huh.' I set out the food that Bathyllus had packed for me on the ground: bread rolls, cheese, pickles and a respectable piece of dried sausage. 'What about the youngsters of the family? Publius and Quintus?'

'Ah, now, we're talking chalk and cheese there, sir. Master Publius, now he's always been a wild one, up to all sorts of nonsense, women, drink, gambling, the lot. Still is. You'd've thought he'd've grown out of it by his age, him being engaged to be married an' all, but no; still in with the fastest set in town, an' spending money like water. 'Cording to Eulalia he an' his father had some rare shouting matches before the old man died. He'll be all right now, though, won't he.'

'Who's Eulalia?'

'That's my mate Simo's girl. She works in the kitchen, one of the skivvies, so she hears all the gossip. Quite a catch for Simo, her being an insider an' all, but he's a good-looking beggar, young Simo, an' he's always been good at pulling the talent. She seems happy enough, anyway.'

Gods, we were really getting a tour of life back-stairs here, and no mistake! 'Quintus is more your studious type, right?'

'Indeed, sir. Nose in a book from no age, young Master Quintus.'

'His bag's history, as I understand it.'

'That's so. Matter of fact he was in thick with the old gentleman as had the house you're staying in. He was a historrorian too. Mind you, 'cording to Eulalia again he'd got other fish to fry in that direction.'

'How do you mean?'

'Sweet on the daughter, isn't he? The Lady Cornelia.'

I stared at him. '*What?*'

'Has been for months. An' it's mutual. Not that there's been any country stuff, mark you, or least Eulalia dun't think so.' He tore off a piece of bread and chewed on it. 'Still, good luck to him, that's what I say. He's a good lad, young Master Quintus. He deserves a bit of luck'

So Quintus Cestius and Cornelia were an item, were they? Things were getting complicated. 'What did your master think about that?' I said.

'Oh, the master din't know nothing about it, or so Eulalia says. If he had done and thought it was serious he'd've hit the roof, the girl being...well, you probably know about that yourself. The mistress dun't know neither, nor no one else. Only reason Eulalia knows is 'cos the chef's girlfriend's cousin is bosom buddies with the Lady Cornelia's maid.'

Score one for the slave grapevine. Yeah, well, I've always said that as information-gathering systems go it has the imperial secret service beat six ways from nothing. Spadix would only be telling me because I was an outsider, and so presumably wouldn't have a vested interest in the matter. I reached absently for the sausage. 'You mind lending me that knife of yours for a minute, pal?' I said.

'Sure.'

He passed it over, and I cut a few slices...

Uh-huh.

'Nice knife,' I said.

He was looking uncomfortable again, and I'd bet for the same reason as last time.

'Yeah,' he said. 'It is.'

'You, ah, found it with the body, didn't you?'

He swallowed. 'Yeah. Yes, sir. Matter of fact I did.' He was watching my face, and his jaw dropped in horror. 'Oh, no, sir, nothin' like that, honest to the gods! It must've been the master's own. He had it in his hand when we found him.'

Yeah, well, that made sense: the thing wasn't a weapon, just the sort of small knife anyone might carry around with them for cutting up dried sausage or similar, the only remarkable thing about it – which was what I'd noticed – being that it had a pricey mother-of-pearl handle. In any case, if he'd been set on murder from the first our chummie would've brought a knife of his own, one a lot bigger, and he wouldn't've been stupid enough to leave it sticking in his victim's body.

Spadix was looking grey, as well he might: theft, for a slave, was a flogging offence at best, and if his owner took special exception to the circumstances – which I'd bet Verania would, if she knew – the poor bugger was for the chop.

I passed it back. 'That's okay, friend,' I said. 'No hassle. But if I were you I wouldn't flash it around. In fact, I'd get rid of it altogether.'

He nodded and swallowed again. I noticed, though, that he put the knife back in his belt-pouch: it was probably the most valuable thing he'd ever owned, or ever would own. He wasn't going to throw it away in a hurry.

'Was there any blood on it, that you saw?' I said. 'When you picked it up?'

'Could of been, sir,' he muttered. 'I din't look.'

Fair enough. Even so, the fact that Cestius had been holding it when he was attacked suggested that he had at least tried to fight back. It was something to bear in mind.

We ate the rest of the meal in silence

10.

It was well into the afternoon when I got home, tired, hot, sticky and soaked with sweat. I stripped off my sodden tunic in the lobby, went straight into the bathroom and had one of the slaves pour cold water over me for five minutes. Then I got dried and changed and went back into the atrium, where Bathyllus was waiting with the wine tray.

'The mistress out, sunshine?' I said, stretching my length on the couch and taking a first restorative swallow.

'Yes, sir. The Lady Cornelia came round this morning to return her hat, and they went out together.'

'Her *hat?*' Oh, yeah, right; the sun-hat that Cornelia's pet monkey had stolen when she'd called in two days previously. That would've pleased Perilla; she'd been hunting for an excuse to make contact with the girl on her own account. 'As you were, Bathyllus. Got it, link made. She say when she'd be back at all?'

'No.' Bathyllus set the wine jug down beside my cup. 'But I think she and the young lady were planning to visit the local sights.'

Uh-huh; that made sense, although since nothing here was any more than a few decades old, and pretty well run-of-the-mill provincial standard at that, I suspected that her ulterior motive of getting to know Cornelia better had taken priority. Unless the heat got to her – which was a definite possibility – she probably wouldn't be back until close on dinnertime.

'What's this wine, by the way?' I'd been meaning to ask, but I'd forgotten every time.

'It's Utican, sir. From a small vineyard that supplies the residence. The governor's aide had a few jars sent over the day we arrived.'

'Is that so, now?' Interesting; it was far better stuff than we'd had at Galba's dinner party. I suspected that had been deliberate as well, and typical of the cheese-paring bastard: don't waste your best wine on tradespeople or inconvenient visitors foisted on you from Rome. I might've been doing him an injustice, but I didn't think so.

'Was there anything else you wanted, sir? Something to eat, perhaps?'

'No, I'll last until dinner now, Bathyllus.'

He left. It'd been a more successful day than I'd expected, thanks to Spadix's little revelation – although whether that was relevant or not only time and further furkling would tell – but a twelve-mile-plus horse ride in the heat of an African summer meant I was completely knackered. I closed my eyes just for a moment and relaxed...

'Hello, Marcus. Been back long?'

'Mmm?' I opened my eyes again. Perilla was taking off her cloak and handing it to Bathyllus. 'Oh. I'm sorry, lady, I must've dozed off. How was your sightseeing?'

'Not terribly interesting, I'm afraid.' She lay down on the other couch. 'However, I did have a very pleasant chat with Cornelia. She really is a very nice girl, and quite talkative when you get to know her.'

'Uh-huh. She confide in you about Quintus Cestius?'

'What?' She gave me a sharp look. 'No! What was there to confide?'

'Only that the pair of them are a secret item. According to one of the Cestius kitchen skivvies, that is.'

I explained.

Perilla smiled. 'Oh, I *am* glad,' she said. 'We don't really know very much about him yet, of course, but judging from what you've been told so far he seems a nice enough young man. And Cornelia needs a bit of romance in her life.'

Gods! She'd only known the girl five minutes and she was already into full mother-hen mode! I stifled a grin.

'One thing, though, Marcus.' A sideways glance, and a hesitancy. 'She is very like Marilla was, when she first came to us, I mean. The way she acts and how she speaks. It's quite frightening. And she won't talk about her father; I tried to get her to several times, but she shied away and changed the subject.'

'She may just not be over his death, like Quirinius suggested.'

'No, that's not it. Absolutely not. You weren't there to see; it wasn't grief, I'm positive of that.' She was frowning now. 'The impression I got wasn't loathing, exactly, but it was something very close.'

Hell; we had to address this problem now. 'Perilla, listen to me,' I said carefully. 'There's an important difference, right? Between this girl and Marilla. Whatever's behind this – and I grant you something is – it's water under the bridge, over and done with. When we sprang Marilla loose from the house on the Janiculan her bastard of a father was still very much alive; Cornelius Albus isn't. Poking around won't do the girl any good, quite the reverse, and it's none of our business. Let her cope with things in her own way. She seems to be doing none too badly.'

Perilla sighed. 'Yes, dear, you're right. Of course you are. Even so–'

Bathyllus buttled in. 'I'm sorry to interrupt, sir, but you have a visitor. Sextus Quirinius.'

'That's fine, sunshine,' I said. 'Show him through. And bring another cup.'

Quirinius appeared a moment or two later, followed by Bathyllus with the extra wine cup.

'Good afternoon, Corvinus. Lady Rufia,' he said. 'I'm sorry to disturb you so close to dinner time, but I thought I'd call in. See how things are going and if there was anything at all you needed.'

'Actually, there is, now you're here, pal,' I said. 'Pull up a stool and have some wine. Which, incidentally, I was meaning to thank you for. It's lovely stuff.'

'The Utican?' He sat, and Bathyllus handed him the filled cup. 'Yes, it is good, isn't it? Very. I'm glad you like it; it's from a small vineyard that's supplied the residence exclusively for over a century. I, ah, don't think the governor will miss one or two jars, but if it's all the same to you we won't mention it to him. Agreed?'

I grinned; he was a nice lad, Quirinius, and totally wasted on a prick like Galba. 'Yeah,' I said. 'I think I can manage that. Agreed.'

'Good. Now. What can I do for you?'

'This might be tricky. I need an excuse to talk to Cestius's two sons. Publius and Quintus.'

Quirinius frowned. 'You don't think they had anything to do with his death, surely?' he said.

'No. I've no reason to, absolutely none. But at the moment they're just names, and that doesn't sit easy. Problem is, I've already had my head bitten off by the widow for asking if I could have a word with them, so I suspect that any sort of official approach would go down like a slug in a salad.'

'Corvinus, you're the emperor's personal representative, investigating Cestius's death on his specific orders. If you say you need to talk to them – or to anyone, for that matter – then refusal isn't an option.'

'Yeah, I know. But pulling rank isn't going to put them into a very co-operative state of mind, is it? Oh, sure, the chances are that neither they or their mother played any part in their father's death' – I had my fingers firmly crossed at this point; me, I wouldn't be making any predictions – 'but talking to them's something that has to be done. There may be information they can give me that they think is innocent but turns out to be important. Understand?'

'Of course.' He was still frowning. 'Well, then. Meeting Publius is simple. He spends most of his evenings at the Honeycomb.'

'That's some kind of club, presumably?'

'Yes. Frequented by the local fast set.' His lips twitched. 'Of whom I'm not one, by the way. Drinking and gambling, mostly. You might add "brothel" to the bag, but the lady who runs the place would take exception to the word. Let's just say there are a few girls on the staff who provide private specialist services to the clientele.'

'And this place is where?'

'In the Aesculapius district, not all that far from Cladus's, as it happens. The name's written up beside the door.'

'I can just walk in?'

'Yes. The club opens after sunset. You'll find there's a one-off membership fee, though. A gold piece, I think.'

'Keep the riff-raff out, yeah?'

'That's the idea. And yes, it is quite exclusive.'

'Fair enough. What about Quintus?'

'Ah. He's more difficult. He doesn't go out much, or at least not in the evenings, and as far as I know he has no set routine. I'm afraid I can't really help you there.'

'No problem.' I might be able to get to him through Cornelia via Perilla, but that connection was clearly not one to spread around. Also, of course, one to be negotiated carefully. 'No doubt I'll manage, and Publius'll be enough to be going on with for the present. Now. Cluvius Scarus.'

That got me a very circumspect look, and Quirinius cleared his throat.

'You've heard about Scarus, then?' he said neutrally.

'Verania's current bit of rough. Yeah, I know who he is. I need to talk to him too at some stage.'

'He's based at the gladiator school near the amphitheatre; that's not far from here, actually, on the edge of town. But you may see him at the Honeycomb as well.'

My eyebrows rose. 'He's a member?'

'Oh, yes. Quite a long-established one, in fact. You know he's freeborn originally, and that he sold himself to the school for five years to clear his debts?'

'Yeah. Yes, I knew that. More or less, anyway.'

'He'd been a member of the Honeycomb for several years before that. And being a successful gladiator brings its own *cachet*; you'll find that where the set he mixes with there is concerned Scarus is very much *persona grata*.'

Uh-huh. Well, that made sense: top-notch race-drivers and sword-fighters are celebrities in their own right, and even if the guy hadn't come from a good family in the first place they'd still have welcomed him with open arms.

'Thanks, Quirinius,' I said. 'Oh, one more name, one that Sextus Gratius mentioned, a guy called Medar.'

'Ah. Yes. The harvester.'

'What puzzles me is that he wasn't pulled in for the killing originally. On suspicion, at least. I mean, he's a prime suspect.'

'Oh, he was. But he claimed to have been working at the time, and his crew backed him up. There being no evidence to the contrary' – Quirinius shrugged – 'well, he was let go. And then the whole thing fell into abeyance, and that was that.'

Yeah, we'd been there already. With no one pushing for a solution to the murder – including Governor Galba – there was no point in testing the truth of his alibi, one way or the other. 'Gratius said he held Cestius responsible for the death of his son.'

'Yes, I've heard that story. But it happened before I came out here, so I've no personal knowledge of the affair.'

'Could you look into it for me? Find me someone to talk to who would know the details?'

'Of course. I'll let you know. What about Medar himself? You'll want to talk to him personally, won't you?'

'Yeah. But he moves around, seemingly. Gratius is tracking him down for me.'

'That's all right, then.' Quirinius stood up, drained his wine cup and set it on the table. 'Well, if there's nothing else you can think of at present I'll leave you to your dinner.'

'Thanks, pal.'

'Don't mention it.' He turned to go, then turned back. 'Oh, incidentally, I meant to give you one more bit of news, purely out of interest.'

'Yeah? What's that?'

'We had another killing yesterday.'

'You had *what*?' I sat up.

'Nothing mysterious. Simply a robbery that went wrong. Only I thought seeing as you're—'

'So who was it?'

'A slave-trader by the name of Justus. Appius Justus.'

'Local?'

'No, he'd only been here for a couple of days. His body was found early this morning in an alleyway near the harbour. His partner says he had a bit of cash on him when he left their lodgings yesterday evening, and his money-belt was missing.'

'Uh-huh. Partner?'

'A freedman. Laenius Cycnus.' Quirinius was frowning again. 'Corvinus, what is this? It was a straightforward mugging. They happen here, not very often and not usually resulting in a death, I grant you, but they're not all that uncommon.'

'Maybe not. All the same, I might chase it up, if that's okay.'

'If you insist, then of course it is. But I can't see why you should bother.'

'Neither do I, really. Even so. Where would I find this Cycnus?'

'He and Justus took a room above one of the harbour wineshops. The one opposite the quay where you landed, in fact.'

'Fine. Enjoy your own dinner, pal. And thanks again.'

Quirinius left, the frown still in place.

'Marcus, what on *earth* are you playing at?' Perilla said when he'd gone. 'The man is absolutely right; another murder it may have been, but it has nothing to do with Cestius's, and so it's no concern of yours.'

'Is that so, now? Well, lady, I bow to your superior knowledge. Me, I don't know at present one way or the other, whether it's connected or not.'

'For heaven's sake! Cestius died two months ago, and this what's-his-name—'

'Appius Justus.'

'Thank you. This Justus has only been in Carthage for five minutes.'

'Three days.'

'Three days, then. Don't fudge. Besides, the motive was obviously robbery. He was probably simply targeted in the wineshop, followed when he left, murdered and robbed. These things happen. As Quirinius said, there's no mystery involved.'

'So where was he going?'

'What?'

'He was a stranger in Carthage, but he went out on his own yesterday evening and got himself killed. It's a fair question: where was he going?'

'How should I know?'

'Exactly. That's the point; me, I don't know either. It's an oddity, and at this stage of the game I can't afford to ignore oddities of any sort.'

Perilla sighed. 'Please yourself, dear. If you want to waste your time chasing wild geese then go ahead.'

'I will. I also intend after dinner going to this club Quirinius mentioned, see if I can find young Publius.'

'Oh, *Marcus!*'

'I may as well do it now. Anyway, I've had my head down for a couple of hours, so I'm pretty much fresh again.'

'All right. Just don't enjoy yourself too much, will you?'

I grinned. 'I'll try not to, lady.'

That might be difficult, mind. The Honeycomb sounded quite an interesting place.

11.

I broke my usual habit and took a chair to the Honeycomb. Sensible: it was a moonless night, very few of the houses had torches burning outside them, and not knowing exactly where I was going I'd almost certainly have got lost. Besides, just in case I needed it I had the equivalent of several gold pieces in my belt-pouch, and I'd no intention of doing a Justus.

The chair lads decanted me outside the club; a largeish corner property in a street just off one of the main drags, with – as Quirinius had said – the place's name written on the wall beside the door and a mosaic of the eponymous lump of filled wax beneath it to help the less literate of Carthaginian society. Not, given the pricey membership fee, there'd be very many of those among the Honeycomb's clientele.

There was a door-slave standing outside who looked like he could break my spine with one hand and was just itching for the chance to prove it. He eyeballed me, then nodded, gave a sketchy salute, and stepped back. I went in.

A decent mosaic in the lobby, with, if I remembered my mythology, Aristaeus the bee-keeper chasing a scantily-clad Eurydice. All done very tastefully. The girl who took my cloak wasn't wearing much more. She gave me a smile and a wooden ticket.

'You haven't been here before, sir?' she said.

'No. This is my first time.'

'Then welcome to the Honeycomb. Just go straight through. Venusta will look after you.'

The place was quietly busy, which was what you'd expect of an exclusive club, although the women there – the male-female ratio was more or less evenly split – were obviously employees entertaining the paying punters. I looked around. Not bad, although definitely a provincial wannabe; the top places in Rome would have it beat six ways from nothing. Single large room, marble-tiled floor with another couple of mosaics, naturalistic this time, walls painted with architectural features and a pair of lively frescos that would've had the strait-laced faction reaching for the whitewash. Lighting by strategically-placed candelabra creating small brightly-lit islands of tables and couches while hiding the nooks and crannies at the edges in shadow; presumably the warm-up areas for the club's third function, with the main event happening up the staircase beside the bar counter at the far end of the room.

The three guys playing dice at the nearest table – from the piles of coins in front of them for pretty high stakes – glanced up at me curiously, then carried on with their game.

'Good evening, sir. Welcome to the Honeycomb. I'm Cassia Venusta.'

I turned round. The woman was at least twenty years older than the cloak-girl, and dressed accordingly. Pretty expensively-dressed, too, and her perfume was understated enough to have cost an arm and a leg. Obviously the club's owner or manageress.

'Valerius Corvinus,' I said.

Her eyes widened. 'The imperial procurator? Well, well. This is an honour.'

I grinned. 'I, uh, don't suppose it entitles me to a deduction in the membership fee, does it?' I said.

She laughed. 'No, I'm afraid not. We will be extra-specially respectful to you, though. I'll instruct the girls accordingly.'

'Deal.' I was beginning to like Venusta. I took a gold piece from my money-belt and handed it over. 'That's bang on, isn't it?'

'Yes, it is. Mind you, you do get a complimentary drink for that. Lydia on the bar will be happy to serve you it.'

'Great.'

'Enjoy your visit, Procurator. And if there's anything you need don't hesitate to ask.'

'I won't. Thanks.' She moved away and I went over to the counter. I noticed that one of the dice-playing trio had renewed his interest.

'What can I get you, sir?' The girl behind the bar counter smiled at me. 'We have quite a range of wines, local, Italian and Greek. The names are on the board there.'

I checked them through. The local varieties weren't familiar, of course, but the Italian ones were all pretty much top-notchers. Good sign.

'I'll try one of the locals,' I said. 'Which would you recommend?'

'The Membressan is good.'

'Okay. Make it a cup of that.' I leaned on the counter while she poured it. 'Is Publius Cestius in tonight, do you know?'

'You've just walked past him.' She nodded over my shoulder towards the dice-players. 'That's him, at the table near the door. The man on the left.'

I half-turned. Yeah, that made sense: the player who'd suddenly developed an interest when I'd given Venusta my name. Well, we might as well get this done and dusted. I took a sip of the wine – good choice, dry but not too dry, and spicier than the wines I was used to – and carried the cup back over to the table.

The guy was still watching me. He didn't look too friendly.

'Publius Cestius?' I said.

'That's me.' Definite reserve there, at the very least.

'Valerius Corvinus. You mind if we have a chat in private?'

He frowned, then shrugged. 'Okay. I was losing anyway. Catch you later, boys.' He scooped up the coins in front of him and replaced them in his money-belt. 'In the corner's best.'

I followed him over. There was a couch, a small table and a stool. He lay down on the couch; I moved the nearest candelabrum closer so we'd have more light and sat down on the stool.

'Now,' he said. 'What can I do for you?'

'You know who I am? What I'm doing in Carthage, I mean?'

'Yeah. You're the snoop from Rome looking into my father's death.'

Hardly a promising beginning, but I couldn't really argue with the description.

'Correct,' I said equably. 'So what can you tell me about it?'

'Absolutely nothing. I wasn't there at the time.'

'I never thought you were.' Not altogether true – the jury was still out on that one, as a possibility at least – but I wasn't under oath here. 'I just thought, as a member of the family, that you might be able to fill me in a little where the background is concerned.'

'What background?'

'Murders don't come out of nowhere, pal. If you look hard enough there're usually some signs that one is building.'

'You've talked to my mother. She'll have told you the chances are he was killed by bandits. For pure monetary gain.' The last bit came out sarcastic as hell. 'End of story.'

I shook my head. 'Uh-uh. According to your factor Gratius that's unlikely. And he wasn't robbed; when he was found he was still wearing

79

his belt-pouch with the cash intact. So let's discount that explanation, shall we?' He just looked at me. 'Thing is, what I can't get my head around is that you, the family, I mean, from what I've seen of you, don't seem to be all that bothered about getting to the truth. Now why would that be? No hassle, I'm just interested.'

'Why do you think?'

'I don't know. That's why I'm asking the question.'

'My father was a gold-plated, hundred-per-cent bastard.'

I blinked. Well, that was forthright enough. 'In what way?'

'In every way. That doesn't mean I didn't like him, mind.'

'Come again?'

'No, I take that back; *like* is the wrong word. You couldn't *like* my father, no one could, and none of us did. *Respect*'s not perfect, but it'll do. We may not have liked him, my mother, my brother and me, but we all respected him. By the gods, we did; he made sure of it.'

'You'll have to explain that.'

He frowned. 'The old man always knew exactly what he wanted. Exactly. And he made sure he got it, every scrap, whatever it took. No compromises, no arguments, no welshing. Not ever. Try to get in his way, whoever you were, family included, and he'd just walk straight over you without a second thought.'

Uh-huh. 'He sounds tough,' I said.

'Oh, he was. But it meant you knew where you were with him, always. Some things he didn't care a straw about.' He gave me a quick sideways look; yeah, his wife's infidelities, for one. 'Other things – well, he'd go to the wall over them. Us, for a start. Quintus and me. So long as we played the part he wanted us to play everything was fine. Pure sweetness and light. Step out of line just the barest fraction or try to go your own way and–' He shrugged again. 'You get the idea.'

'Yeah,' I said. 'Yeah, I think I do.'

'So you can see why we couldn't care less that he's dead, or who killed him. It means we can finally breathe.'

'Will it change things at all?'

'How do you mean? What sort of things?'

'The decision to go back to Italy, for a start. Now you're due to inherit.'

'No.' He shook his head. 'No, I'm happy with that, always have been. Carthage is okay, but it's a dead end. I've got ambitions. Political.'

'And the engagement?'

'The girl's from a consular family. Not one of the top ones, and only the suffect version, but her father's got influence in the senate.'

'You've met her, I assume. You like her?'

He looked at me in surprise. 'Vettia? Of course I've met her; I was over in Rome in the spring, sussing things out, having a look at the future in-laws and letting them have a look at me. She's okay; no great beauty, mind, and not my type, boring as hell, but the dowry's good, and like I say her dad's got political clout. I'm going to need that if I'm to get on.' He grinned. 'You can't have everything, can you?'

'No, that's true enough.' Yeah, well, and I'd just been starting to feel sorry for him, too. It just went to show. 'What about–?'

Someone had moved between us and the lamps. I looked round and up.

'Who's your friend, Publius?' the man said.

Big-boned, solid muscle from the neck down and probably up as well, the stance of a prize-fighter and just radiating Attitude with a capital 'A'. Shit; this just had to be Verania's current bit of rough, Cluvius Scarus: Quirinius had said he was a member.

'Fuck off, Scarus,' Publius said. 'This is a private conversation.'

Spoken with real venom. Interesting: clearly there was no love lost there.

The guy ignored him, hooked over another stool with a negligent foot, and sat down.

'Actually,' he said to me, 'I know who you are. Valerius Corvinus, right? The emperor's lap-dog from Rome.'

'More or less,' I said. We were going to be great buddies, Scarus and me; I could see that now.

He gave me a long stare, then turned back to Publius. 'I told you I'd be in tonight,' he said. 'Let you get your revenge. Or try to.'

'That depends,' Publius said; his hands were clenched into fists. 'Whose dice will we be playing with this time?'

Scarus's face darkened. 'You want to watch what you say, sonny boy,' he said quietly.

'Or else?'

'Or else I might tell Mummy on you.' He gave a sudden bark of laughter.

Publius stood up. 'Some other night,' he said. 'I've had enough of dice for the moment. I'll see you around, Corvinus.'

And he left. Scarus watched him go, smiling. Then he turned back to me.

'He's a bastard,' he said conversationally. 'You probably noticed. And he doesn't like me.'

'Yeah, well, I just can't understand that at all, friend,' I said. 'Still, there's no accounting for taste.'

Another bark of laughter, and he slapped me on the arm. It was like being hit with an oak plank.

'Maybe there isn't, at that,' he said. 'You want a drink?'

'Got one, thanks.'

But he was already signalling in the direction of the bar. 'Hey, Lydia! A cup of the usual for me, and a refill of whatever the Roman's having. My bill.' He turned to face me again. 'Now. You'll want to talk to me, no doubt. Decide whether it was me that did it. Killed the old man, I mean.'

Sod this for a game of soldiers. 'Did you?' I said.

'No. I couldn't have, could I? The day it happened was one before a fight day. We spend that training, or working out routines if the guy who's paying just wants a good show to please the punters, with no deaths. The whole team, sunrise to sundown with an hour's break for lunch. You can check if you like.'

Yeah, I would. Not that I thought it wouldn't square up when I did: some alibis you can't fake, and that one sounded pretty much cast-iron.

Bugger.

He was watching me, and grinning. 'Spoiled your evening, have I?' he said.

'Uh-uh. I'm glad of the information. It means I can look elsewhere.'

'Of course, I'd be a natural suspect, I know that. I was screwing Cestius's wife; still am, for that matter. Which is why Sonny Boy there hates my guts.' The drinks came over. He winked at Lydia, took his own cup and raised it. 'Cheers. To a successful investigation.'

'Thanks.' I didn't drink.

He lowered the cup. 'Come on, Corvinus! I'm trying to be nice.'

'So what happens now?' I said. 'You and Verania becoming a permanent item?'

'Marriage, you mean?' He stared at me. 'Nah! No chance! She might bed a sword-fighter, but that lady wouldn't marry one, not if she wanted to keep her reputation with her high-class friends. And if she's planning to go back to Rome – which she is – then it's even more unlikely. Not that I'm crying: we'd get tired of each other sooner or later, there's plenty around to take her place, and marriage would take all the spice out. Besides, she's too fond of getting her own way for my liking.'

'Like her husband?' I said. 'He know about you two, by the way?'

He shrugged. 'Presumably. I never asked. But I doubt if Verania made any secret of it. The boys knew, certainly.'

'And he didn't mind? Cestius, I mean.'

'Obviously not. We never had occasion to talk, so I wouldn't know.'

'He have anything going for him in that line himself?'

Scarus laughed. 'Him? No. Or if he did Verania's never mentioned it. Cestius just wasn't interested in sex of any kind. Power, now, that was a different thing. You know he didn't retire from politics in Rome altogether voluntarily?'

'Yeah, I did, as a matter of fact.' Claudius had told me something about that when we talked.

'Bastard was lucky to escape before he got the order to slit his wrists, that's the way Verania tells it, anyway. You ask me, it rankled. What we had here was a top-notch mover and shaker *manqué*.' He must've seen my expression, because he grinned. 'Come on, Corvinus! Just because I signed on for a gladiator and look the part doesn't mean I'm a complete thicko! Cestius got off on power; here he could be a big fish in a small pond and boss everyone around, whistle and watch them jump. He loved it. My guess is that's what got him killed. If you're looking for a motive you can have that one on me, free of charge.' He stood up. 'Well, I have to be off; other wannabe dice-players to skin now Publius has run away scared. It's been a pleasure talking to you. Come and watch me fight some time, okay?'

And he was gone.

Interesting.

12.

I was up late next morning, and Perilla was ahead of her usual time, so for a change our breakfasts overlapped: mine, consisting of my usual bit of bread, dipping oil and small bowl of cheese and olives, hers consisting of a three-egg omelette, half a bushel of fruit, and several rolls with honey. How she manages to put away as much as that first thing without bursting at the seams or putting on serious poundage is one of nature's greatest mysteries.

'Well, dear,' she said, quartering another pear and removing the core, 'how was your evening? Hugely enjoyable, apparently, judging by the hour you got home and the over-obvious wine-fuelled efforts you were making not to wake me.'

I grinned. 'Don't be catty, lady. It wasn't all that late, barely after midnight, I had less than half a jug, and the way you were snoring your socks off I couldn't've wakened you up this side of the Winter Festival.'

'Marcus, I do *not* snore!'

'Tell that to the neighbours.'

She ducked her head to hide a smile. 'All right. So. Was the visit a success?'

'Yeah, I'd say that. I managed to talk to both Publius Cestius and Verania's gladiator pal Scarus.'

'Did you, indeed?' She reached for the honey-pot. 'And?'

'Publius is your typical man on the make. Selfish as hell with, I suspect, about as many scruples as a Suburan landlord. Perfect credentials for the wannabe politician, in other words; he should go down a bomb in Rome. Mind you, from what I've seen of his mother and from what he told me about old Cestius it would've been a miracle if he'd turned out any different.'

'What exactly *did* he say about his father?'

I told her. 'The guy sounds a real horror. A total control freak with a vindictive streak a mile wide. Scarus suggested that that was why he was killed, that he'd finally pushed someone just a little too far, and as a working theory that has a lot going for it.'

'You think that someone could have been Publius?'

'It's possible, but I doubt it. Not on present showing, anyway. The recent changes to his life – going back to Italy, the whole betrothal business, starting out on a career – may've been his father's ideas to begin with but he seems quite happy with them. In fact, completely in favour. The push, if there was one, might've been to do with something else entirely, mind; Spadix's contact in the kitchen said the two men had had some furious arguments recently, so there had to be some serious bone of contention. In which case he'd be well in the frame.'

'His gambling?'

'Maybe. I get the impression that where gambling's concerned he's quite definitely a loser. Even so, Cestius was well enough off to mop up a few gambling debts without breaking sweat too much, and that's what rich daddies are for, after all; they may complain like hell, but they know themselves that it's nothing out of the ordinary. Things would've had to have got pretty bad between the pair of them before they justified murder, at least, they would've had to if we were talking normal father-son relations, which this time we evidently aren't. Besides, in other ways Publius was the perfect blue-eyed boy, bringing home the family bacon.' I shook my head. 'Ah, hell. The simple answer is that I can't decide about him one way or the other. We need to know more than he's giving us himself, and where that's going to come from I've no idea at present. Put a question mark over him for the time being.'

'Fair enough. How about Scarus?'

'He's even more complicated. I thought at first he was your usual muscle-bound bonehead, but he isn't; he thinks things through and he can be objective about them. His relationship with Verania, for example. He's perfectly up front about that, sure, but he's got no illusions about it being made permanent.' I frowned. 'At least, that was the impression he was trying to give because naturally it would mean that he'd no motive for killing Cestius, either on his own account or as a favour to the prospective widow.'

'You don't believe him?'

'Perilla, that is a guy I wouldn't believe if he told me the sun would rise tomorrow. He's smart. I'll bet you taking the opportunity of getting his oar in first and talking to me before I could talk to him was deliberate. He was careful to give me an alibi up front for the day of the murder, too.'

'What was that?'

'That he'd spent it, all of it, at the gladiatorial school, getting ready with the rest of the team for a fight the next day. Oh, sure, I'll check that out – he's too good a prospect just to cross off the suspect list on his own say-so – but I'll be surprised if it doesn't square. Pity; apart from this guy Medar he's the best bet we've got so far where motive's concerned. And of course given his line of business he'd have no compunction about carrying out the actual killing.' I used the last crust of bread to mop up the remainder of the oil and ate it. 'There was another interesting feature of the conversation, too, although it probably doesn't have anything to do with the murder.'

'Namely?'

'Just something he said to Publius, before the guy got up and left. They'd had a bit of a spat, with Publius practically accusing Scarus of cheating at dice, and Scarus threatened to, quote, "tell Mummy on him".'

'But , Marcus, there's nothing odd about that. Snide and nasty, I grant you – the implication that Publius was no more than a naughty child under his mother's thumb – but hardly dripping with significance.'

'Well, maybe not. It was just a feeling. For all his faults, Publius didn't strike me as a mummy's boy. For a start, when he was talking about his father he bracketed his mother, his brother and himself together on more or less equal terms, and like I say as far as the engagement and move to Rome are concerned there were no signs of arm-twisting; quite the contrary. Scarus was needling him, sure, no argument, but for that to work you have to target a genuinely weak spot. No, me, I think it was a real threat disguised for my benefit as a put-down, and Publius recognised it as such. Which was why he left straight off without any comeback.'

Perilla sighed. 'I'm sorry, dear,' she said, 'but without some proof to back it up that is simply too far-fetched. Perhaps it was just a nasty reminder that he and the mother were on intimate terms. In any case, tell her what? Publius is a grown man, in fact now his father's dead he's officially head of the family and heir to most of the estate. If he's no mummy's boy, as you say, then why should he worry about his mother's lover threatening to tell tales?'

'I don't know.' I shrugged. 'Maybe you're right. Still, there was something going on beneath the surface, that I'd swear to.'

Perilla smeared the last vestiges of the honey onto the remainder of her roll. 'Fair enough,' she said. 'So. What are your plans for today?'

'Yeah, well, I'm a bit stuck at present,' I said. 'There's Medar, of course, he's the biggie, but I'll have to wait until Gratius finds him for me. Given that he ever does, because if the guy was responsible for Cestius's death and has the sense of a newt he'll've legged it out of the province and be staying away for as long as it takes. I still have to talk to the other brother, Quintus, but I'm not sure how to manage that. I was hoping you'd be able to help there.'

'Me? How?'

'Through your pal Cornelia, of course. You'll be seeing her shortly?'

'Yes. Later today, actually. But her relationship with Quintus Cestius is supposed to be a secret. I can't just–'

'You'll find a way, Aristotle, I'm sure. Think about it. Meanwhile' – I stood up – 'I think I'll go down to the harbour, see if I can have a word with what's-his-name, the assistant to the slave-dealer who was found dead yesterday morning. Laenius Cycnus.'

'Oh, Marcus! I told you, that is a sheer waste of time! It was a straightforward mugging and robbery, nothing out of the ordinary, Quirinius said, even if the man was killed in the process. It has nothing to do with you, or with the Cestius case. Can't you think of anything more useful to do?'

I grinned. 'Uh-uh. Unless you have any bright suggestions, lady, that's all that's currently on offer. And for all we know, it's relevant in spades. I'll see you later.'

There was only one wineshop that fitted Quirinius's description; not a particularly salubrious one – although that's pretty much standard for harbour area wineshops anywhere in the empire – but no doubt the fact that it was close to where Justus's ship was moored made up for that. I pushed open the door and went in.

'Morning, sir.' The guy behind the bar was stacking wine jars. 'What can I get you?'

'I was looking for a Laenius Cycnus,' I said. 'He and his boss had a room here, I understand.'

'Ah.' His expression went serious. 'The murder, right? Terrible business, that. You'd be from the authorities, yes?'

'Yeah.' Not strictly true, of course, but I didn't think Quirinius would come down too hard on me for misrepresentation. Let alone sit-on-your-hands Sulpicius Galba. And it would simplify things in the long run. 'He still here?'

'He's staying here, aye, until after the funeral. But if you're looking for him this minute you'll probably find him at his ship.'

'And where's that, do you know?'

'Quay Six. That's to your right as you go out the door, third quay along. The "Dolphin".'

'Thanks, pal.' I half-turned to go, then changed my mind. 'As you were, no hurry. I'll have a cup of wine while I'm here.' I glanced up at the board and went for a name at random. 'Tubernucan?'

'Tubernucan it is.' He reached up a jar, and poured. I laid the necessary coins on the counter and took a sip...

Uh-huh. Maybe not Tubernucan in future, then, unless this was a particularly bad example, which given the place and the low price was eminently possible. Cat's piss came to mind. And it must've been a pretty sick cat.

'So what was he like, this Appius Justus?' I asked, shifting the cup to one side where it couldn't do any more harm.

'In himself? Big man, well-built, late fifties. Heavy beard. Italian, from his accent.' The barman hefted the jar back into its cradle. 'Pretty rough-spoken, but polite enough. And he didn't haggle over the price of the room, neither.'

Evidently, from the man's satisfied tone, sufficient to raise Justus to the status of Ideal Tenant.

'He a regular?' I said.

'Here in Carthage, you mean? I'd not seen him before myself, sir, but that don't signify. It would've depended on where his ship was berthed, which quay, like. Plenty of other places to put up around here.'

Yeah, that was true, if you weren't too fussy. Given that you wanted to stay close by the harbour renting a whole room above a wineshop would be one of the pricier options; there'd be a fair number of spare beds on offer in the private properties near the waterfront that you could get for a quarter of the price, if you didn't mind the risk of sharing them with the local fleas.

'So what happened, exactly?' I said.

'You mean the murder? Can't tell you much about that, except that it was two nights ago. He and his mate had a bite to eat, then he goes out on his own. He can't've got far, though, because old Prescius who lives in the alleyway just back of us found him on his doorstep the next morning with his throat cut and his purse missing.'

'He didn't say where he was going?'

'Not to me, sir. Why should he? Your Cycnus'll know, if anyone does. You'll have to ask him.'

Yeah; that was about the sum of it. Well, there wasn't much more I could do here.

'Thanks, friend,' I said, turning. 'See you around.'

I found the 'Dolphin' where the wineshop owner had said she'd be, the middle ship of three moored to the quay. There was no one around, but a gangplank linked the ship itself to the quayside and I stepped aboard.

I'd never been on a slave-ship before. No difference to the usual small merchantman, mind – single-masted, with a raised part-deck at the stern with the steering-oar and everything else open for cargo – except that there was a rail running the whole length of each side of the boat inside the curve of the hull, with short chains and manacles attached. It smelled, too, of old urine and faeces; not strongly, but you could tell the stink had become a part of the woodwork. Nasty. Oh, sure, slavery's a fact of life: the world couldn't get along without it, and society would grind to a halt. But that doesn't mean you have to like being brought face to face with the sordid realities.

Hell. Well, I could either hang around to twiddle my thumbs here or go elsewhere, maybe find a more upmarket wineshop, and try again later.

The smell and the general ambience didn't make the choice too difficult. I was re-crossing the gangplank when there was a shout from further along the quay. I looked over to see a guy in a freedman's cap hurrying towards me.

'You looking for me, sir?' he said. Late middle-aged, small and scrawny, with – like a lot of sailors, shaving at sea being the problem it was – a substantial beard. 'Laenius Cycnus?'

'Yeah, as it happens,' I said. 'Valerius Corvinus. Sextus Quirinius, the governor's aide, asked me to look you up.' Another white lie, of course, but what the hell. 'You got a minute to tell me about things?'

'Sure. Come aboard.'

'Uh...perhaps not,' I said. 'Maybe we could go back to the wineshop where you're staying? It's not all that far, and we can talk in comfort.'

Relative comfort. And it wouldn't include another cup of bloody Tubernucan, either.

'Suits me.'

We walked back.

'You're travelling empty?' I said.

'Yeah. We sold our last cargo in Syracuse, before we made the crossing. The plan was – still is, for that matter, even with poor Titus gone – to head west along the coast, see what we could pick up along the way.'

'That your usual route?'

'Nah, first time south of Sicily. We usually work the Sicilian east coast, then up through the straits to Italy as far as Ostia, picking up cargo as we go. Maybe selling a few en route if we're overstocked and the prices are good. Mostly buying in that direction, though: it's a poor area, and a buyer's market.' He must've noticed the expression on my face. 'Look, someone's got to do it, right? Most of the time we're doing the merchandise a favour. The rate those country buggers breed more than half of the youngsters we get would've starved to death or died of disease before they hit their teens, and those'd be the lucky ones. The rest are old by thirty if they make it that far, worked out. At least this way they've the chance of a half-decent future.'

'Very altruistic.' I wasn't being fair, I knew that; like I say, slavery is one of life's unalterable facts, and I couldn't get by without the bought help myself. Besides, from the cap he was wearing chances were he'd been that route personally, and he hadn't done too badly in the end. There's a lot to be said on both sides.

'We treat them better than most, while we've got them, sir,' he said carefully. 'Most traders do, the reputable ones at least. After all, like I say, they're merchandise. At the end of the day it's in our own best interests.'

'Yeah, you're right,' I said. 'I'm sorry; I apologise.'

'That's okay, I'm used to it; slave trading's not what you'd call a cosy profession. No bones broken.'

We'd got to the wineshop, and I led the way in.

'Ah, you found him,' the barman said.

'Yeah.' I turned to Cycnus. 'What'll it be?'

'A cup of the usual would be welcome.'

The barman grunted and hefted a flask. 'You, sir? Same as before, the Tubernucan?'

'No, I think I'll pass this time round. It's a bit early in the day for me.' Simple rule: never, ever tell a wineshop owner that his wines are crap. It doesn't do a lot for customer relations, and some of them can get seriously miffed. I put the coins down on the counter. 'Over there in the corner be fine?'

'Perfect.' Cycnus picked up his cup and took it to the corner table. We sat.

'Now,' I said. 'Tell me.'

Cycnus swallowed a mouthful of his wine, whatever it was, and smacked his lips. 'That's better,' he said. 'There's not much to tell. We'd been here for two or three days and we were getting ready to move along the coast. Titus said he'd got something to do in town, and not to wait up for him. He went out and that was the last I saw of him alive.'

'He say what the something was?'

'Someone he needed to see.'

My interest sharpened. 'He give you any indication of who that might be? Or why he needed to see them?'

He shook his head. 'No. None at all. Not even if it was a man or a woman. Tell you the truth, he'd been pretty cagey ever since we'd got here, going off on his own without a word of explanation before or after.'

'That was normal behaviour for him?'

Another shake of the head; a definite one. 'Uh-uh. Twelve years we've been partners, Corvinus, he was like my brother, and he'd never acted like that before. Never. It didn't start just recently, either. He hadn't been himself the whole way down from Ostia.'

'What was his mood like?'

'Come again?'

'He seem more cheerful than usual? More worried?'

'Not worried, definitely not that. Cheerful...no, that's not quite it either, although it's close.' Cycnus frowned, thinking. 'Satisfied. Or maybe smug's better. Smug about sums it up.'

'"Smug"?' Odd word to choose. 'About what?'

A shrug. 'No idea. But it was like he'd heard something that showed he'd finally been proved right all along, or that something bad had happened to an old enemy of his. Something deservedly bad, if you get my meaning.'

'Yeah. More or less.' Interesting.

'Well, that's good, because I'm buggered if I do.' He swallowed some more of his wine. 'Anyway, it doesn't signify, does it? Wherever he was going he got himself robbed and killed on the way there, poor devil, and that's an end to it.'

Uh-huh. Maybe, but I wouldn't be taking any bets. My gut feeling told me that this hadn't been a wasted trip in the slightest. Quite the reverse. 'So when did you start out from Ostia?' I said.

'About a month ago. Middle of August or thereabouts.'

Right. And Cestius had been killed, what, a month before that. Plenty of time, in other words. The news of his death hadn't reached Lepida – and so Claudius – until a bit later, mind, but that was down to sheer couldn't-care-lessedness on Verania's part; the sailing fraternity, being frequent and long-distance travellers by profession, have their own grapevine, and news items, especially the lurid sort such as the murder of an ex-praetor, can travel pretty fast via quayside wineshop gossip. There was no reason, none at all, why Appius Justus couldn't've heard about Cestius's death before he set out.

Why the hell it should matter to him, mind, was another thing entirely. If it did. And even given that, why should he take the trouble to come all the way to Carthage on the strength of it? Because six got you ten that, whatever his reasons for making it were, the change to his usual trading route had been no coincidence.

To see someone, of course; that was obvious. The questions of who and why, now, those were the real buggers to answer. Yet another little mystery to be solved.

'You'll be on your way soon, then?' I said.

'Yeah. Nothing to keep me and the lads – we've a crew of three – in Carthage. I've arranged the funeral for tomorrow, and if the wind's right we'll be off the day after.'

'You mind if I come? To the funeral, I mean.'

He looked at me in surprise. 'Not at all; glad to have you. There'll just be us and the undertakers' men. The ceremony's set for the third hour.' Half way through the morning, in other words. 'The cemetery's on the Utica road, I understand.'

'Fair enough. I'll see you there, then.'

I left.

13.

So where to now? It was still an hour shy of noon, far too early to be heading back, and besides Perilla had said she was meeting Cornelia, so she wouldn't be home. Maybe it was time to check out Scarus's alibi, for all the good it would do: it was plausible, and he'd been far too cocky for it to have been an outright lie. Still, I might as well go through the motions.

The gladiator school, I knew, was on the far side of town, near the amphitheatre. No great distance, but then nothing was in Carthage, if you kept within the city boundaries. Either I was getting used to the heat, or it was a kinder day, with a fresh wind blowing off the sea; in any case, I quite enjoyed the walk, and off the main drag in comparison with Rome that time in the forenoon the streets were practically empty. I bought a sesame bread ring from a guy with a couple of dozen of them on a stick and chewed on it as I went along.

I found the amphitheatre first, and took a look inside just out of interest. Definitely provincial quality: pretty small, certainly in comparison with the ones back home, and hardly more than a developed natural depression in the ground separated off from whatever was going on by a high wall and ringed with a bank of wooden benches, with more upmarket stone seats for the local dignitaries. There was no one around. Well, at least today wasn't a fight day, however often they had those here, so I could be pretty sure of getting someone at the school to talk to.

It was a hundred yards further up the road I was on, right on the edge of town: a major complex behind a high wall with a single gate. There didn't seem to be anyone on duty outside, and the gate wasn't barred, so I pushed it open and went in.

Those places are pretty much standard: a block of buildings housing the men's sleeping cubbies – you can hardly call them 'bedrooms' –, a communal dining hall and kitchen, equipment stores, latrine and so on, and a large practice yard. Plus, most schools have basic hospital facilities with a doctor, usually an ex army man, on the permanent staff: injuries, wounds in particular, are common for obvious reasons, and like Cycnus had said it makes sense to keep your stock in prime condition. Find yourself in need of a surgeon and you're miles better off in a gladiatorial school than you would be anywhere else, barring a legionary base.

The comparison holds good in other ways, too. Like an army camp, a school is a self-contained unit, with the all-male inmates living together every minute of every day, sunrise to sunrise. Oh, sure, there're exceptions. If the real stars, guys like Scarus, want to jump the wall and do a bit of tomcatting or whatever then a blind eye is most definitely turned; but in general discipline is as strict as it would be in a legion, the one important difference being that when it comes to fighting your best mate might be the bastard doing his best to kill you. Me, I'd think living with guys you knew one day might put a sword through your gut just to entertain the crowd, or you might have to do it to them, would be pretty stressful; but professional sword-fighters seem to take it in their stride.

The residential part was deserted, but there were a fair number of people about in the yard beyond: two or three pairs sparring, chaser against net-man, wearing loincloths, no armour and with practice weapons, and a few loungers in the portico chatting or throwing dice. No sign of Scarus, for which I was grateful: if I was going to check up on him then I didn't want him breathing down the back of my neck while I did it.

I went up to one of the loungers.

'Morning,' I said. 'The trainer around?'

'On his lunch break.' He jerked his thumb in the direction of the open doorway to my left. 'That's his office there.'

I went inside.

The guy behind the desk with the plate of bread, cheese and olives in front of him wasn't big, but what there was of him was solid muscle. Some trainers, like the doctors, are ex-army, legion centurions mostly, taking the closest civilian job they can get to what they're used to. Others were in the business themselves and been given the sword-fighter's equivalent of the military discharge diploma, a wooden practice sword with their name and years of service carved into the blade. That, evidently, from the example hanging on the wall behind him, was what we'd got here.

'What can I do for you, sir?' he said.

'Uh, this is kind of delicate.' I closed the door behind me. 'The name's Corvinus. Valerius Corvinus.'

He grunted. 'The imperial procurator just arrived from Rome.'

'Yeah, that's right.' Well, if he knew who I was it made things a lot easier. 'Looking into the murder of the ex-praetor Decimus Cestius.'

'And?'

'I just wanted to check up on something. One of your lads. Cluvius Scarus.'

'Scarus?' The barest of pauses. Then: 'What about him?'

'There's just a chance he might have been involved.' His eyes shifted; yeah, well, if Scarus's liaison with Verania was no secret elsewhere it'd hardly be one inside the school. 'According to him, he spent the day of the murder here, getting ready for the fight the following day. Would that be right?'

'If we'd games on the next day then yeah, it would be. Standard practice, no one leaves the premises the day before a fight.'

'And did you? Have games on?'

'Depends. What date are we talking about?'

'Mid-July. The Ides.'

'In that case, sure, that fits.'

Damn. 'You're certain? It was quite a while ago, after all.'

He gave me a long, slow look, reached for the bread, tore off a bit, dipped it into the olive oil and ate it. All very leisurely, without taking his eyes from my face. I felt my balls clench. Finally he said: 'The day after the July Ides is a local festival. There's always a fight on that day every year, this year not excepted. So yes, procurator, I am absolutely one hundred per cent cast-iron certain. That good enough for you?'

Hell. That was that, then. Still, it'd been worth a try.

'Thanks,' I said. 'That's all. Sorry to have disturbed your lunch.'

I turned to go.

'Hold on.' I turned back. He was frowning.

'Yeah?'

He opened his mouth to say something, then closed it again and shook his head. 'No. It's nothing. Have a nice day.'

Uh-huh. He might be able to take me apart with one arm tied, but he was a lousy liar.

'Look,' I said carefully. 'This is official, right? I'm under instruction from the emperor himself, and he can get very tetchy if he knows that someone has been fucking around with one of his reps. Now. If you're hiding something vital to my investigation and I find out about it later then believe me you are so far up shit creek that even a paddle and a full set of sails wouldn't do you any good. So tell me.'

He cleared his throat. 'Half way through that morning Scarus says he's pulled a muscle in his shoulder, right? I tell him to rest it up for a while under the portico, but he says he'd rather go back to his cubby and rest it there. Which he does. He doesn't show up again until late afternoon.'

Glory and trumpets! We'd nailed the bastard! 'Thanks, friend,' I said. 'Very helpful.'

I turned to go again.

'Wait.'

I looked round. 'Yeah?'

He was scowling. 'You just remember, *friend*,' he said. 'Scarus is the best chaser I've got, best I've seen for years for that matter. So if you think he killed Cestius then you make damn sure you have your facts right before you do anything about it. Understand?'

'Yeah. I understand.' I opened the door. 'Thanks again. Have a good day yourself.'

14.

Perilla was home by the time I got back, sitting out on the terrace. She wasn't alone; Cornelia was with her, and a young man in his early twenties.

Uh-huh.

'Oh, good, I was hoping you'd be back early, Marcus,' Perilla said. 'You remember Cornelia, of course. And this is her young man Quintus Cestius.'

Well done, lady! Brilliant! 'Hi,' I said.

'You've been wanting to talk to me, I understand. About my father.' Chalk and cheese, Gordius had called the guy and his elder brother, and I could see what he meant. It wasn't that they looked all that different, although Publius was more heavily-built and rounder in the face; it was the at-first-sight impression they made. Publius had been in-your-face brash, the typical lad-about-town brimming with self-confidence and egotism; his brother had the same self-confidence, or at least he seemed perfectly at ease and comfortable with himself, but there was a settled calmness to him that Publius didn't have. Despite the fact that he was three years younger, I'd bet Quintus was the more adult of the two.

'Yeah, I have,' I said. Bathyllus came up beside me carrying another wicker chair. I sat down. 'Nothing formal, just a few questions and a chat.'

'Go ahead, then.'

No more, only that; completely relaxed. I noticed that Cornelia was watching him closely.

'He, uh, could be quite difficult,' I said. 'According to your brother.'

'My father, Valerius Corvinus, was an egotistical, lying, manipulative swine.'

I blinked. He hadn't raised his voice or changed his tone, and the assessment was delivered as a simple statement of fact. 'Egotistical' and 'manipulative'; yeah, well, no surprises there, and no doubt 'swine' fitted, too; but 'lying'... That was odd. Still, maybe now wasn't the time to pursue the matter.

'Is that so, now?' I said.

'You want the truth of it, there you are. I'm delighted he's dead, and I hope he's roasting in hell.'

Jupiter! This guy didn't pull his punches, did he? Interestingly, Cornelia hadn't batted an eyelid; in fact, I wouldn't swear to it on oath, but I had the impression that she'd given a slight involuntary nod of agreement. Perilla didn't react either, but maybe she'd been made aware of his feelings on the matter earlier.

'That a general assessment, or are you basing it on anything specific?' I kept my tone matter-of-fact, to match his.

'Yes to the second, as it happens. But that's a family affair, and I'm sorry but it's no concern of yours.' He smiled, possibly to take the sting out of the words.

'You don't think maybe that's for me to decide?'

'No. In any case, I doubt if it had anything to do with his murder.'

Murder. Not 'killing' or 'death'. That was interesting, too; I couldn't remember either his brother or his mother using the word. 'You *doubt* it?' I said.

'Yes. Very much so.'

Gods! Ordinary self-assurance was one thing, but his variety you could've bent iron bars around. 'Fair enough,' I said mildly. 'We'll leave that for the present. Anything you can tell me about the actual death?'

'No.' Again, just the simple negative.

'You, uh, were occupied yourself that day, were you?' The question had to be asked at some stage, and I might as well get it over. 'Just for the record.'

'He was with me,' Cornelia said quickly. 'It was the day after my father's funeral. We took a picnic along the coast to a quiet cove I know of and stayed there all day.'

Uh-huh. Well, as far as alibis went, I'd heard better. Still, it might've been more suspicious if, like Scarus, they'd offered something more convincing. 'Right,' I said. 'Moving on. Have you any idea who might have done it? Any enemies your father had, that you know of?'

'I'm not pointing any fingers, if that's what you mean.'

Not exactly a straight answer to the question, but I supposed all I was going to get. 'Your father's factor, Sextus Gratius, mentioned the leader of one of the itinerant harvester gangs. A man called Medar.'

'That's not likely,' Cornelia said. 'That he was responsible, I mean. I know Medar well. He wouldn't murder anyone, not even Quintus's father, and he'd good–' She stopped.

'And he had good reason to do that,' I said. 'I know. Gratius told me about that side of things too.' She and Quintus exchanged a quick glance that I couldn't quite read; at least, that was the impression I got, but it was so fleeting I could've imagined it. 'About the death of his son.'

Did they both relax? Again, I couldn't be sure.

'Gratius is a garrulous old woman,' Quintus said, but there was another of those half-apologetic smiles. 'Believe me, Corvinus, Cornelia is absolutely right. Medar wouldn't have done it, whatever the provocation.'

Uh-huh. I hadn't met the guy myself yet, of course, but it wasn't something I'd be rushing to take on trust. It was interesting to know, though, not only that both of them admitted to knowing him but were obviously on close and very friendly terms. The social gap alone would've made that unlikely, under ordinary circumstances. Which suggested that the circumstances weren't ordinary at all.

'So,' I said. 'Moving on again. Did your father know about you and Cornelia? Being an item, I mean?'

'No. Neither of our fathers did. None of the rest of my family, either.'

There was something there again; the way he said the word "family" sounded...I wasn't sure how it sounded, but it wasn't pleasant. Not pleasant at all. 'They would've objected?' I said.

'Yes, they would. Strongly.'

Odd. Or partly odd, anyway. 'Uh...forgive me, Cornelia,' I said. 'I can see why Quintus's parents might've been against the relationship' – she lowered her eyes – 'but your father, well, frankly he's a different matter. I'd've thought someone like Albus would've viewed Cestius's son, the son of an ex-praetor, as quite a catch.'

Her eyes came up again. She looked like she was going to be sick. Quintus put his hand out and grasped hers.

'Cornelia's father,' he said, very carefully, 'would have been just as opposed to a marriage as mine would. More so, in fact.'

'Yeah? And why would that be, now?' His lips set in a hard line. 'Come on! It's a reasonable question.'

'Maybe it is, but it's one that I have no intention of answering. I'm sorry, but there you are.'

Bugger; we'd hit the stone wall again.

'Okay,' I said. 'Even so, if the pair of you are serious both families will have to know eventually. In fact, since you're planning to go back to Rome shortly they'd have to be told pretty soon.'

'I've no intention of going back to Rome; I never have done. And now Cornelia's father is dead there won't be any opposition to a marriage on her side.'

I sat back. 'You're staying in Carthage?'

'Yes. Why not? I like it here, it's been home to me for most of my life, and I certainly wouldn't want to live anywhere near either Publius or my mother.' He must've noticed my expression, because he smiled. 'Well? Would you? You've met both of them; you must've formed an opinion, and I'd be very surprised if it differed much from mine. Besides, it makes marriage with Cornelia a great deal easier.'

Yeah, both true; but still, there'd been more than simple familial dislike beneath the words. A lot more. 'Do they know that either?' I said. 'Your mother and brother, that you're not going back, I mean?'

'No. I was leaving off telling them until the last minute, together with the news of our engagement. There's no point in causing trouble before you have to, is there?'

'So what are you going to do for a living?'

'Oh, my father's will is more than generous, and if Publius agrees – there's no reason why he shouldn't; he'll have far more than he needs to make a success of things in Rome – I'll take part of my inheritance in land. We won't be all that rich, certainly not at first, but with Cornelia's money and my own we won't starve, not by a long way.' He shifted in his chair. 'Now, Corvinus, I really have told you all I can. Very little in total, I know, but if I've been reticent on some matters I give you my word it's because they have no connection with my father's death and are therefore not your business. Besides' – he smiled again – 'I'm taking you at *your* word, that this is an informal chat, not an interrogation.'

'All right, pal,' I said. 'Grilling over. If you want to call it that.' I turned to Cornelia. 'No monkey today, I notice.'

'Ptolemy?' She was still holding Quintus's hand, quite unselfconsciously. 'No, I only brought him with me last time because I thought he'd like to see the house again. Generally when I go out I leave him at home. It's much safer.' She smiled. 'Whatever interest hats hold for him, he really is terrible over them. It's bad enough when they belong to

102

someone you know – Perilla's, or Gratius's, that I had to return to him at father's funeral, for instance; that was *really* embarrassing – but at least then you can give them back when you get them off him. The problem is that he's just as likely to snatch one from a passer-by in the street, and there's nothing to be done then but grovel.'

'Couldn't you put him on a leash, dear?' Perilla said.

Cornelia turned to her. 'Oh, no! That wouldn't do at all, he'd hate that. It's best just not to take him out in the first place. As I say, I almost never do.'

Interesting: she seemed, today, a completely different girl from the one I'd seen before. That smile, for a start. And she was a lot more...'lively' fitted, but I supposed a better word would be 'normal'. It had everything to do, I suspected, with Quintus being there: despite the fact that there didn't seem any purpose to it now, their two hands were still clasped together.

Well, good luck to them. It didn't stop there being several large question marks hanging over what the guy had just been telling me, though. Or rather not telling me.

He stood up, followed by Cornelia.

'We have to go,' he said. 'Cornelia told her aunt that she was showing Perilla round the sights this morning, and while that was mostly true she'll have been expecting her back before now. It was nice meeting you, Corvinus. After a fashion.'

'You too,' I said.

'I'll be in touch again soon, Cornelia,' Perilla said, netting herself another smile.

We watched them leave.

'Well, Marcus.' Perilla turned to me. 'What did you think?'

'About Quintus? He seems okay, on the surface at least, if a tad disconcerting. And your Cornelia is obviously completely smitten.'

'Yes, she is.'

'How did you manage it, by the way? Get Quintus to come and talk to me, I mean.'

'Oh, that was easy. I just told Cornelia, as a *fait accompli*, that I knew about her relationship with him and that I wholeheartedly approved of it. Which I do. You must've noticed the change in her when he was here from the last time.'

'Yeah. Yes, I did, as it happens.'

'Anyway, after that it was easy. She was most concerned, of course, that I wouldn't give the secret away, but once I'd made a promise on that score she was quite happy. Delighted, even. The fact that I don't belong here was important, too; I suspect that she's been longing to share with someone for some time, but couldn't bring herself to take the risk. Most of all, I think, she wanted to show him off.' She smiled. 'She really is very young for her age.'

'Uhuh.' I was frowning; this was going to be tricky. 'Look, Perilla, before I go on to the next bit I want your word that you won't jump down my throat as soon as I start, right? That you'll let me argue it through.'

'Argue what through?'

'Just give me your word, okay?'

She sniffed. 'Very well, dear. You have it. Although why on earth you should–'

'I think there's a possibility that young Quintus, with or without the connivance of Cornelia, was responsible for Cornelius Albus's death.'

'*What?*' Perilla stared at me. 'Marcus Valerius Corvinus, that is absolutely the stupidest, most idiotic thing I've ever heard in my entire–!' I held up a finger, and she stopped dead. 'All right. Explain. But it had better be good.'

'Yeah, well, like I say it's only a possibility. Maybe, now I've met the guy, not as likely a one as I'd originally thought, I'll give you that. All the same, the theory holds together as far as it goes.'

'Very well. I'm listening.' Stiff as hell, and her ears had gone pink, which is always a bad sign. Even so.

'First off. We've been through this part before. When we first met Cornelia she reminded us both of Marilla when I sprang her from her father's house on the Janiculan. Yes?'

'Yes, she did. Strongly. But as you said– '

'I know what I said. Just wait. Marius had been abusing Marilla, sleeping with her, for years. According to him, she was his...what did he call her? Something in Punic.'

'His Ta'anit-pene-Ba'al. His "Lady, Face of the Lord".' She frowned. 'But Marcus, Sextus Marius was mad. That's crucial.'

'Oh, sure. No arguments there. Only he wasn't doing it completely out of madness, was he? He believed – genuinely believed – that with her he'd breed a magical son, like the Phoenician folk-hero who grew up to destroy the country's enemies. To wit, in this instance, Rome.'

She sighed. 'Marcus, dear, I'm sorry, but this really *is* complete nonsense. First of all, as I say, Marius was insane, which explained the delusion in the first place. Secondly–'

'We don't know that Albus wasn't. After all, Marilla's father got away without anyone noticing it for years.'

'Secondly, Marius had a reason for hating the Romans, or what passed for one in his own mind: he was a Spaniard, of Carthaginian descent. Cornelius Albus was Roman.'

'Come on, lady, don't fudge! You don't know that for a fact, and nor do I. Oh, sure, he had a Roman name, but after two centuries that means nothing. All we know for certain is that he was local, which means that his family might've lived here since Carthage was a viable proposition. After all, his interest in Carthaginian history – which, incidentally, in case you hadn't noticed, he shared with Marius – must've come from somewhere.'

She was quiet for a long time. Then she said, 'All right. Let's admit it as a possibility.' Then, when I grinned: 'Not this mystical nonsense; once in a lifetime is quite enough for that. The sexual abuse, now, that's another matter entirely. You may well be right about that, and in fact I'm very much afraid that you are. Still, as you said when I tried to broach the subject with you before, dreadful though it may be it's past history, and the man is dead. Which does *not* mean that Quintus was responsible for killing him, let alone Cornelia. It doesn't even plausibly suggest that his death was any more than the accident it appeared to be.'

'Okay. So let's look at the scenario from the other side. Cornelia's. She's been stuck for the gods know how long in an incestuous relationship with her father. Maybe like Marilla she can't see a way out, maybe she's just grown to accept it as normal, but–'

'Hold on, Marcus. There's a difference. Marilla had no one to turn to, no friends, no close relatives, and she was being kept a virtual prisoner; Cornelia had both, not least the aunt and uncle who took her in after her father's death, and as far as we know before he died she was free to come and go as she pleased. Besides, she was in her late teens. She'd know perfectly well what was happening, even if she hadn't been aware of it as a child.'

'Yeah, well, that's my point, isn't it? Oh, as far as her friends and relatives were concerned, once she did realise the situation she was in she might just be too ashamed to tell them. But Quintus, now, he'd be different, wouldn't he?'

'Possibly. I don't see that it automatically follows, but–'

'It'd explain why they kept their relationship a secret from her father as well as his, and why they're so sure now that he'd've been against an engagement. It wouldn't've just been *their* relationship, *their* engagement: he couldn't've risked her spilling the beans once she was free of him and leading a normal life. Like Marilla again. There'd be an aspect of sexual jealousy into the bargain.'

Perilla was twisting a stray lock of hair, something she always did when she was thinking things over.

'You're beginning to convince me,' she said. 'Stop it.'

'It makes sense, doesn't it?'

'Yes, I'm afraid it does. In theory, at least. You're about to say that Quintus – with or without Cornelia's help or knowledge – engineered her father's "accident" to resolve matters. As indeed it has done.'

'That's more or less it, yeah. It would've been easy enough. Everyone knew the old man was getting shaky, and a fall downstairs wouldn't rouse any suspicions at all.'

'The problem is that if you're right then my sympathies are completely with the young couple. Cornelius Albus would have fully deserved to die. And there is a certain ironic justice in the fact that, like Sextus Marius, he was killed in a fall.'

'True. I hadn't thought of that.' Marius hadn't so much fallen as been thrown from the top of the Tarpeian Rock, mind, and as the result of due legal process and sentence. Still, it was a fair parallel. And for what it was worth I had to agree: if the theory held good then the bastard had only got what was coming to him. 'It might explain the rape story as well.'

'How do you mean?'

'Just an idea. The charge would've been brought by Albus himself as the victim's father, yes?'

'Naturally it would. So?'

'The case never came to trial, but the result was effectively to pull Cornelia out of the marriage market, at least for the time being. And at the very stage when Albus might be expecting offers for her. If he was lucky she might even end up on the shelf permanently.'

She stared at me. 'You're saying that the whole thing was a complete invention by Albus himself?'

'It's possible, yeah. Under the circumstances. And that he forced Cornelia to back the story up.'

'But, Marcus, the perpetrator was actually identified; Lautia told us that, at Galba's dinner party. What was his name again?'

'Marcus Virrius. Yes, I know.' I frowned. 'Maybe that's something to check up on, if I get the chance.'

She gave me a sideways look. 'You don't think that perhaps this is one time to let sleeping dogs lie?'

I shook my head. 'Uh-uh. Oh, I agree completely: if Albus was what we think he was then he's better off dead, whatever happened. But we don't know yet that his death *didn't* have anything to do with Cestius's murder, and if there's a chance that Cestius's son was involved then I have to follow it up. I may not altogether like it, but there you are.'

She sighed again. 'Yes. Of course you do. Still, for Cornelia's sake I really, *really* hope that you're wrong.'

'Yeah. So do I. But I've a nasty suspicion, this time round, that I'm bang on the nail.'

'Incidentally, you still haven't told me about the rest of your day.'

'Oh. Right. True. For a start, we've broken Scarus's alibi.'

'*What?*'

'Yeah, that was my reaction too. Oh, sure, officially he was at the gladiator school all day like he said, but in fact there's a window of about six hours, from mid-morning to late afternoon, when he was out of everyone's sight, ostensibly resting up a shoulder strain in his cubby. Plenty of time, if he'd arranged things in advance, to get on over to Cestius's picnic spot, shove a knife into him, and be back without anyone knowing he'd been gone. The timing fits, too. So chummie is still most definitely in the frame.'

'What about the other matter? The slave-dealer?'

'Now *that* was interesting.' I gave her the details. 'I've said I'm going to the funeral tomorrow. It'll be my last chance to see his partner before he leaves, and he may've remembered something more that's relevant.'

'Marcus, I know I've said this before, but don't you think a connection between this Justus's death and Cestius's murder is unlikely? For all sorts of reasons. I mean, all you've got to hang a theory on is the fact that seemingly he came to Carthage to see someone from his past, and was being very secretive about it.'

'That about sums it up, yeah.'

'Well, then! For goodness' sake!'

'Perilla, I don't know, right? It's just a feeling, that's all. But I've learned over the years not to ignore feelings. There's generally something behind them.'

'All right, dear, you know best. At least, so you keep telling me.' She looked up at the sun. 'It's getting quite close to dinner time. I think I might change out of these clothes; today's been hot and sticky, and you really need to wear fresh in the evenings here.'

'Yeah. Good idea. I might put on a new tunic myself. Maybe have a cold drench first.'

She shuddered. 'If you must. Only don't expect me to join you. Dinner's out here, on the terrace.'

'Fine.'

Well, I reckoned it'd been a pretty good day, all told; certainly an eventful one.

We'd see what tomorrow brought.

15.

I had a fairly leisurely breakfast again the next day, although I was still ahead of Perilla; according to his partner Cycnus, Justus's funeral had been arranged for half way through the morning, and if the cemetery was just outside the city limits on the west-bound Utica road then I didn't have far to walk. Walk, I would, because I'd decided against wearing a mourning mantle; these things weigh a ton, and they're hot and uncomfortable enough under normal circumstances, let alone at the height of a North African summer, plus the fact that I'd never even met the guy. Besides, I doubted if Cycnus and the rest of the crew would be in full mourning gear, either.

So I was sitting on the shaded terrace twiddling my thumbs when Bathyllus came through to announce a visitor. Sextus Gratius.

'Hi, pal,' I said, when he appeared. 'Take a seat. You want a drink?'

'Thank you.' He sat in the other wicker chair. 'Some plain water would be good.'

'Okay.' I nodded to Bathyllus, who went in to fetch it. 'Now. What can I do for you?'

He smiled. 'It's more what I can do for you, sir. I was simply going to leave a message, but I'm glad I've caught you in in person. I've found the harvester. Medar.'

I sat up straight. 'Hey! Great!'

'Actually, he isn't all that far from here. He and his family have set up camp a mile or two to the west of town, just off the Utica road.'

'That's absolutely perfect. I was going out that way myself this morning, as a matter of fact.'

'Excellent.' Bathyllus shimmered back with the water. Gratius drank some and set the cup down. 'As I said, I'd assumed you'd be away from home, so I haven't made any arrangements. But I could have Spadix meet you at whatever time you choose and take you the rest of the way to Medar's camp. Would that be satisfactory?'

'Yeah. Perfect. The fourth hour should be plenty of time, at the burning ground; I don't know where that'll be, exactly, in the line of tombs, but he should be able to find it.'

'Excellent.'

'Oh, and I'll be on foot, so get him to bring a spare horse again.'

'I'll do that, sir.' He made to get up.

'Hang on, Gratius,' I said. 'There's one more question, and since you're here anyway you might be the best person to answer it.'

He sat down again. 'Yes, of course. If I can.'

'Cornelius Albus's death. What do you know about that?'

He frowned. 'I don't see what you mean.'

'How did he die, exactly? Do you know the circumstances?'

'Only from what his major-domo told everyone later, sir. He'd come through from discussing the dinner menu with the chef in the kitchen and he found the old man lying at the foot of the stairs with his neck broken. That's all there was.'

'He was alone in the house? Albus, I mean? Except for the slaves?'

'Yes. According to Chilo – that's the major-domo – he'd been working upstairs in his study all morning.'

'He didn't have any visitors at all?'

'Visitors? That I can't say; you'd have to ask Chilo. It's possible, of course it is, but why should it matter?'

I ignored the question. 'You, uh, didn't see him yourself that day, then? You being a close friend of his?'

'No, sir.' He was still frowning. 'I'd dropped in two days previously to return a book, but that was the last time I saw him alive.'

'How about his...you called him Albus's protégé. Quintus Cestius.'

'As I said, I can't answer for anyone else. You'd have to ask Chilo.'

'And his daughter? She was out too?'

'Elissa? Cornelia Alba, I should say, now. Yes, she was, that I do know. Visiting a friend.' The frown had deepened. 'Valerius Corvinus, I'm sorry, but what *is* your interest here?'

I shrugged. 'Maybe nothing. They got on well, did they? Albus and his daughter?'

He hesitated. 'There was a certain coolness between them, on her side, at least. I'd no idea why. But she was at a difficult age, and...well, I think by now you'll know the other circumstances.'

'Yeah. Yes, I do.'

'Perhaps that would explain it. She's a strange young lady, Cornelia. As, again, you'll no doubt know for yourself.'

'So where would I find this major-domo – Chilo – if I wanted to talk to him?'

'I really can't say. Before you came he was always here, of course, looking after the place, even when Elissa – Cornelia – moved to her uncle's. Cornelia would be able to tell you, naturally, if you're really interested.' He gave me a curious look and half-opened his mouth to speak again, but obviously decided against it. Then he stood up. 'I'll make the arrangements with Spadix. The cemetery, fourth hour, with a spare horse.'

'You've got it, pal. Many thanks.'

He left.

I found the burning area no bother, largely because I was slightly late, the pyre was already well alight, and you could see the plume of smoke practically from the city's western gate. Smell it, too, once you got much closer, although fortunately only in gusts. As Cycnus had said, it was a very low-key ceremony, with just him, his three-man crew, all dressed like me in simple tunic-and-cloak, and the undertaker's men, plus a single flute-player.

He was watching the flames; Justus was already gone and it was only a question of waiting until the fire died down. He turned briefly as I came up and nodded to me. For a while we stood in silence.

'One good thing, though,' he said eventually. 'He's being burned properly, and buried on dry land. That's always the fear: that the ship'll go down and the fish will get you. He'd have been grateful.'

'How long were you partners, did you say?' I said.

'Twelve years. Thirteen come January. A long time.'

'And before that?'

'We were both in the business, in a small way, him doing better than me, working the Italian coast in a ship of his own out of Ostia. Not the "Dolphin", we pooled our cash and bought that together. A real gut-bucket of a thing she was, thirty years old and leaked like a sieve. It was taking most of his profits to keep her afloat, and he decided to cut his losses. Me, I was a junior partner with another man, but he died and his heirs sold up. The new owner preferred to ship non-human cargo, we didn't get on too well and I'd a bit of money saved, so I left at the end of the season.' His eyes were still on the pyre. 'You haven't caught the bastards who did it?'

'No,' I said. 'Not yet.'

He shrugged. 'Well, that's how things go, I suppose. Can't be helped, it wouldn't bring him back in any case, and we're off tomorrow, wind permitting.'

'You don't have any more of an idea now of why he wanted to come to Carthage?'

'No. How do you mean?'

'I just thought that whoever he wanted to see might've heard the news and got in touch. Maybe come here, to the funeral.'

'No. That's still a mystery, always will be, now, far as I'm concerned. It might've been a woman, though.'

My interest sharpened. 'What makes you think that?'

'Oh, not from anything he said. I told you, he never let on one way or another. But Titus always did have an eye for the women, and he was a good-looking devil. Never had any problems on that score.'

'He didn't mention anyone in particular?'

'Nah. Love them and leave them, that was his way. But he couldn't let them alone, and it was mutual. Must've had one in every port between Syracuse and home when he was younger.'

'Home being Ostia, right?'

'That's it. For both of us. Got a wife and kids there myself, as it happens, grandchildren too, five at the last count. Not Titus, 'leastways not officially. And he never mentioned having any kids of his own. Bloody amazing, that was, if it was true; he got around enough to have a whole raft of them.'

The head undertaker's man came over.

'We're about ready to put the fire out now,' he said to Cycnus.

'Fine.' Cycnus turned to me. 'Me and the lads are going back to the wineshop when we're done here, give Titus a decent send-off. You'd be welcome to join us for a cup or two.'

'Thanks, pal, but no.' Given what might be poured into the cups I blessed the fact that I had a genuine excuse. 'There's a man I've got to see, up the road a bit.'

'Fair enough. If you do get the murdering bastard you've a friend in me for life.' He held out his hand. 'Thanks again for coming.'

I shook. 'You're welcome. And you never know, I might get him at that.'

'Morning, Corvinus. How's the boy?'

I turned. Cluvius Scarus.

'Yeah, well, that's very interesting,' I said. 'I was just thinking about you.'

'Were you indeed? Anything specific?'

'Nothing that won't wait. So why are you here?'

He smiled. 'Maybe I just like funerals.'

'Yeah. Right.'

'Actually, I wanted to have a private word with you. I called in at the house and your major-domo said you'd be out here.' Then, to Cycnus: 'You mind?'

'Not at all. I'll see you around, Valerius Corvinus. Don't forget, now. And if you do catch the man I might just hear about it through the grapevine.'

'Fingers crossed, friend,' I said. I turned back to Scarus. 'Over there be all right?' I nodded towards one of the big family tombs a dozen yards away by the roadside.

'Perfect.'

We walked on over.

'Okay, I said. 'I'm all ears.'

He sat down on the low wall around the tomb. 'Pettius tells me you've sussed out that I wasn't being entirely truthful about where I was the day Cestius was killed.'

'Pettius being the trainer, I assume.' He nodded. 'Yeah, that's right. If not being entirely truthful means that you were lying through your fucking teeth.'

'Oh, but I wasn't. That's the thing I wanted to explain before you jump to any unwarranted conclusions.'

'Fine. Very conscientious of you. So what's the story now?'

He pulled up a stem of grass and put it between his teeth. 'I was there, right enough. At the school, in my cubby, like I told Pettius I would be, from mid-morning to late afternoon. But I wasn't alone, and I wasn't exactly resting.'

'Uh-huh. So no strained shoulder-muscle, then?'

'No, I'm afraid not. Now *that* was a lie, if you like, pure and simple. I'd made a prior arrangement, you see.'

'To meet Verania.'

113

'You've got it. "Meet" isn't the right verb, but we'll stick with it. The lady gets off "meeting" in an all-male environment, the seedier the better. Something about the smell of the place, I think. She doesn't have the chance to do it very often, naturally enough, and that day was perfect: no one around or likely to be, everyone busy in the exercise yard. We were there "meeting" for the whole of the time. At least, up to the middle of the afternoon; I'm not that good.'

'You, uh, can't produce any witnesses, then.'

He laughed. 'No, I'm afraid I can't. Understandably so. You could ask the lady herself to confirm, of course, but if you were to try that you'd be a braver man than I am.' He stood up and threw away the chewed grass stem. 'Well, that's all I wanted to say to you. Enjoy the rest of your day.'

He turned to leave.

'Okay,' I said. 'So what about three evenings past. You got a story for that as well?'

He turned back slowly. 'What?'

'The guy who's just been burned was mugged and killed three nights back, at the docks. Robbed, too, but I reckon that was a blind.'

He stared at me. 'Corvinus, you are out of your fucking skull! Why the hell would I kill someone I've never met? I don't even know the man's name.'

'Justus. Titus Appius Justus. He was a slave-trader.'

'Fine. Whatever. The question still stands.'

'Because Verania told you to. Why I'm not exactly sure yet, although I have my theories. But I'll find out in time, and when I do you, sunshine, are in serious schtook. The lady as well.'

He shook his head, smiling. 'You're fantasising. I haven't been near the docks for months. And I haven't killed anyone recently either. Except in the line of duty, of course. I'll see you around. Have a nice day.'

He walked off in the direction of town, and I watched him go. Yeah, well, I was glad I'd rattled the bastard's cage, anyway. And when it got back to Verania, as no doubt it would, pretty damn quickly, it might give his girlfriend something to think about, too.

Spadix turned up ten minutes later on his mule, leading my half of the transport arrangements behind him.

'Valerius Corvinus, sir,' he mumbled, not quite meeting my eye. Obviously still nervous about being shopped for liberating the master's penknife.

'That's me, sunshine,' I said, mounting up. 'Let's go. Is it far?'

'Coupla miles. But the camp's off the road, down a track, like.'

'Uh-huh.' We rode for a while in silence. Then I said: 'Your kitchen friend. Or rather your mate's one. What was she called again?'

'Eulalia.'

Chatty in Greek; or close enough, anyway. I hoped she lived up to her name. 'You think I could meet her?'

He shot me a sideways glance, and I grinned to myself. *Meet.* Right; unfortunate timing. 'Just to talk. I need a bit of information pretty badly.'

'What sort of information?'

'Sorry, pal, that's classified.' His brow creased. 'Means I can't tell you.'

'Fair enough.' Thank the gods for someone with total curiosity burn-out. 'Sure, no problem. Arranging it might be tricky, though.'

'I'm in your hands, Spadix.' Another frown; keep off the metaphorical language, Corvinus! 'Ah...you tell me the where and when and I'll be there.'

Another conversationless stretch of riding, lasting a good five minutes; I could almost hear his brain grinding away at the problem. Finally he said:

'Early afternoon'd be best. The cook, he gets his head down then for a coupla hours before he starts on dinner, an' there isn't much doing. You know the setup, sir? Of the house, I mean.'

'Uh-uh. Not in detail. I've only been there once, and it's a big place.'

'Okay. Kitchen garden's behind the wall at the corner. First corner you come to along the road from town. There's a gate in it. You with me?'

'More or less. I will be, when I see it.'

'That'll be open. That stretch of garden's my patch, me an' Simo's plus another coupla mates. No one else around, ever, an' I can square them, no problem. There's a shed there that Simo an' Eulalia use for...well...' He stopped and shot me another sideways glance.

'Where they meet. Right. Got you.'

'She'll see you there. I need time to arrange it, mind. Day after tomorrow suit?'

'Yeah. The day after tomorrow's fine. Early afternoon, yes?'

'Seventh hour's best.'

'Two days' time, seventh hour, in the shed. We have a deal.'

'She won't get into no trouble over this, will she?'

'No, I guarantee it. And she'll come out well ahead of the bargain, that's a promise.'

'Okay.'

Let's see if we couldn't get a bit of corroborative evidence here. If only for my own satisfaction.

Medar's camp was a ramshackle collection of sailcloth tents, washing hanging from lines stretched between the poles, and a few smouldering cook-fires. There were a fair number of people around, women and kids, mostly, the women sitting in small groups chatting to friends while they got on with the day's chores. Conversation gradually died away as eyes and faces were turned in our direction.

Not that I could see much of the latter, mind; we might only be a couple of miles from town, but we'd shifted cultures with a vengeance. Greek women in general, and some of ours, especially upper-class ladies, wear veils when they're out in the streets, sure, but the things are pretty much light-weight and semi-transparent. Those veils were neither; they were designed to cover and hide. The chunky gold bangles and earrings that most of the women were wearing had an exotic look to them, too, and the eyes that watched us with more suspicion than interest were heavily outlined in black.

There was a knot of men lounging by the tent to my right. As I dismounted, one of them got up and ambled over.

Forget the interest; the look he gave us was pure suspicion.

'Hi,' I said. 'Is Medar around, by any chance?'

'Wait here.'

That was all; not exactly a cheerful welcome full of good fellowship and bonhomie, but then under the circumstances I hadn't been expecting one. I waited, while he ambled off again and disappeared into another of the tents. It was a good couple of minutes before he reappeared with a much older man.

Medar must've been a big, powerful man in his day, and even in late middle age he looked as though he could lift me off my feet with one hand and crack walnuts with the other. He'd clearly been pickled in Egyptian natron then left out in the sun for a lifetime to dry out, and his belter of a nose could've been modelled on the business end of a trireme.

The pattern of old scars on his cheeks – regular and identical on both sides, so probably made deliberately – and the hard, piercing black eyes that had been fixed on me all the way over from the tent didn't qualify him for Least Villainous-Looking Suspect in the Case prize, either.

'Yes?' he said.

Obviously no great wordsmiths, these itinerant harvesters. 'The name's Valerius Corvinus,' I said. 'I'm looking into the murder of Decimus Cestius.'

He grunted. 'Are you, indeed?'

'I'm told you had a' – I hesitated – 'a cause for disliking him. I thought I'd better hear your side of the story.'

'"Disliking"? The man killed my son. Let's be clear from the start, I hated his guts. But I assume, since you're here, that you've been told that already.'

'Yeah, I have,' I said. 'Still, like I say, I haven't heard your version of things yet. You want to give me it, or should I just fuck off?'

That got me a straight, searching look. Then he grunted again, clapped me twice on the shoulder and turned.

'We'll go somewhere more private,' he said. 'Follow me.'

We were walking towards the tent he'd come out of. When he passed a small group of women he said something to one in a language I didn't recognise. She stood up and moved off.

'I told her to bring us wine,' he said. 'You won't mind that?'

'Uh-uh,' I said. 'Not at all.' What with the walk to the cemetery and the two-mile horse ride I could've murdered half a jug.

'Good.' He held open the tent flap. 'Go in. Make yourself comfortable. It means sitting on the floor, I'm afraid, but there are plenty of cushions.'

Interesting. Forget the monosyllabic knucklehead, this guy sounded educated. Certainly more at home with words than I'd've expected an itinerant harvester from out in the sticks to be. I ducked my head and went inside. It was pretty spartan, no furniture, none at all, except for a chest that I assumed held clothes and personal possessions. Cushions, like he'd said, with the covers in bright geometric patterns. The same went for the carpet that covered most of the beaten earth that the tent was pitched on.

I sat, as best I could. Medar settled opposite me.

'Now,' he said. 'What do you want to know?'

'Maybe it'd be best if you just took me through it. The incident of your son, I mean.'

'Mm.' He frowned. 'Adon, his name was. You know it? Adonis, it comes out in Latin.' Ah. Right. 'He was well-named, a lovely boy. Eighteen when he died.'

'So what happened? What had he done?'

'Nothing. That's just it; he had done absolutely nothing. That day – it was two years ago, at the start of the grain harvest – I had a message from this man Cestius, wanting to talk to me about hiring my people to bring in some of his crops. I'd some other business elsewhere at the time he gave me, so I sent Adon instead. When–'

He stopped; the tent-flap had opened and the woman had come in carrying a tray with a jug and two cups. She set them down, Medar gave her a brief nod of acknowledgement, and she went out again. He poured and handed me a cup. I sipped...

Good bloody Jupiter and all the gods in heaven!

Medar was watching me, a half-smile on his lips. I hesitated, then deliberately took a proper mouthful and swallowed.

Date wine; this just *had* to be date wine. Even the Tubernucan I'd tasted in the harbour wineshop hadn't been this bad, not even close. And Quirinius had been right: German beer had it beaten hands down.

'You like it?' he said.

'It's...different.' *Sweet and holy gods!*

He laughed and took the cup from me. 'Fair enough, Corvinus. You've shown that you have good manners for a Roman, and I won't push you too far. Well done. I told Maryam to wait a few minutes and then bring us some proper stuff. Now. Where was I?'

'You sent your son to a meeting with Cestius.'

'Yes.' The laughter disappeared from his face. 'That, I've regretted ever since. If I hadn't, if I'd gone as Cestius asked, he might still be alive. I might be dead myself, mind, but that's the natural order of things, that fathers die before their sons. So. When Adon got there, Cestius was in his study. He'd evidently just closed his strongbox, because when the slave showed Adon in he was on the point of removing the key from the lock. There was a small book cubby beside the box. He took out one of the book-rolls, put the key in its far end, and replaced it. Then he turned back to Adon.' I frowned and opened my mouth to speak, but he held up a hand. 'Wait, please. I'm telling you what happened, exactly as Adon told it to me later.'

Uh-huh; I knew what was coming, that much was obvious. What wasn't obvious, a long way from it, in fact, was what in hell Cestius had been playing at, and why.

'The meeting lasted barely five minutes, just a request to be in such and such a place on such and such a day, at the usual rates. Cestius could just as easily have made that his original message. Adon left. The next day men came from the big house. They searched Adon's tent, found three gold pieces, and took Adon away.'

'He was charged with robbing Cestius's strongbox,' I said.

Medar nodded. 'According to Cestius, he'd been seen outside the villa late that evening. The claim was that he'd broken in during the night, used the key to open the box, and taken what money there was inside. Not that there was much, no more than a few hundred sesterces' worth; Cestius, it seemed, had had a number of expenses in the days previous to the robbery, and hadn't brought his store of ready money up to its usual level yet. There isn't much more to tell. Adon was put on trial, with Cestius himself on the bench, found guilty and sentenced to be flogged. He must've had some sort of weakness inside, because half way through the punishment he collapsed and died.' He paused. 'There. You know now as much as I do about the matter.'

Shit; there were so many holes in that story you could've used it as a colander. If Medar was telling the truth – and my gut feeling told me that he was – then what the fuck had been going on? Because it was clear that something had been.

The woman Maryam came back in with another jug and two fresh cups. I caught a brief glimpse of two very speculative black-rimmed eyes as she set them down on the tray, and then she was gone.

'My daughter,' Medar said, pouring. 'Or one of them.'

'You have other sons?' I said.

'Three. All older than Adon. But he was my favourite, the best of them.' He shrugged. 'The Lady gives, and the Lady takes away. It's fate; what can you do?'

He handed me a cup, and I drank. Not the best wine in the world, not even close, but at least it had been made from honest grapes. 'You're telling me it was a stitch-up,' I said. 'Your son was framed.'

'I'm telling you nothing, except the facts. Make of them what you like.'

'So why? Why should Cestius do it? Why would he bother?'

'That I don't know. I genuinely have no idea, none at all. But yes, the whole thing was a deliberate invention on Cestius's part, from start to finish. You understand now why I hated him. Still hate him.'

Not a question; a statement. And yes, I understood perfectly well. Even so, I had my job to do.

'Okay,' I said. 'Let's talk about two months ago. The day he was killed. You were in the neighbourhood at the time. Or am I wrong?'

'We were working about a quarter of a mile from where he was found, yes.'

'You know he was there, at all?'

'Of course. He'd ridden over to check up on us that morning, the way he often did.'

'And that was the last time you saw him?'

'That's right. We finished off for the day at sunset and went back to camp.'

'Which was where?'

'Practically next door to where we were. You've seen how we manage things; it makes sense to set the camp up as close as possible to wherever we're working. That means we can use the whole day to get whatever it is done without having to travel.'

'And you were with your harvesting gang the whole time?'

Medar smiled. 'Corvinus, I could tell you that and they'd back me to the hilt, even if no one had seen me at all from sunrise to sunset. They're family, all of them. Family sticks together, it's all we've got.' He paused. 'Your answer is yes. Of course it is.'

'Uh-huh.' Well, if he was lying at least he was being open in acknowledging the possibility. Which, I supposed, was the best way of getting the lie believed. Certainly I hadn't a hope in hell of proving otherwise. 'Fair enough,' I said. 'I don't suppose you or any of your people saw anything amiss that day?'

'You mean, did we see anyone out here who might've been the killer?'

'Yeah, that's more or less it.'

'You think I – or any of us – would give him away if we had?' He smiled again. 'Or her, of course. I assume you're keeping an open mind on that score.'

'You might.'

'We wouldn't.' That came out flat, and he wasn't smiling now. 'I told you; family. Adon was one of us, and Cestius murdered him. If they knew the identity of that man's killer every man, woman and child in this camp would be proud to shake his hand. Swear later by Ta'anit, Ba'al and every god in your pantheon that they'd never laid eyes on him into the bargain. Her. What you like.'

'You're not being very helpful,' I said mildly.

'I've no intention of being helpful. What I am doing is giving you truth. If that's not enough for you I'm sorry, but it's the best I can do.'

'Okay. Leave it there.' I took another swallow of the wine. 'Incidentally, I understand you know young Cornelia Alba.'

'Yes, very well. I've known her all her life, in fact. Have you a reason for asking?'

'No. I'm just curious.'

'Really? And why should that be?'

'Well, not to put too fine a point on it, you're not exactly in the same social bracket, are you? And you're not part of the Cornelius household, which would be another reasonable explanation. In fact, as far as I can see the only other one. So, yes, I'm curious.'

'Her father was a close friend of mine. We'd been friends for years, since before she was born.'

'The same argument holds good. Or does answering the question constitute being helpful?'

He hesitated. 'You never knew Cornelius Albus, did you?'

'No. Of course I didn't.'

'His family has lived hereabouts for generations. Oh, they were pure Roman, in fact a cadet branch of your top-ranking Cornelii, but they arrived not long after Carthage was destroyed and settled in Utica, which had always taken the Roman side. They've had close ties with the province ever since.'

'That happens. So?'

'Albus was a very clever man, a scholar, interested primarily in history; which, his family being who they were, meant the history of this area, of Carthage in particular.'

'Yeah, that I did know.' I was getting just a tad impatient here. 'Again: so?'

'His interest in things local went beyond the academic. Cornelia's mother was one of us; a cousin of mine, in fact.'

I sat back. '*What?*'

'Her name was Arishat.' He was watching me closely, half-smiling. 'Oh, it was no disgrace, Corvinus, at least not as far as Albus was concerned. We may live in tents now and hire ourselves out as casual labour, but our family line goes back to the Carthaginian *shophetim*, the hereditary rulers of the city. When Carthage fell and was destroyed those of us who survived fled south to Mactaris. We've come down in the world since, yes, a long way down; but we are still who we are. We still remember.'

Jupiter! 'So Cornelia is family, right?' I said.

'Indeed. As her father was, by marriage. The fact that her mother died at her birth doesn't change that.'

I shook my head. Gods alive! This had really buggered up the case; or if not exactly buggered it up because there was precious little at present to do that to, then at least dragged it off screaming in a fresh and unexpected direction.

Medar was still watching me closely, his mouth pulled into that same half-smile.

'But I'm forgetting the rules of hospitality,' he said. 'Another cup of wine.'

Before I could answer he had picked up my half-empty cup with his left hand, filled it from the jug, and passed it over. I glanced down as I took the cup from him...

'That, uh, wouldn't be an old knife wound you've got there, would it?' I kept my voice level.

'This?' He frowned at the puckered scar an inch or so above his wrist, running from the base of his thumb to the first joint of the index finger. 'Yes, as a matter of fact it is.'

'Care to tell me where you got it?'

'In a knife fight, about two months ago.' His voice was bland, but his eyes challenged me.

'Is that so, now?'

'Yes. I was trying to stop it and got cut for my pains. You know the sort of thing, two young men arguing over the same girl. It happens quite a lot in a small community like ours.'

'I'm sure it does.' Shit. He was playing games with me here; I knew it and he knew I knew it. I felt suddenly tired. I set the cup down again and stood up. 'Thanks for your...help.' I paused before the word, and stressed it. 'I should be getting back.'

He got to his feet as well. 'It's been a pleasure meeting you, Valerius Corvinus,' he said. 'I can't say I hope you find your killer, but believe me I bear you no ill-will.'

'Yeah. Right.' No doubt jaundiced-sounding as hell, sure, but in a cockeyed way I did believe him. 'Oh...one more question before I go. You know Cestius's second son as well, don't you?' I slipped it in as casually as I could.

'Elissa's fiancé, young Quintus,' he said calmly. 'Fiancé as far as he and she are concerned, at least. Yes, I do. Not well, but I've met him, through her. I'm surprised, though, that you know anything about the relationship.'

There was a question in his own voice, but I ignored it. 'What do you think of him?' I said.

'Corvinus, the son is not the father, nor is he responsible for the father's actions. I've nothing against Quintus Cestius; on the contrary, I have a great deal of respect for him, a very great deal. Elissa couldn't have made a better choice.'

'Uhuh. Well, thanks again, Medar. I'll see you around.'

'No doubt. I look forward to it.'

Spadix was waiting where I'd left him. I mounted up, and we rode back to town, my head buzzing all the way.

Gods!

16.

Perilla was upstairs in Albus's study when I got back, working her way through a sheaf of paper sheets that lay on the desk in front of her and sorting them into various piles. She looked up as I came in.

'Oh, hello, Marcus,' she said. 'Did you have a good day?'

'Not so's you'd notice.' I put the wine jug and cup I'd brought with me on the low table and stretched out on the reading couch beside it. 'What's going on?'

'Nothing, really. I'm being nosey. Or rather, it's not as bad as that, because none of this is private or confidential, and I did ask Cornelia if it would be all right to browse though her father's library.' She frowned. 'Actually, to be fair, I am stretching things a little. I happened on a collection of notes, presumably by Albus himself. He seems to have been working on a book covering the years of the third Carthaginian war, from the Carthaginian side.'

'Uh...."happened on"?' I said.

She coloured. 'Well, yes, true, they were out of sight in the bottom drawer of the desk. But it wasn't locked, and some of the details are fascinating. Where he got them from, I don't know; not from any author that I'm familiar with.'

'Maybe he made them up.'

'Marcus, whatever else he may have been he was a conscientious historian. Historians don't do that sort of thing.' I just looked at her. 'Or perhaps they do, some of them. But I'm sure not in this instance.' She set down the sheet she was holding. 'So. What was wrong with your day?'

'To begin with, Cluvius Scarus has wriggled off the hook. At least he hasn't, quite, but it'll be difficult proving otherwise.' I told her about his new alibi, for what it was worth.

'You don't believe him?'

'Come on, lady! We've been through this before. He's already tried one bluff that didn't work, now he's trying another. And he's right: I don't exactly relish the prospect of asking Verania to confirm that at the time her husband was killed she was being screwed in a gladiatorial school dorm.'

'But we'd decided that neither Scarus nor Verania had a motive for murder, hadn't we? Or not a particularly strong one, anyway. Cestius

125

didn't seem to care about his wife's infidelities, while on Scarus's side it's highly unlikely that, with her husband dead, Verania would legitimise things with a marriage.'

'Yeah, well, we only have Scarus's own say-so on the second point, don't we? As for Verania, maybe she had other reasons for wanting Cestius out of the picture.'

'Such as?'

'I've no idea.' I wasn't going to tell her, yet, about the other suspicions I had re Scarus and Appius Justus: she'd only have poured cold water on them, which was fair enough, because suspicions were all that they were, at present. Time enough when I'd talked to Spadix's friend Eulalia. Or so I hoped. 'Even so, it's a possibility.'

'All right. What about this man Medar? Did you manage to talk to him?'

'Yeah.' I rubbed my chin 'Now that was interesting. You know anything about the...what did he call them? The *shophetim*.'

'Yes, of course. What we call the suffetes. They were the old Carthaginian rulers, a cross between hereditary kings and our elected consuls. The name meant "Judges". So?'

Judges, eh? 'Seemingly, Medar's descended from them. Or rather, not just him, his whole tribe. That possible?'

She was staring at me. 'I don't know, dear; not for certain. On the one hand, the suffetes were elected from among several noble families, so the number of candidates can't've been prohibitively small. And after the destruction quite a few survivors did flee to Mactaris and establish themselves there.'

'Yeah. Medar told me that.'

'On the other hand, any Carthaginian nobles would've been singled out for capture or execution by the Roman authorities. Hasdrubal, the last suffete, was strangled in the Tullianum after Aemilianus's triumph, and his wife and children were already dead, so that line was certainly extinct.' She frowned. 'Marcus, I agree about this being interesting, but I don't see the relevance.'

'Albus's wife – and Cornelia's mother – was one of the family. Medar's cousin, name of Arishat.'

'*What?*' I'd really rocked her this time. 'You're sure?'

126

'Well, no, of course I'm not; I'm only repeating what Medar told me. But he'd no reason to lie, and in any case it'd be too easy to check.' I gave her the details, including the background info on Albus himself. 'You see the implications?'

'No, I can't say that I do, altogether.'

She was being intentionally obtuse, I could see that from the way her jaw had set. It was pretty obvious why, too.

'Okay,' I said equably, 'then I'll spell it out. Medar is big on family, for, you'll now appreciate, very strong reasons. He had his own quarrel with Cestius, again with good reason – we'll come to that later – to do with the death of his son, and then it transpired that the bastard was mixing it with another relative by getting in the way of her choice of husband.'

'Marcus, Cestius didn't know about Cornelia's relationship with Quintus.'

'*Potentially* getting in the way of it, then. Don't quibble. It was only a matter of time before he did know, and since he was planning to go back to Italy before the start of winter time was running out fast.'

She ignored me. 'Added to which,' she said, 'whatever Albus's reasons for being so were, he was opposed to the match as well. Or would have been if he'd known in his turn. And as Cornelia's father and head of the family he could've stopped it off his own bat.'

'Yeah, I hadn't forgotten that.' Quite the contrary. Shit, we had to go very, very carefully here: this wasn't a subject that the lady was disposed to be rational about, and she wouldn't like this particular theory one little bit. 'So the combination of factors pushes Medar over the edge, and he kills Cestius. Maybe he didn't plan things ahead, but circumstances provided him with his best chance, so he took it.'

'You can't know that.'

'No.' I was still being patient. 'Even so, it's by far the most likely solution. Medar had motive in spades; he had the opportunity, because he knew Cestius was alone and in the neighbourhood that day, and he'd also know where to find him. Plus of course he had the means. The whole bag, in other words. Hell, when we talked he practically admitted that he'd done it, even deliberately let me see a cut on his hand and told me he'd got it in a knife fight at the time of the murder.'

'So have Quirinius arrest him.'

We were getting to the tricky bit now. 'Actually, there's a chance things may be a bit more complicated than that,' I said.

'Oh? In what way?'

'It's, ah, possible that when he talked to me Medar wanted to attract all the suspicion to himself.' I glanced at her. Perilla was no fool, and her mouth had set in a hard line. 'Oh, sure, he'd be the one to do the actual killing, no argument, but he might've wanted to protect someone else who had a vested interest in Cestius's death.'

'Marcus, if you're implying that Quintus and Cornelia were involved, separately or together, then you are totally wrong! We've discussed this! It's impossible!'

'Uh-uh.' I shook my head. 'We haven't discussed it at all. The point at issue before was Cornelius Albus's death, not Cestius's. And if I remember rightly you were beginning to come round on that score. Or at least to accept the possibility.' She opened her mouth to say something, then closed it. 'Look. This is just a theory like any other, okay?' A bloody good one, in my view, but I didn't have to labour the point; when she was in a more rational frame of mind – if that ever happened – she'd see that for herself. 'It may be completely wrong; it probably is. But we won't be doing ourselves any favours if we ignore it.'

'All right.' Stiff as hell. 'Carry on.'

I took a swallow of wine; that had been a sticky moment, but at least it seemed we were over the worst part, getting the lady to listen 'Actually, there's not a lot to say. It's all about removing the obstacles to the marriage. Albus – well, we've talked about him; if I'm right, the accident was rigged' – I used the passive deliberately – 'to free Cornelia on her side, and the bastard only got what he deserved. Cestius was more difficult, but just as important: because the family was scheduled to go back to Rome in a few months at most, Quintus was going to have to tell his father that he wouldn't be travelling with them, and why. Which, knowing what we do about Cestius, would've meant a major row, most likely ending with Quintus being disinherited. As things are, the lad's not only free to stay and marry who he likes but he comes into his full share of the estate, which according to Verania will be pretty substantial. That's a fairly hefty motive for murder in anyone's book, especially considering that it wouldn't be his hand on the knife.'

'Wait a moment, dear. I agree that Quintus and Cornelia would benefit from Cestius's death, there's absolutely no doubt about that; but there's no reason for them to be cognisant, is there? Let alone directly involved? Medar may have decided to kill the man without their knowledge as...well, as a sort of advanced wedding present.' I winced. 'After all, you did say that he had excellent reasons of his own for hating him, connected with his son's death.'

'Yeah. Yeah, that's possible, I suppose.' Unlikely, mind: for the theory to hold water, it had to be both fathers or neither. And if Quintus, with or without Cornelia's help, had already zeroed Albus then... But like I say, now was not the time to force Perilla into a corner. If she wanted to believe her pair of lovebirds were squeaky-clean innocents, or at least comparatively so, I wasn't going to argue the toss.

'What exactly were they, by the way?' she said. 'Medar's reasons?'

'Oh. Right.' I cleared my throat; at least we were moving onto safe, neutral ground here. 'Now *that* is really weird.' I told her what Medar had told me, about the business with Cestius's strongbox and the subsequent arrest and trial.

'But it makes no sense at all!' she said when I'd finished. 'You're saying that Cestius deliberately showed Adon where he kept the strongbox key.'

'Not only that,' I said. 'The likelihood would've been that that was a spare, hidden away for emergencies with not even the trusted bought help knowing where it was, while Cestius kept the original on him. Under normal circumstances he would've been using that. So why didn't he?'

'Obviously so he could claim that the boy had known the location of a key when he carried out the burglary. In other words, that the whole thing was a set-up.'

'Right. It had to be. Plus the fact that, according to Medar, the box only held the equivalent of a few hundred sesterces. That's only a handful of gold pieces at best, and three were recovered from Adon's tent when it was searched. If it was a genuine burglary Cestius had got off pretty lightly. You ever hear of someone as wealthy as that letting the contents of their strongbox get that low? Even if they had had a few unusual expenses recently?'

'But why would he do it? I mean, if it was deliberate, which it must have been, then he must have had a definite reason.'

I shrugged. 'The original intention – again according to Medar – was that it'd be Medar himself who got caught. If Cestius had had a personal grudge against the guy and was setting him up then it might've made some sort of twisted sense, don't ask me what sort or how. But it was the son who came to the meeting, not the father, so why go ahead with the plan?'

'Perhaps because he realised that it might hurt Medar more if Adon was implicated in his place.'

'Yeah, actually that would make a lot of sense,' I said. 'The fact that it was his son that got caught up in the scam and not him obviously weighed pretty heavy with him, and for Adon to have died as a result made things even worse. We're still short of a motive on Cestius's part, mind. If it's relevant, which it may not be.'

'Medar himself didn't have any suggestions?'

'Absolutely none. He's as much in the dark over the whys and wherefores as we are, as far as I can tell genuinely so. Which makes the whole thing even more of a puzzle.'

'So where do you go from here? As far as the case is concerned?'

'I thought I might ask Quirinius to point me in the direction of the Virrius family.'

'Who?'

'You remember. The guy who was supposed to have raped Cornelia. Marcus Virrius?'

'For heaven's sake, Marcus! I thought we'd agreed to leave that side of things alone!'

'Not as far as I recall. And I've a feeling it may fit in somewhere.'

She sighed. 'Very well. I do think, though, that you're causing unnecessary trouble, both for yourself and others. Grief, too, if you mean to contact the young man's family. However, you're the emperor's representative, not me. Do whatever you like.'

Gods! I hated it when she turned long-suffering. And it wasn't even credibly in character.

'Look, lady,' I said. 'In case you haven't noticed I'm floundering here. I can't afford to ignore any avenue, whether it seems immediately relevant or not. And I don't play favourites, either. So cut me some slack, okay?'

She ducked her head to hide a smile. 'All right,' she said. 'I'm sorry. No doubt everything will come out in the wash eventually; it usually does. Just don't expect me to be supportive all the time.'

I got up, collected the wine jug and cup, then leaned over and kissed her.

'Fair enough,' I said. 'Deal. I'll let you get on with your intellectual snooping.'

I went downstairs.

17.

I checked in with Quirinius next morning and got the Virrius family's address, one of the up-market middle class houses in the eastern part of town: Marcus Virrius Senior was, according to Quirinius, one of the city's most prominent tradesmen, a pillar of local society and a leading figure in the local senate.

I hadn't exactly been looking for a rapturous welcome, and I wasn't disappointed. Virrius and his wife were both at home, and the atmosphere when the slave showed me into the atrium was cold as a glacier.

'Valerius Corvinus, sir.' The guy fixed me with a look that could've done service as an ice-pick. 'And what can I do for you?'

'Ah...like your door-slave probably explained, I wanted to ask you about your son Marcus,' I said. No invitation to sit down, note: Virrius himself was standing foursquare by the ornamental pool in the centre of the room, while his wife sat in a chair to one side glaring at me like Tisiphone the Fury on a bad day. 'He no longer lives here, I understand, but–'

'You've been misinformed. I have no son Marcus.'

'Yeah, well, I do realise that you've disinherited him. All the same I was wondering if–'

'Marcus has been no son of ours for the last two and a half years. We have had no contact during that period, nor do we wish to have. Furthermore, I have no intention whatsoever of discussing any detail of his past conduct with you, if that is the reason for your visit. Now, I am extremely busy at present and if you'll excuse me' – he signalled to the slave, who was still hovering – 'Sestus, show Valerius Corvinus the door, please. A very good day to you, sir.'

'Now just one fucking minute, pal–' I began.

Tisiphone gave a Furies-like hiss, and Virrius drew himself up to his full five foot nothing.

'You will please leave,' he said. 'Now.'

Faced with implacable opposition like that even Mercury, messenger of the gods, would chuck in his wand and bugger off back to Olympus. There wasn't a lot I could do, for the present, at least. I left without another word.

There was a girl – a young woman, rather, maybe fifteen or sixteen – hanging around in the lobby just beyond the entrance to the atrium. I nodded to her and was walking past when she reached out and tugged at my tunic sleeve. I stopped.

'Wait outside,' she whispered. 'Give me five minutes.'

Hey! Maybe we were getting somewhere after all!

I hung around twiddling my thumbs on the street corner where I could keep an eye on the front door, but there must've been a back entrance to the house because she came up on my blind side.

'Valerius Corvinus?' she said. 'I'm Virria. Marcus is my elder brother.' She glanced towards the house, where the door-slave had taken up position again on his stool. 'There's a shrine in the next street. It's usually deserted; we can talk there.'

'Fair enough.' I followed her.

The shrine was the usual arrangement: an altar with a covered niche for offerings, set in its own small patch of ground behind a wall and a gate. We went inside and she turned to face me.

'Marcus didn't do it,' she said.

I blinked. 'What?'

'Interfere with that girl. Cornelia Alba. At least, I suppose that's what you wanted to talk to my parents about.'

'Ah...yeah.' I was frowning. 'Yes, it was. You seem pretty certain of that.'

'I am.'

'Care to tell me why?'

'Because she wasn't his type, not at all. Marcus is exactly what they say he is. He's a gambler, a wastrel, he gets into fights, and he's too fond of wine. Women, too. But the women he goes with are always safe.'

'"Safe"?'

'Professionals.' She had reddened slightly. 'You know the kind I mean. Or wives with complaisant husbands. Women with...experience. Not wholesome, wide-eyed innocents from good families like Cornelia Alba. He'd never have risked going anywhere near someone like that, not in a million years, and besides she would've bored him to tears inside five minutes.'

'He tell you this?'

She hesitated. 'No. How could he? The...what he was supposed to have done happened a month or so after father had disinherited him. He wasn't

134

living with us then, in fact I didn't know where he was living, not even that he was still in Carthage.'

'Uhuh. How did he get disinherited in the first place? Do you know?'

'The gambling, for the most part. Both my parents are very strait-laced, particularly where gambling's concerned, and Marcus had run up debts on several occasions without telling them until he had to. My father had given him final warnings several times. But then there was the–' She stopped.

'There was the what?'

'Nothing. I'm sorry, it's nothing. Really.' Her eyes avoided mine.

'Come on, Virria!' I said. 'Spit it out!'

Another hesitation, far longer this time. Then she said: 'A ring went missing from my mother's jewellery-box, quite an expensive one, although she hardly ever wore it. She suspected her maid at first, naturally, but the woman had been with her for years, and she swore blind she hadn't taken it. Anyway, the thief turned out to be Marcus. There was a dreadful row and Father told him to leave the house and not come back.'

'So where is he now?'

Her eyes flickered. 'I've no idea,' she said. 'I told you: the last time I saw him was over two years ago. All I know is that he isn't in Carthage any longer.'

'Virria.' I was patient. 'When we started this conversation you were talking about your brother in the present tense. So you may not have actually seen him face to face in that time, but you've kept in touch. So where is he?'

Long silence. Then, very quietly: 'Utica. He has a small stud farm outside the town, on the Carthage road.'

'Fine. He wouldn't be using his real name, though, would he?'

'No. He's Marcus Mandonius.'

'Great. Thank you. Uh...he did tell you it wasn't him after all, right? With Cornelia, I mean.'

'No. He admitted it.'

I blinked. 'Come again? I thought you said–'

'He was lying. I told you: she wasn't his type. He would never have gone with her.'

'So why would he lie?'

She shook her head. 'I don't know. But he did.'

135

There was absolute conviction in her voice. Gods, we'd got a real puzzle here, and no mistake! 'Okay,' I said. 'Thanks. You've been very helpful.' I half-turned to go. 'Oh...one more thing. When was the, uh, business with Cornelia exactly? Do you know?'

'Two days before the Nones of June.'

'That's...pretty exact.'

'It was my fourteenth birthday. You will be seeing Marcus, won't you?'

'Yeah,' I said. 'That's the plan, anyway.'

'Give him my love.'

So; it would seem that I was in for a trip over to Utica. Which meant going back to Quirinius at the residence, as my official minder, to check on the best way of doing it.

He was still in his office, working through a pile of invoices.

'Utica?' His eyebrows rose. 'Why on earth would you want to go there?'

'You mind if I keep that to myself at present, pal?' I said.

'Not at all, that's your privilege. I am curious, though, particularly since you've just asked me for the address of Marcus Virrius's father.' He eyed me speculatively: he was no fool, young Quirinius. 'Which, if you don't mind my saying so, was odd in itself. You think the rape case two and a half years ago had some relevance to Cestius's death? Because if you do then I'm damned if I can see the connection.'

'Nor can I,' I said easily. 'It's just another avenue that needs to be followed up. Probably a complete dead end.'

'You do know that the case against Virrius is still technically open? Since he'd fled Carthage before the trial and gone into voluntary exile, as it were, that would normally put the lid on things. But if his whereabouts did happen to become known then it would be up to Cornelia Alba's uncle, as her present head of family, to decide whether to continue the prosecution.'

'Yeah. I'm aware of that.'

'Hmm.' He shrugged. 'Very well. You know your own mind, and as an imperial procurator you're entitled to keep your own counsel. When were you thinking of travelling?'

'As soon as possible. I've a commitment tomorrow afternoon' – that was the appointment with Eulalia – 'but I'm free after that. How long would it take?'

'By road it's fifty or sixty miles, so a good two days. Better to go by ship. It might take just as long, depending on the wind, but it'd be more comfortable. I'll arrange things for you.'

'Thanks. That would be great.' I turned as if to go, then turned back. 'Oh, incidentally. You happen to know where I can find the Cornelius property's old major-domo?'

'Chilo?' The eyebrows rose again. 'What do you want with him?'

'Not me this time; my own major-domo, Bathyllus. He was wondering which dealer the wine in our cellar came from so's he can replace what we've used when we leave.'

'Oh, I'm sure that won't be necessary. Cornelia Alba will be more than happy for you to make full use of–'

'Uh-uh. Point of honour, both with him and me: always restock your host's cellar before you go with his own choice of wine. That way you don't feel guilty about making a hole in it.'

He grinned. 'Very laudable. Albus freed Chilo in his will and he married a long-term lady friend with a pastry shop near the racetrack; that's in the south-west corner of town, just before you get to open country. They live above the shop, although it should be open at this time of day in any case. There's only one possible candidate, I think, but if you can't find it ask for Silvilla's.'

'Will do. Thanks again, Quirinius. And let me know as soon as you've arranged the Utica trip, right?'

Time for a quiet word with the major-domo re Albus's 'accident'.

Open the shop was, with a large woman in her late middle age behind the counter. I bought a couple of nut-and-honey pastries for the look of things, then asked if Cornelius Chilo was at home.

'No, sir, I'm afraid he's not at present,' she said. 'Was it something important?'

Damn! 'Not really,' I said. 'I just wanted a word with him to do with the Cornelius house. My name's Valerius Corvinus.'

Her face cleared. 'The procurator! Oh, my! I'm sorry, sir, yes, of course. He's out at the moment, like I say, but he's only gone round the corner to make a delivery. He should be back any minute, if you don't mind waiting.'

'Sure. No problem.' I leaned my back against the door jamb. 'You've been married for long?'

'Not long, less than two months. But Chilo and me, we've known each other for years.'

'Less than two months? That must've been just after his old master died. Cornelius Albus?'

'Yes, sir. That's when Chilo got his freedom, in the will, like.'

'Did you know the old man yourself?'

'Oh, no. I never saw him. I used to have a stall in the market, and Chilo used to drop by in passing if he was over that way, for a pastry and a chat. That was when my first husband was alive, mind, so there was no funny business. Then Titus died and, well, here we are.' She looked past me through the open door. 'That's Chilo back now, sir.'

I turned. An old guy in a freedman's cap was crossing the road towards us. He came into the shop and gave me an enquiring look.

'Hi,' I said. 'Valerius Corvinus. I'm staying in your old master's house at present.'

'Oh, yes, sir. The gentleman from Rome. Of course.' He looked worried. 'Is anything wrong?'

'Absolutely nothing. We're very comfortable. Just a couple of administrative points I need to check up on.' I glanced outside at the sun. 'Uh...you fancy a cup of wine while we do it?'

'Well, it's a little–'

'Oh, go on, Chilo,' his wife said. 'I can manage here. And it's not often you get an invite from a representative of the emperor, gods bless him.'

'Fair enough. There's a wineshop I use just up the street, Valerius Corvinus. It's nothing special, but–'

'It'll be fine. Lead on.'

He did. Actually, when we reached the place I was quite impressed, at least by the setting: two or three tables in a small private courtyard shaded by a trellised vine and a stand of palm trees.

We sat down and the owner came over. Table service too. Or maybe we were just privileged.

'You want to order?' I said to Chilo. 'Make it half a jug.' That should give me time, and if it did turn out to be rot-gut we'd just have to put it down to the perils of the profession.

138

'Half a jug of my usual, please, Felix,' he said to the owner. The man went off. 'Zarytan, sir. From just beyond Utica. It's quite respectable, for a local wine.'

'Suits me.' Well, we might as well get the bread-and-butter excuse out of the way straight off, in the unlikely event of word getting back to Quirinius and arousing his entirely-justified suspicions about my motives. 'Actually, wine's what I wanted to ask you about. Or not me; I'm just passing on the question from my major-domo. What supplier do you use? Or did you use, when your master was alive?'

'Tarrius Milo, sir. In the Market Square district. But your major-domo should know that already; I left a list for him and the chef giving the names and addresses of all the suppliers we dealt with, on the kitchen table.'

'Ah. Fine. Probably a glitch in communication between the pair of them, then. And it clears up all the other points I was going to raise. No harm done.' The owner came back with the half jug and two cups. I paid, poured for both of us, and sipped. Not bad; not bad at all. 'So. How long were you with your late master?'

'Over forty years, sir,' Chilo said proudly. 'I was left to him in his father's will. I was his major-domo for just under half of that.'

'He easy to work for?'

'Oh, yes. A very pleasant gentleman. A bit' – he tapped his temple with his index finger – 'you know, at times. Obsessed with the old Carthaginians, he was, breathed, ate and slept them, you might say. You can be too clever for your own good, that's my view.'

'Uh-huh. He get on well with his daughter?' He frowned. 'It's just that I've heard her mother died in childbirth and he never remarried. That makes things difficult sometimes, with no other woman in the house.'

'Oh. Oh, yes, sir. They were very close. At least, until the...' He hesitated. 'The business with young Marcus Virrius, if you've heard about that.'

'Yeah, I have.' I picked up my cup and took a swallow, then said casually. 'What exactly happened there, do you know?'

'Not in detail. The...it happened outside the house. The mistress came back that day in a terrible state, hysterical, you know? She asked me where her father was, I told her in his study, and she went straight up. She was up there for about an hour, and I could hear them arguing even downstairs.'

'"Arguing"?'

139

Long silence. Then he said, quietly: 'Forgive me, sir. The word slipped out, and I shouldn't have used it. It's not my place to comment.'

Shit; we'd hit the Code of the Major-domos. I hated to use the strong-arm approach, but if I was going to get any more out of him I'd no alternative.

'Look, Chilo, you know who I am, right?' I said.

'Yes, sir. Indeed I do.'

'Just to make it clear. I'm charged by the emperor in person to investigate the murder of Decimus Cestius some two months ago. Now. That job involves me asking questions, sometimes awkward ones that the person I'm talking to would rather not answer. I don't know whether your late master's affairs have anything to do with Cestius's death, but at present it looks as if they might, and in any case I can't afford to ignore the possibility. So give. You said Albus and his daughter were arguing.'

'Yes, sir.' Barely a whisper.

'You happen to hear what about? Any of the details?'

His eyes came up. '*No*, sir! I was very careful not to.'

Bugger; from the genuine indignation in his voice he wasn't lying, either. Well, it couldn't be helped. 'And then?'

'The mistress shut herself away in her room for two days. Wouldn't come down, wouldn't eat. The master tried to persuade her to come out and talk to him but she wouldn't open the door. And when she did come downstairs she'd hardly speak to him. It was like that, more or less, for the whole two years until he died. She wouldn't speak a word to him that wasn't necessary, and apart from at mealtimes she kept out of his way.'

Gods! Well, at least we could dismiss the abuse theory. Whatever Cornelia had against her father – something major, that was clear – it only dated back as far as the rape. And from what Chilo was saying Albus himself couldn't've been responsible for that after all. Which, taken together with what Virria had told me, raised some interesting questions.

'Okay,' I said. 'Moving forward to the day your master died. You notice anything peculiar or unusual happening around then?'

'I'm sorry, sir. I'm not with you.'

'Anything out of the ordinary. The way your master was acting, for example. Or something he said. Unaccustomed visitors to the house, going out at odd hours, that sort of thing.'

That got me a straight look. I suspected that Chilo had tumbled to the fact that maybe my interest in Albus's death wasn't only curiosity, and he was beginning to see the implications.

'No,' he said. 'He was just as normal. But then, sir, the master was very...maybe the right word is "secretive". I don't mean in a nasty way, mind, he wasn't sly, he just didn't let on about what he was thinking, kept himself to himself all the time. And as I told you his work was everything. Most days he didn't even come downstairs to eat, just had something brought up on a tray.'

'He have any visitors at all?'

'Oh, no, sir, hardly any. He didn't go out visiting himself, as you'd imagine, and he'd very few acquaintances, let alone friends. There was young Quintus Cestius, of course, the master was very fond of him, and Sextus Gratius, he'd been a close friend for a long, long time. They were in and out most days. Practically no one else, barring the man Medar.' He sniffed. '*Not* a gentleman, that one. An agricultural worker, in fact.'

Delivered in a tone which was the equivalent of the metaphorical ten foot pole and gloves. Yeah, well, major-domos are all alike, when you got down to it, arch-snobs, the lot of them; Bathyllus could've given your average blue-blooded Roman matron lessons. And the Disapproving Sniff was practically a job requirement.

'Medar?' I said.

'Yes, sir. You know him?

'Yeah. Yeah, we've met. And, to be fair, he did say that he and your master were old friends. Even so, he didn't tell me he was a regular visitor to his house.'

'I understand your surprise, sir, and believe me I share it.' Another sniff. 'Medar is hardly the type of man you'd expect someone like Cornelius Albus to encourage. However, I'm sorry to say he was actually family, a relative of the master's late wife.'

'Uhuh. That I did know too, as it happens. So his visits were pretty frequent?'

'They became so, sir, especially in the month before the master died. In fact, the last was the day before his accident.'

'What about the day of the accident itself? You mentioned Quintus Cestius and Sextus Gratius. Did they happen to drop in at all?'

'Not Gratius, sir; he hadn't been for two or three days. Quintus Cestius, yes, about half way through the morning.'

'He stay for long?'

'An hour or so, I think.'

'You *think?*'

'Yes, sir. That was how long he usually stayed, anyway. I was busy elsewhere in the house, and he let himself out.'

'So you didn't see him leave?'

'No. He must have gone before the early afternoon, though, because of course that's when the master had his accident, and he was alone in the house.'

'Right. Right.' Jupiter! 'What about the young mistress? She'd gone out earlier, I understand.'

'Yes, sir. To meet a friend. Just before Master Quintus arrived.'

'You happen to know which friend?'

'No, I'm afraid I don't. She didn't tell me, and she certainly wouldn't have told her father.'

'Fine. And she wasn't back until...?'

'Mid-afternoon. About an hour after I found the master.'

'She seem upset at all? About the death?'

He hesitated, and looked uncomfortable. 'Yes, sir. Yes, of course she did. That goes without saying.'

Too slow, and unconvincing as hell. 'So your master had had no other visitors that day?'

'There was just the one, sir. Quite early on. But you could hardly call him a visitor. He was only there for a few minutes, and the master insisted on talking to him in private in the lobby rather than taking him upstairs to the study, which was his usual practice.'

'Yeah? And who was that?'

Another hesitation, and a sideways look. 'Actually, sir, it was your murder victim. Young Master Quintus's father.'

I sat back.

Gods!

18

Perilla was still on her academic bean-feast in Albus's study when I got back. The separate piles had grown in number and thickness, and she'd obviously found a fresh cache somewhere or other, because the sheaf of unsorted incunabula immediately in front of her didn't seem to have got any smaller.

'Hello, dear,' she said as I stretched out on the couch and put the usual welcome-home jug and cup on the table within easy reach. 'These notes of Cornelius Albus's are absolutely fascinating. He hadn't arranged them in any sort of order, unfortunately, chronological or otherwise, but I'm doing that as I go. I must ask Cornelia what she intends to do with them. I'm no expert, but even I can see that it fills in quite a few gaps, and there's easily enough material here for a proper history. Did you know, for example, that during the final siege of the Byrsa there were some nine hundred deserters from the Roman army on the Carthaginian side? Nine *hundred!*'

I grinned; the lady was clearly happy as a pig in muck. Weird, but there you go; whatever turns you on.

'Surprisingly,' I said, 'no.'

'And that Hasdrubal's wife, the one who led the defence and threw her children down from the walls into the burning city below before committing suicide herself, was called Elissa? I don't think she's given a name anywhere else.'

'That's the same name as Albus gave his daughter.'

'Yes. So, considering who her mother was, possibly one passed down the suffete female line. Of course, the original founder of Carthage – our Queen Dido – was Elissa too. There's a certain irony in the fact, don't you think, that the line of rulers began and ended with a woman of the same name.'

'Your Elissa – the one who committed suicide – wasn't in charge. That was her husband.'

'Don't quibble, dear. Hasdrubal had sold out to Aemilianus in exchange for his life. A temporary reprieve, yes, but still. He wasn't on the Byrsa, and those who were – Carthage's last defenders, including his wife – regarded him as a traitor. Elissa was in command. I'd say giving her the title of ruler would be the fair thing to do, don't you?'

'You're the budding historian, not me,' I said equably. 'Incidentally, it might not be a good idea to mention to Cornelia that you're going through her father's notes, if you haven't done already. Have you?'

She coloured. 'No. In actual fact I haven't. I'm sure she wouldn't mind, though. Why should it matter?'

'No reason that it should, really. But just to be on the safe side keep away from the subject for the present, okay? Unless she raises it herself.'

'Very well, Marcus. If you insist.' She looked relieved. And no arguments, notice, not the shred of one, let alone a demand for an explanation. Evidently the lady's academic urges had been tussling with a feeling of guilt re furkling through what, despite her claims to the contrary, were Albus's private papers, and so far the former had won out hands down. This way she could justify the fact to herself by shifting any incoming blame onto me for possible future use. I grinned to myself: you can't live with another person for twenty-odd years without picking up on some of their little foibles. And that one was pure Perilla. 'So,' she said. 'How did your interview go with Marcus Virrius's father?'

'It didn't. But I had a very interesting chat with the daughter.' I told her what Virria had told me.

'She said that her brother had actually admitted to the rape?'

'Yeah, but–'

'Then that would seem to settle the matter, wouldn't it? As for Virria's own opinion, that's the product of wishful thinking typical in a girl of her age. She obviously idolised him, because of his imperfections rather than in spite of them – typical again – which meant that he couldn't possibly have done it. Therefore he didn't.'

'Come on, lady! That's sophistry!'

'No, it isn't. It's common sense, combined with a knowledge of human nature. The adolescent female side of it in particular.'

'Do you want a trip to Utica or not?'

'Pardon?'

'I've asked Quirinius to arrange it. Only for me so far, but there's no reason why you shouldn't tag along for the ride. The sail. Whatever.' She was frowning. 'The place is older than Carthage, right?' I prompted. 'And because it was on our side in the last Carthaginian war when Carthage was flattened our boys left it alone. So it's probably chock-full of things to see, Punic temples, tombs and so on. Of course, if you're not interested–'

The frown lifted, and she grinned. 'Marcus Valerius Corvinus, you are a devious, conniving rat completely devoid of any moral scruples.'

'True.'

'How long would we be away?'

'Quirinius says all being well probably two days there, two back. If I find Virrius straight off I can be finished in five, easy. But under the circumstances I'm willing to compromise.'

'Eight days and you have a bargain.'

'Seven.'

'Very well. Seven. Actually, I'll be quite happy to get back to this.' She indicated the pile of papers. 'There's still a great deal to be done, and as I said because Albus was treating events from a Carthaginian viewpoint it's fascinating. So. How was the rest of your day? After your talk with Virria?'

'Oh, now, that was even more interesting. It seems we were completely wrong about Albus's relationship with Cornelia, for a start.' I told her about my conversation with Chilo.

'Oh, I am glad!' she said. 'That we haven't got another Marilla on our hands, I mean. Still, it's puzzling, isn't it? What could she and her father have been arguing about, and why should it have had such a drastic long-term effect? After all, he did prosecute Marcus Virrius, and it wasn't his fault that the young man escaped punishment by running away.'

'Yeah.' I rubbed my chin. 'Actually, I've got my own theory about that.'

'Namely?'

I told her.

She stared at me open-mouthed. 'You think *what?*' she said. 'Marcus, that is *insane!* It goes against all the evidence, and you haven't the smallest scrap of proof to back it up. Nor are you likely to get it.'

'No, I know,' I said. 'Not here in Carthage, anyway. Which is why I have to go to Utica. It'd explain why Cestius Senior sharked up the prosecution of Medar's son Adon, though, wouldn't it? And what Cornelia had against her father. Just leave it as a possibility for the present, okay?'

'Perhaps we'd better.' She sniffed. 'However, I'm afraid you've overreached yourself this time.'

145

'Maybe so. Nevertheless.' I took a large swallow of wine; the next bit was going to be *really* tricky. 'Meanwhile you do see the implications of what Chilo told me about Albus's death, yes?'

'I'm not stupid, Marcus,' she said tartly. 'Neither do I allow my personal feelings and opinions to cloud my judgment. You think Quintus Cestius never left the house at all that morning. That, either completely on his own initiative or more probably with Cornelia's connivance, he waited for an opportunity to decoy the old man out of his study and to the head of the stairs and then pushed him down them.'

'Yeah,' I said. 'That about covers it. It would fit in with Cestius Senior's visit earlier as well.' I took a deep breath. 'Not to mention, ah, the timing of his own murder two days later.'

'Oh?' she said. 'How so?' Her protestations of impartiality notwithstanding, the lady was sounding distinctly tetchy, and there was a definite tang of ice in the air.

'Come on, Perilla!' I said. 'The only proof we have that neither Cestius nor Albus was aware that their son and daughter were an item, immediately prior to their own deaths at any rate, comes from what the pair themselves have told us, right? So what if they're lying? Say Cestius had found out somehow, very recently, that his son had taken up with Cornelia and had gone round first thing that day to have it out with Albus? Who, of course, knows nothing about it himself but would be equally opposed. Quintus and Cornelia would have to act quickly, and where both parents were concerned. Albus is easy: Quintus is a frequent visitor, so the old man won't be suspicious if he turns up later that morning, in fact he'll welcome the opportunity to have things out with him. When–'

'Hold on, Marcus. Surely he would've wanted to see both Quintus and Cornelia together? So why didn't he?'

'Because Cornelia had already gone out.'

'Yes, but Albus wouldn't have known that at the time, would he? They never talked. So the natural thing for him to have done, under the circumstances, would've been to go and tell Chilo to fetch her into the study. Which, of course, he didn't, because otherwise Chilo would've mentioned it to you. In fact, after he'd learned of the affair from Cestius Albus would've pulled Cornelia in for questioning straight away, whether he knew Quintus was coming round that morning or not. And Chilo didn't say that he did that either.'

146

Shit; she was right, of course. Even so. 'Look,' I said, 'maybe he had his reasons, okay? Remember, the two of them – Albus and his daughter – had barely exchanged a word, civil or otherwise, for over two years. That's a hard habit to break, even if the circumstances were special. Besides, if I'm right about his past dealings with Cestius then Albus hated the man's guts; note the fact that Chilo told me he'd hardly allowed him past the threshold, and the visit only lasted five minutes. So why should he go over the top, alienate his favourite protégé and put the cap on his relationship, or lack of one, with his only daughter, just on Cestius's say-so? I'd reckon keeping things low key, checking out Cestius's claims with Quintus first before he took matters any further, possibly even trying persuasion on the couple, would be exactly what he would do.' I frowned. 'In fact, when he left his study to go downstairs he might've had just that in mind and been on his way to find Cornelia, leaving Quintus behind him in the study. Which might make the lad's decision to kill him a heat-of-the-moment one rather than premeditated. That suit you better?'

'Hmm.' She was twisting a stray lock of hair. 'You could be right, I suppose. It all makes sense, in theory at least.' Hey! Score one for the boy! 'Even so, there is still one major problem.'

'Yeah? And what's that?'

'If Quintus did push Albus downstairs then how did he get out of the house?'

'How do you mean? Through the front door, of course.'

'In that case he'd be taking quite a risk, wouldn't he? If the murder was premeditated. After all, Chilo couldn't have been far away–'

'He was in the kitchen, discussing the dinner menu with the chef, remember. That's–'

'– and there had to be other slaves around as well. Albus would probably have cried out as he fell, and he'd certainly have made a racket falling down the wooden staircase. Quintus would have to get downstairs himself, past Albus, across the lobby to the front door – which would probably have been bolted, at least – and outside, all before someone came to investigate. That would be quite difficult, wouldn't it?'

Hell's teeth. 'Uh...yeah,' I said. 'Yes, I suppose it would.'

'There you are, then. As I say, a problem. Ideas?'

147

'He could've slipped back into the study. Or Cornelia's room would've been on this floor, all the bedrooms are. He could've waited in there until she was able to smuggle him out.'

'For how long? Cornelia didn't get back, according to Chilo, for several hours, so he'd be running the risk of discovery for all that time. And following Albus's death the house would be in an uproar, with people coming and going downstairs constantly. Perhaps upstairs, as well. And there would've been more of them than usual, the undertaker's men, for a start. Don't forget, Quintus only had to be found on the premises for his guilt to be obvious. As I say, the risk involved would be considerable.'

'And if he hadn't planned the murder? If it was just a spur-of-the-moment thing? There'd be nothing he could do about that, and he'd still be stuck.'

'Then if you're right – as I fully admit you may be – we'll just have to hope that that was what happened and he was simply very lucky; that he managed to slip out eventually, or that when Cornelia came back and found him she was able to arrange something.'

'Fair enough,' I said. 'Shelve the whole boiling for the present in the theory category, okay?'

She smiled. 'Agreed.'

'Moving on to Cestius's murder.'

The smile disappeared. 'Oh, *Marcus!*'

'If I'm right about the reason for his father's visit to Albus – which I think I am – it puts Quintus, and probably Cornelia by association, slap bang at the top of the suspects list. At least as the instigators; I still think Medar did the actual killing.'

'Reasons?'

'Come on, lady! It's obvious! As a father, Cestius was a completely different kettle of fish from Albus. As soon as he found out his son was contemplating a marriage he disapproved of the first thing he'd do wouldn't be to go round to the girl's father and tell him what was going on; it'd be to haul the boy onto the carpet and chew his balls off. If that's not an unfortunate metaphor under the circumstances. Closely followed, Quintus being Quintus and as stubborn a bugger as you're likely to meet, by the threat of estrangement and disinheritance at the first opportunity. Only, again, as with Albus, the opportunity doesn't arise, because Quintus arranges with Medar to zero him two days later. Or, of course, does it himself, you take your pick, because his alibi that he spent a romantic morning and afternoon with Cornelia at their private cove wouldn't even make it to the starting line.'

'How did he know?'

'How did who know what?'

'Quintus. That his father would be riding out that day to the very part of the estate where Medar was working.'

'Jupiter, Perilla, *it doesn't matter*, okay? It's irrelevant. Quintus had decided that his father had to die asap. That time of year, Cestius rode out most days to some part of the estate, he made no secret of where he was going, and if Quintus was prepared to do the killing himself he'd have plenty of opportunity. Cestius'd have no suspicion that his life was in danger from his son – why should he? – and Quintus could easily have got close enough to do the job at his leisure, whenever the opportunity arose. Maybe pretended that he'd had a change of heart and was prepared to give Cornelia up but wanted to talk things over first. The fact that his father chose Medar's stretch of country to head for that day need simply have been a coincidental bonus.'

'Medar would surely have had to know, though. That Cestius had to die, and there was some urgency about it.'

'Sure he would. So what's wrong with Quintus riding out there in the course of the morning and telling him? It wouldn't even matter if his father saw him in the process, or, for different reasons, any of Medar's kinfolk did, because later his father would be dead and none of the harvesters, on Medar's own showing, would give him away.'

'Hmm,' she said again, as she had when I'd finished explaining my theory re Albus. Only this time, just that and nothing more. I grinned; got her! When Perilla doesn't come straight out with an objection it means she can't think of one. And the fact that she didn't add anything in the way of a comprehensible Latin sentence as a rider to it meant she didn't like admitting it one little bit.

'Actually,' I said, rubbing it in, 'that's something we can confirm, if we're lucky. That Cestius knew last thing about the Quintus Cornelia pairing. I'm booked in to have a word with a lady called Eulalia tomorrow afternoon. She works in the Cestius house's kitchens, and it seems she's a natural for picking up the domestic gossip. If Quintus and his father did have a spat just before Albus died she might remember hearing about it.

Then we can–' There was a knock on the door and Bathyllus came in. 'Yeah, what is it, sunshine? Not dinner-time yet, surely?'

'No, sir. Sextus Quirinius is downstairs. It's about your trip to Utica.'

Hey! Great! 'Tell him I'll be right there.' I turned to Perilla. 'You want to come down?'

'No, dear. I'll carry on with this, if you don't mind. I may as well get some serious work done before we set off on your little jaunt.'

Stiff as hell; she really does *not* like to come out second best in a discussion, Perilla. Fortunately for domestic harmony, that doesn't happen too often. Even so, a rare joy to be savoured. I was grinning all the way to the atrium.

Quirinius was perched on one of the couches.

'Hello, Corvinus,' he said. 'I just dropped by to say your journey to Utica is all arranged. Leaving at the second hour the day after tomorrow, if that's convenient. Winds permitting, of course, but they're generally reliable at this time of year.'

'That's great.' I set the wine jug and cup that I'd brought down with me on the low table. 'You have time for some wine?'

'No, honestly, it's just a fleeting visit.' He stood up. 'I should be in a dozen other places at the moment. Anyway, I've managed to commandeer the governor's official yacht for you.'

'Have you, indeed?' I said. 'Does Galba know?'

The barest twitch of the lips. 'Actually, no. But he hardly ever uses it, particularly not in high summer. And it'll cut the crossing time in half. How long were you planning to be away?'

'Seven days in total should be ample time. And Perilla will be coming with me, if that's okay by you.' Not that I was going to let on that most of the slack was for the purpose of the lady's sightseeing jag. Yeah, well, there had to be some perks to the job of imperial procurator, and if we got back to find Sulpicius Galba hopping up and down venting his enraged spleen on the quayside then that'd just be too bad. 'The boat'll wait around for the return trip?'

'Yes, of course. Accommodation's no problem when you get there. We do have a small official residence – the city was the provincial capital until Carthage was rebuilt – but as you can understand it's very old and not often used, and there's no permanent staff. When the governor goes through on business he usually stays with an ex-mayor of the town, a

150

gentleman by the name of Titus Statius. I'm sure he'd be delighted to put you and your wife up; in any case, I've sent a courier to give him the message that you're coming, so you should be expected.'

'Marvellous. Thanks again, Quirinius.'

'I'll send a carriage for you half way through the second hour. If there's anything else just let me know.'

He left. Well, that was that side of things done and dusted. And I was looking forward to having a word with young Virrius.

Meanwhile there was that interview with Eulalia.

19.

The sun had just moved into its eighth-hour slot when I reached the Cestius family mansion. Like Spadix had said it would be, the first gate I came to in the perimeter wall was unbarred. I pushed it open and went through.

There was a youngish slave hoeing between two rows of lettuces. He stopped, grounded the hoe, and stood watching me with a look that was more than half way to a scowl. Obviously the lady's boyfriend, on hand to make sure the word 'meeting' didn't have any of its Spadixian connotations.

'Valerius Corvinus, sir?' I turned. The guy himself was coming towards me, together with a mousey wisp of a thing that had to be the *femme fatale* in person. 'You din't have no problems finding your way, then?'

'Uh-uh,' I said. 'This Eulalia?'

'Yeah.' The girl dropped me a curtsey, but I'd caught the quick, speculative look before she lowered her eyes. Not so mousey after all, then; Spadix's pal Simo was right to be worried. 'Shed's this way, if you want to use it. Like I said, this time of day we'd be safe enough out here in the open, but you might prefer the privacy.'

'Perfect.' That got me another glare from Simo, and I could almost hear his teeth grinding. 'Lead on, pal.'

The shed was little more than a lean-to built against the back of the wall. I opened the door and went in. There was a pile of straw in one corner with a few sacks on top – obviously where the couple had their meetings – and a miscellaneous collection of tools and assorted gardening-related odds and ends.

'I'll leave you to it, then,' Spadix said. 'Plenty time, don't you worry. An' Simo an' me, we'll keep an eye peeled out front, just in case.'

He closed the door behind him, leaving the two of us facing each other in the dim light that came through the cracks in the woodwork.

'You're the gentleman from Rome,' Eulalia said. 'The emperor's friend. Yes?'

'Yeah. More or less. Now, what I wanted to ask you was–'

'Me, I've never been outside Carthage.' She went over to the pile of straw and sat down. 'Must be nice to see a bit of the world.'

'Pretty much so, yes. Now about–'

''Course, if anyone was to offer me the chance to do it, well,' – she leaned back – 'I'd be very grateful.' She leaned back a bit more. 'Really, *really* grateful.'

Mousey, nothing, nowhere near it; we'd got a proper little scheming Cleopatra here, and no mistake. Mind you, I didn't blame her for trying. If you're a kitchen skivvy with nowhere to go but up and a boyfriend who hoes lettuces for a living you go full tilt at any opportunity that offers itself.

'Look, Eulalia,' I said. 'I just want some information, okay? About the time your master died. You think you can manage that without trying to jump me?' She scowled, sat up and folded her arms deliberately across her inconsequential bosom. 'Good. Well done. On the plus side' – I took a half gold piece out of my belt-purse and laid it on an upturned bucket – 'I'm not asking for any freebies here, and there'll be no comeback. That I guarantee. Fair?'

Her eyes went to the coin, the scowl disappeared, and the arms uncrossed. 'Fair,' she said. 'What do you want to know?'

'First off. Your young Master Quintus. Was he on good terms with his father?'

She gave an unmouselike snort. 'With that old devil? 'Course he wasn't. Mind you, that was nothing special, none of them was. They gener'ly kept out of one another's way altogether if they could, the whole boiling, because when they din't they fought like bloody cats.'

'Yeah, I'd already got that impression. But I'm thinking especially about latterly.' Her expression clouded. 'Uh...immediately before the old man died. They have any specific disagreements that you know of? Quintus and him?'

'What's "specific" mean?'

Bugger; we were venturing onto the thin ice of linguistic competence here. 'Particular,' I said. 'Outside of the usual.'

'Oh. Right. Yeah. Yeah, actually, they did.'

Jupiter! 'Namely?'

'Must of been, oh, three or four days before it happened, 'least 'cording to my friend Leuce. She works above stairs, does the cleaning in what was the old master's part of the house. Which was what she was doing at the time, like. Master Quintus, he comes belting upstairs from the front

154

entrance with a face like bloody thunder and asks her where his father is. Leuce tells him in his study, an' he leaves her standing an' barges through the door without so much as a knock.'

'Did Leuce hear what the quarrel was about?'

'No. She tried to listen in, o'course, but they're solid oak two inch thick, them doors, an' the pair of them was keeping their voices down. All she got before the young master slammed the door in her face was he called his father an effin' crupulous liar.'

I translated. *Unscrupulous*. Right. And *liar*; Quintus had used the same word to me about his father, or close to it, when we'd talked. The difference was that now I knew why, or at least I thought I did.

The 'unscrupulous' fitted, too.

'Was there anything more?' I said.

'Not that Leuce saw. She made herself scarce straight off 'cos believe me you din't want to be nowhere near the old master when he was in that sort of a mood.'

Yeah, well; I wasn't all that disappointed: after all, like I say, I had a fair idea already about what had been going on behind the closed door. Still, it was good to have the theory confirmed. And, of course, to know that the quarrel had happened in the first place. It appeared that young Quintus had some serious questions to answer.

'Okay,' I said. 'Moving on to something a lot more recent, maybe about six or seven days ago.' I crossed my fingers. 'You happen to know if your mistress had a visit from an Appius Justus at all?'

'Never heard of him.'

'Sailor type, big beard. About the same age as she is.'

'Oh. Him. The pincher.' She giggled.

'Ah..."The pincher"?'

'That's what Xanthippe called him, the randy old sod. He never give his name, not that Xanthippe heard, anyway.'

'Who's Xanthippe?'

'The mistress's maid. She told Leuce – they're best friends, if you get my meaning, Leuce an' her, well, that's no one's business but theirs – an' Leuce told me.' Uh-huh; score another point for the bought-help grapevine. 'Must of been about that, six or seven days ago. He was only here the once, mind, not that Xanthippe's crying. 'Cording to Leuce she's still got a black and blue patch the size of a sesterce on her you-know-where. Me, I've no sympathy. Stuck-up cow.'

'Right. Right.' Gods! 'So, uh, what did he want, do you know?'

Eulalia shrugged. 'Search me. He turns up at the door late on, like, after the lamps is lit, an' gives Crescens a note an' a silver piece to deliver it to the mistress.'

'Crescens being the door-slave?'

'Yeah. 'Course. Anyway, Crescens passes it to Xanthippe an' Xanthippe takes it on up.'

'She know what was in it?'

'Nah, it was sealed, wasn't it? Not that it would've made a blind bit of difference, mind, 'cos for all her airs an' graces that cow can't tell one bloody word from the next.'

'So what happened then?'

'The mistress sends Xanthippe back down hell for leather to fetch him up. Pale as a ghost, Xanthippe said she was, in a proper state. So Xanthippe does, which was when the bastard pinches her on the what's-its-name. She'd of turned round an' smacked him if she'd dared, but she din't want to risk it 'case he was one of the mistress's friends an' got her into trouble for it.'

'Uh-huh. She, ah, overhear what went on between them?'

'Nah. The mistress sent her out of the room an' warned her that if she snooped she'd have the skin off of her back. So she went straight downstairs an' stayed there until he'd gone.'

'Which was when?'

''Bout half an hour later, 'cording to Crescens.' Eulalia grinned. 'Must of been a fast worker, Xanthippe said, or the mistress was losing her touch. Mind you, she usually likes them younger.'

'And you say that was the only time he came?'

'Yeah. Just that once, far as I know.'

'So that was the end of it? Again, as far as you know. Or as far as Xanthippe knows, that is.'

'Sure. The mistress was in a foul temper for a coupla days after, though, Xanthippe couldn't do a thing right.' She gave me a covert glance. 'So who was he, then, that you're so interested? Not the one that did for the master?'

'No, just someone new to Carthage, an Italian slave-dealer. In fact he was killed himself a couple of days later.'

'A slave-dealer, right? No bloody loss there, then. I'll get Leuce to tell Xanthippe. She'll be mad she din't clock the bastard one when she'd the chance after all.'

There was real venom there. Yeah, well, I supposed it was understandable.

'Fair enough,' I said. I picked up the half gold piece and gave it to her. 'Thanks, Eulalia. You've been really helpful.'

'You're welcome.' She palmed the coin and stood up. 'An' if you, like, change your mind about things, you know what I mean, well, you know where to find me, don't you?'

'Sure I do. Thanks again.'

I opened the shed door and went out to face the accusing stare of the lady's boyfriend.

Yeah, well, that was another little mystery cleared up, then. And if I didn't miss my guess it gave Verania a prime reason, in retrospect, at least, for stiffing her husband.

When I got back home it was to find Perilla in our bedroom supervising the packing for the trip to Utica the following day.

'Marcus, I thought I'd thrown out that old green tunic of yours before we left Rome,' she said. 'So what is it doing here in Carthage, at the bottom of your clothes chest?'

Bugger. I set the jug and wine cup that I'd brought up with me on one of the side tables.

'Ah...'

'Packed in error, madam.' Bathyllus passed her a folded cloak, and I breathed again. Not so much as a pause or a batted eyelid; saved by the duplicitous major-domo.

'Yes, well, it certainly is *not* coming to Utica with us.' She tossed it onto the bed. 'Bathyllus, we'll finish this later, if you don't mind.' He left. 'So, dear. How was your talk with what's-her-name?'

'Eulalia.' I pulled up a stool, and sat down. 'Very informative. For a start, when he said that his father knew nothing about his relationship with Cornelia Quintus Cestius was lying through his teeth.'

'You're sure?' she said sharply.

'Absolutely.' I told her what Eulalia had told me, about the father-and-son quarrel.

'Yes, but Marcus, the girl's friend also said she didn't hear any of their actual conversation.' Perilla put the folded cloak into the travelling chest. 'For all we know, the argument could have been about something else entirely. And what she *did* hear, that Quintus called his father an unscrupulous liar, doesn't fit the situation at all, does it?'

'Sure it does. At least, it fits with the theory re the "family affair" he refused to go into details about when he talked to us, and for that to work knowledge on the elder Cestius's part that Cornelia and his son were an item with no secrets from each other is a *sine qua non.*'

'Very well.' Perilla sniffed. 'So assuming, for the present at least, that you're right – and I *mean* assuming – then what are the implications?'

'Come on, lady! We discussed these! That Quintus, off his own bat or in collusion with Medar, killed or was complicit in the killing of his father to safeguard his own future. The only differences are that now we know that it wasn't the father who started the ball rolling but the son. And that we also know that there was another element involved which may, or, as Quintus insisted, may not have had any relevance to the old man's murder a couple of days later but sure as hell qualifies as a prime contributory motive.'

'Think we know.'

'What?'

'As you said, dear, that part's only a theory at present. I'll admit that it looks extremely likely now that just before his death Cestius Senior found out about his son's relationship with Cornelia, and that the information may well have come from Quintus himself in the course of their argument, but the rest remains pure supposition. We only *think* we know it.'

Gods! The woman could be picky when she chose! And she was clearly still hell-bent on defending squeaky-clean young Quintus, even if it did go against all reason. 'Fine,' I said. 'Have it your own way. In any case, judging by the rest of what Eulalia told me we have another front-runner suspect altogether.'

'Yes? And who's that?'

'Verania. At least, her as the instigator, with Scarus as the actual perp.'

'Really, dear!' She sat down on the bed. 'We've been through that. Why on earth should Verania want to murder her husband? Not as a result of her affair with Scarus, certainly; we know Cestius couldn't have cared less what she got up to in that direction.'

'Not her affair with Scarus. The one with Appius Justus.'

'*What?*' She goggled.

'Publius isn't Cestius's son. Or at least one of the lads isn't, but Publius is favourite by a mile.'

'How the *hell* do you know that?'

I grinned; the lady only swears when she's seriously rattled. 'It's the only explanation that makes sense.' I told her what Eulalia had told me, about Justus's evening visit and how Verania had seemed to react to it. 'My bet is that he was threatening to blackmail her, and that she had Scarus kill him.'

'Your rationale, please.'

'Okay.' I poured myself a cupful of wine. 'To begin with, all the circumstantial stuff fits. Twenty-six years ago, which would be the time in question, Verania and her husband were in Rome and according to his later partner Cycnus Justus was running a slave-trading business based in Ostia. Again according to Cycnus, Justus had an eye for the ladies, and he was just the type Verania would've found attractive. So–'

'How would they have met?'

'Jupiter, Perilla, I don't know! Maybe she was in Ostia shopping for bought help. Maybe she was between lovers and trawling. Maybe she fell off the quayside into his fucking boat and everything progressed from there. Does it matter?'

'Possibly not. And don't swear.'

'Anyway, the upshot was she made a mistake and got pregnant. No great problem: she was married, she could easily engineer things so that Cestius would think the child was his. In any case – '

'There are ways to end a pregnancy, you know. Dangerous and illegal, yes, but none the less. She wouldn't have *had* to go through with it.'

'True. But then we don't know the full circumstances, do we? Maybe Cestius had been pestering her for an heir; remember, they'd already been married for a good four years, at least, before Publius showed up. Or maybe she just didn't want to take the risk of triggering an abortion. Now could I possibly sodding carry on, please?'

'I suppose so, dear. If you must.'

'Thank you. In any case, then, from what I know of Verania, and from what Cycnus told me about Justus, I wouldn't imagine the affair went on for all that long. Neither was into long-term relationships, and when one of them got bored – probably Verania, judging by her track record – that was the end of it. Amicable separation, no hassle on either side. The chances are that Justus never knew she had had his child at all. Of course until recently, that is.'

'And how would that have come about? They were from totally different social strata, Verania had been living in Carthage for the past fifteen years, and from what you told me, or from what Justus's partner told you at least, during that time he hadn't been south of Sicily.'

'Yeah, well, that'd be because of the engagement, wouldn't it? Between Publius Cestius and Vettius Rufus's girl.'

'Marcus, don't you think that it's a little unlikely that an Ostian slave-dealer would be up to date with events in the Roman social calendar?'

'Not when you consider that news of the match would be linked to the much-more-lurid news of an ex-praetor's murder, no. And given he'd known the guy in question, or known his wife, at least, it'd only take a passing mention of that in a wineshop by one of his seafaring cronies to jog his interest. Then a bit of thought on his part, comparison of dates and ages, maybe a bit of sleuthing, would've been enough for him to put two and two together.'

She sighed. 'I'm sorry, dear, but all this really is extremely tenuous. After all, as you said, the affair had to have happened over twenty-five years ago, and for the first ten of these Verania would still have been in Rome. With, of course, the child. Don't you think that if Justus had been up to entertaining the idea of blackmail he would have had his opportunity long since?'

I shook my head. 'Maybe not. You said yourself; the two of them moved in completely different circles. For all Justus would know about her current life Verania might as well be on the moon, and he'd be travelling for most of the time himself. Also, going by the impression I got of him from Cycnus, at heart he wasn't really the blackmailing type: a serial womaniser, sure, but the love-them-and-leave-them-laughing sort. Nothing really nasty.'

'That's another objection, surely.' Perilla leaned back against the headboard. 'The blackmailing. What would be the point of blackmail now, when he knew the woman's husband was dead?'

'There'd be plenty of point. Verania's son was poised to marry into a strait-laced consular family. How do you think Rufus would've reacted if he'd found out his daughter was engaged to the son of a slave-dealer? Also, Justus was getting on in years. The temptation to add substantially to whatever he'd managed to put away for his retirement would've been pretty strong.'

'Hmm. All right. Fair enough, I suppose.'

Grudging as hell, but still. 'Besides, all these whys-and-wherefores don't matter; the bottom line is that Justus did make a special trip to Carthage to call on Verania, he wasn't a welcome visitor, and a couple of days later someone cut his throat in an alleyway. My conclusion is that the guy was threatening blackmail, the most obvious reason being the existence of an old affair, and Verania got her lover Scarus to take him out.' I took another mouthful of wine. 'Pretty reasonable, I'd've thought.'

'Yes.' She was twisting a lock of hair. 'Yes, to be fair I suppose it is, at that. Actually, though, there is another possible angle to it that would make the theory slightly less unstable.'

'Yeah?' I said cautiously. 'And what's that?'

'If Publius Cestius were directly involved, *propria persona*.'

'Okay, Aristotle,' I said. 'All yours, you have the floor. The bed. Whatever.'

'There's not much to add, really. And I'm afraid it does involve some degree of coincidence.'

'No problem. Coincidences happen. Go on.'

'When he talked to you Publius said he'd been in Rome earlier in the year meeting his future wife and her family, yes?'

'Yeah. Spring, he said, so presumably right after the sea-lanes opened in March.'

'So if the ship that brought him docked at Ostia rather than Puteoli then Justus may well have seen him. Which is where the coincidence comes in. We don't know, of course, whether Publius took after his father physically to any great extent, but if he did then at age twenty-five any similarity would be quite marked. Certainly clearly enough for Justus to notice it and take the trouble to find out who the young man was. After which naturally,

161

it would only be a question of his, as you say, putting two and two together.'

I sat back. Shit; she was right. It wouldn't have gone the other way, mind: if there was a resemblance then a clean-shaven Justus arriving in Carthage, where Publius Cestius was so well known, might've caused a bit of speculation, but the guy from all accounts had been heavily bearded; and that, plus the fact that he was twice his son's age, would've put recognition well on the safe side of unlikely. I'd never seen Justus's corpse, which was a pity; shave off the beard and for all I knew he might've been, no pun intended, a dead ringer.

'It would certainly explain a lot of things, wouldn't it?' Perilla went on. 'How he made the connection with Carthage, for a start. There is the problem of why, in that case, he didn't come straight here, but if as you say his mind didn't automatically turn to thoughts of blackmail perhaps that isn't too much of an obstacle; in fact, if he wasn't really the criminal type what may have led him to get in touch might simply have been the news of Verania's husband's death.' She was still twisting the stray lock of hair. 'What I'd be really interested to know, though, is whether he revealed who he was to Publius. Because if he did then...well, the implications are obvious, aren't they?'

Uh-huh; sure they were. 'If he did,' I said, 'then Publius – and his mother, when he got back to Carthage and told her – would know they were living on borrowed time. Justus could turn up at any minute and spill the beans to Cestius Senior. Whereupon the chances were that Cestius being Cestius the pair of them would be out on their ears before they could spit, Verania divorced and Publius disinherited, with both his marriage plans and his future political career sent straight down the tube. A casual affair would've been one thing, Cestius could've shrugged that off, but discovering that for the past twenty-odd years he'd been rearing another man's bastard would've–' I stopped.

'Marcus?' She frowned. 'What is it?'

Oh, gods! 'Scarus knew,' I said. 'Knows. And Publius knows he knows.'

'Are you being deliberately obscure, dear, or what? Only–'

I waved her to silence. Jupiter! 'That day at the Honeycomb, when I was talking to Publius and he came over and interrupted us,' I said. 'He had some sort of hold over Publius, that was obvious from how easily he

162

got rid of him. And when Publius had gone he called him a bastard. I assumed at the time, naturally enough, he was being metaphorical, but he wasn't, he was being absolutely literal, knowing full well I wouldn't twig. Typical Scarus: private joke, laugh in your sleeve, take the piss out of the dumb Roman.'

'Ah. That would make sense. And if Scarus knew then it could only have been through Verania.' She pulled at the lock of hair. 'So which of them do you think would have committed the actual murder? Cestius's, I mean. Publius or Scarus?'

I shrugged. 'Jury's out on that one, and frankly I don't think it matters at the moment: Verania's hand might not have been on the knife, but six gets you ten that if the theory holds good whichever of them did it she was the instigator. Certainly, given that Scarus's alibi for that morning is the lady herself, both Scarus and Publius had the opportunity. Me, all things being equal, I'd go for Publius: keep it in the family, as it were, and the same arguments about Quintus being able to get close enough to his father to do the business would apply to him. Plus it would explain Scarus's hold over him. On the other hand, he hasn't got the seasoned killer's track record that Scarus has. So, like I say, the jury's out.'

'What about your Appius Justus? Which of them would have killed him?'

'Same answer, and for the same reasons. All that's fairly certain – at least, I think it is – is that Verania set it up, told Justus to come back for the money in a couple of days, and then had either her son or her lover nail him when he left his lodgings.'

'So. Are you going to face her with it?'

'Uh-uh.' I shook my head. 'I don't see how I can at present. Oh, sure, the theory holds water, better than, but that's all it is, a theory. We've no actual proof, and without proof the lady would just laugh in my face, certainly where her husband's death is concerned. Besides, on balance the chances are that I was right in the first place and Cestius's killer was either Medar or Quintus.'

'Hmm.'

A comment wordless in nature but richly redolent of disapproval. I ignored it and carried on.

'Justus, mind, is another thing entirely. Okay, fine, we know, or think we know, that the motive was to cover up Verania's affair with him and its result, but as far as the authorities are concerned it was a simple mugging that ended in a death. On the other hand, the killing was recent and it was done practically in the middle of town as opposed to out in the sticks, so it's wide open to investigation and the compilation of evidence, technically, at least.'

'So?'

'Come on, Perilla! I'm an imperial procurator, which means I have clout. For the emperor's direct rep to accuse a pal of his mother-in-law of zeroing her ex-praetor husband without a shred of proof to back the accusation, particularly when her alleged motive is to cover up her high-flyer son's illegitimacy, is one thing; pulling in a no-account gladiator with a dodgy reputation for questioning on a charge of mugging a low-class slave-dealer is something else entirely. I wouldn't even have to worry about justifying the arrest, because even if it was me doing the asking Galba wouldn't think twice about giving the okay. And he wouldn't be too picky about me proving my case, either.'

'That's hardly fair, is it? After all, you don't know for certain that Scarus *did* murder Justus.'

'I never said it was fair. But it is the way of the world. I bet you not even Sextus Quirinius would bat an eyelid, and young Quirinius is as honest and fair-minded as they come. Besides, the chances are it wouldn't come to that. Just the threat would be enough to loosen the bastard's tongue, particularly if I showed him I knew the surrounding circumstances.'

'Verania would back him up, surely.'

'You think so? Remember, unlike in Cestius's case there's nothing to connect her with Justus, and Scarus's past history and the robbery motive would be enough on their own to put him down. Enough for a social snob like Galba, anyway. And if he threatened to uncover the whole boiling to the authorities it'd be his word against hers, with Galba doing the listening and getting hotter and hotter under the collar every second re jumped-up provincial thugs bad-mouthing their betters. Verania would be safe enough, Publius, too. She'd drop Scarus without a second thought.'

'So what is your plan, exactly?'

'Simple. As soon as we get back from Utica I get the crooked bastard into a corner somewhere and explain his options to him. If Verania doesn't owe Scarus any favours then it's mutual, particularly if the killer in both instances was Publius. Oh, sure, his evidence might not weigh in for much at the end of the day, but at the very least I'll have it myself, to use as best I can.'

She got up off the bed. 'Yes, well, dear, apropos of that we won't be going to Utica at all if I don't get on with the packing, will we?'

True. I grinned and stood up myself. 'Fair enough,' I said. 'I'll leave you to it.'

'Good. Send Bathyllus back up.'

I collected the jug and wine cup and went downstairs.

At least things were finally moving.

20.

We got to Utica just short of mid-day two days later. It turned out much as I'd expected from Quirinius's description of the residence, old, faded and slightly seedy. Which was perfectly understandable, since not only had it lost its provincial capital status fifty-odd years previously, and so imperial interest in terms of new public buildings and facilities, but its harbour was silting up even faster than Ostia, meaning that now most of the shipping trade went through Carthage taking the town's prosperity with it. Hardly just, considering that the place had been on our side, and suffered for it, during the Carthaginian wars, but then history doesn't play favourites.

Old and faded pretty much described our host, too, although I wouldn't've added the 'seedy': Titus Statius might be well into his eighties, and thinned practically to a shadow, but he was one of the snappiest dressers I'd ever encountered, as was his wife Visellia, who was almost as old as he was. Not a bad guy, either, by any means, and bright as a button.

'You'll be Messalla Corvinus's grandson,' he said to me when he'd finished showing us the suite of rooms in his house that we'd be staying in for the duration.

'Yeah. That's right, I am.' To say I was surprised was putting it mildly: Grandpa Marcus had died when I was eight, and to my knowledge he'd never been closer to Africa than Egypt. 'You knew him?'

'Not really. I only met him the once, when I was very young, at a dinner party with my father in Rome. It must've been about seventy years back, when he was City Prefect for all of five minutes.' He chuckled. 'The official line was that he'd resigned because he didn't feel he was right for the job. Which I suppose is fair enough, if you take into account that his actual expressed opinion was that he was buggered if he could see the point of it to begin with, and told the Divine Augustus so to his face. My father had a lot of time for Corvinus; "perfectly civilised", he called him. It's a pleasure to have his grandson under my roof. Not to mention' – he turned to Perilla – 'his protégé Ovidius Naso's daughter.'

'Stepdaughter.' Perilla smiled.

'Indeed. I stand corrected. Him, I never met, I'm sorry to say, but I'm a great admirer of his verse. Superior even to Valerius Catullus's, in my view, although my wife would disagree.'

'Certainly quite as scandalous.' Visellia smiled. 'Not that that's a criticism. I remember as a girl smuggling a copy of his "Art of Love" into my room disguised as a commentary on Euripides's "Alcestis". My mother never did find out.'

'Now, Corvinus.' Statius cleared his throat. 'Of course you'll have your official business to attend to here, so please feel free to come and go as you please. We dine very early and very simply, I'm afraid, well before sundown – one of the penalties of advanced age – and although you're perfectly welcome to do the same you may find it both impractical and inconvenient. Euthias will be delighted to make separate arrangements if you prefer; just let him know your requirements, for that and for everything else.'

'Thank you,' I said. 'Perfect.' Euthias, of course, was Statius's major-domo. I was glad, now, that we'd decided not to bring Bathyllus: short stay or not, having two major-domos, at least one of whom was a card-carrying control freak who brooked no rival, in the same domestic environment was like putting two king bees into the same hive. Sooner or later – and probably very much the former – it was sure to end in tears, if not actual bodily harm.

'And in the meantime, if she likes,' Visellia said, 'I'd be delighted to show Rufia Perilla around Utica. There's the temple of Astarte, of course, that's very old, or part of it is, four hundred years or more. The priestesses there still go in for ritual prostitution, although naturally it's not what it was in the past. Terribly commercialised, I'm afraid, like everything else these days.'

'Really,' Perilla said faintly.

'Yes, unfortunately. Still, it *is* traditional, and it's always sad to see old traditions dying out, don't you think? The chief priestess is an old friend of mine, and great fun. I'll introduce you.'

'That would be marvellous. I look forward to it.'

'Excellent.'

Well, that was the lady taken care of for the immediate future. In spades. I smothered a grin and turned back to Statius.

'You happen to know of a stud farm out the Carthage road, run by a guy called Mandonius?' I said.

He shook his head. 'No, I'm afraid not. I don't get much beyond the city boundaries at all these days, and my interest in horse-riding has long been academic. But no doubt Euthias will.' Yeah, that I'd believe: the major-domo isn't born, or whatever creative process those guys undergo to waft them into existence, who doesn't know everything there is to know about names and addresses within at least a five mile radius. 'If you're going out that way you'll need a horse yourself. Unless you'd prefer a carriage?'

'No, a horse would be fine. First thing tomorrow morning, if that's okay.'

'I'm sure it will be. I'll have Euthias arrange it. Now, we'll leave you to settle in. You'll dine with us today, at least?'

'Yes, of course,' Perilla said. 'Thank you.'

'Fine. Take your time; I've put dinner off until the tenth hour, but it can be later if you'd prefer.'

'No, the tenth hour will be perfect.'

'We'll see you later, then.'

I had an even more skimpy breakfast than usual very early next morning before setting out for the stud farm where his sister had said Marcus Virrius – aka Marcus Mandonius – hung out. Good choice of time: away from the coast, the area around Utica was even hotter than inland of Carthage. It was a lot less intensively cultivated, too, and once I'd got past the stretch of tombs beyond the city gate the road was bordered with a succession of farms and vineyards: prosperous enough, from the looks of things, but clearly the property of ordinary farmers rather than big landowners. Plus of course the ubiquitous palm trees.

Euthias had said the place was a mile from town, adjacent to the road, and he was bang on: a pair of fields with half a dozen horses grazing, and a low-slung building with a yard and stables to the side at the end of a short cart-track. I rode up to them and dismounted.

A youngish guy, late twenties early thirties, was standing in the yard talking to an elderly slave. He looked up as I came over. I noticed the resemblance at once: same features as the sister, but in a masculine face. You could see he'd have no problems with women. Not of any type.

169

'Marcus Virrius?' I said.

To give the guy his due, he barely even blinked. He turned to the slave, spoke a few words to him, and then, as the man nodded and walked away, turned back to me.

'Some mistake here, friend,' he said. 'The Marcus is right enough, but the family name's Mandonius.'

'Uh-huh.' I waited until we were properly alone. 'Your sister told me to give you her love.'

He stood absolutely still for a moment, just watching me. Then he shrugged.

'Okay,' he said. 'We'll talk inside.'

He led the way towards the house, opened the door and then stood aside for me to pass. I'd been expecting a pit, but although the place was pretty basic – a living room with a door at the back leading, presumably, to an inner bedroom – it was clean and tidy. There was even a vase of fresh flowers on the table.

He came in after me and shut the door behind him, just as the room's other door opened and a girl's face looked out. Rather more of her than her face, actually, and with just as much, or as little, covering. Virrius jerked a thumb at her and she ducked back inside, closing the door behind her.

'Now,' he said. 'Sit down and tell me who you are and why the hell you're here.'

I pulled up a stool while he perched on the edge of the table.

'The name's Valerius Corvinus,' I said. 'The emperor sent me from Rome to look into a murder a couple of months ago in Carthage. Of an ex-praetor by the name of Decimus Cestius. You knew him?'

'Yeah. I did, as it happens.' Not so much as the bat of an eyelid: I continued to be impressed. 'Total bastard. But if you think I killed him you're completely wrong. I haven't been anywhere near Carthage since I left the place two years ago.'

'Yeah, I know. That's not why I'm here.'

'So?'

'I wanted to ask you about Cornelia Alba.'

He grinned. 'Really? And you've come all this way to do it?'

'Uh-huh.'

'Then you've had a wasted journey, pal. I had the girl, I was found out, and I ran before the trial. That's why I'm here.' He stood up. 'And *that* is all there is. So off you pop, I've got work to do. Give my love to Virria.'

I didn't move. 'No. You didn't,' I said.

He looked blank. 'Didn't what?'

'Have the girl.'

He was staring at me, hard. 'What the hell do you mean? Of course I did, I'm sodding telling you! You talked to Virria, and she confirmed it, right?'

'She said you'd admitted it to her, yes.'

'And Cornelia Alba herself. She say any different?'

'No.'

He threw up his arms. 'Then what the *fuck* is your problem? You think I'd admit to something I didn't do?'

'Yeah. That's exactly what I think.'

I hadn't raised my voice, and I hadn't moved. He gave me another long stare, pulled up a stool and sat on it.

'Okay,' he said. 'I'm listening. Let's have the explanation.'

'You were a friend of Cestius's son Publius, yes?'

'"Friend" is putting it too strong. We knew each other, sure.'

'Fair enough. Different term. You were gambling mates.'

'We had the occasional game of dice together over a jug of wine, along with two or three other guys, yes.' For the first time, he was beginning to look uneasy. 'So what?'

'Only Publius wasn't all that good at it, was he? Gambling. Not as good as you, at least. Maybe it was lack of skill, maybe it was bad luck, maybe it was something else, but–'

'I never cheated,' he said sharply. 'That's something I don't do.'

'Fine. Anyway, the upshot was young Publius ended up owing you a fair amount of money. Much more than he could pay, and he was already on his last warning from his father.' I waited, but he didn't speak. 'So under the threat of turning the whole boiling over to Cestius Senior you persuaded him to get the money another way. He "borrowed" the key to his father's strongbox, at least long enough to take an impression and have a copy made, took out the cash he needed, and gave it to you. How am I doing so far?'

'Go on.' He leaned his back against the edge of the table and folded his arms.

'The thing was, the guy had just got himself into another spot of trouble, an even worse one. I don't know the exact circumstances, and they don't really matter, but he'd just raped, or at least seriously interfered with, young Cornelia Alba. Cornelia had told her father, and Albus had gone hot-foot to Cestius, demanding that he put matters right by arranging a wedding or else. Cestius couldn't have that: he might not have had the Vettius family in his sights quite yet, but he wanted more for his boy than marriage to the daughter of a no-account provincial. He gets Publius into his study and faces him with the rape claim. Publius admits it, and Cestius Senior hits the roof.

'Okay. Now we get to the bit I'm not altogether sure of. Obviously, Cestius already knows about the missing money, but Cestius is no fool: he also knows his son, and as a result he's put two and two together to make the correct four. Or maybe Publius, to save his own skin, comes up with the idea himself and makes a clean breast of things. I don't know which, if either, is right, but again the details don't matter. What does matter is that father and son between them cook up a plan whereby you'll take responsibility for the rape in exchange for being let off the hook where your part in the robbery is concerned. Plus, no doubt, notch up a whacking great extra payment to compensate you for your trouble, because when you do your pre-arranged runner you're going to need a substantial sum to set yourself up elsewhere.' I paused. 'How am I doing now?'

He was still sitting back with his arms folded, but now he was smiling gently. 'Not bad, I'll admit that,' he said. 'No point in pretending otherwise, seeing you've got this far. Not a perfect account of what happened, but you've got the gist, at least.' He shifted slightly. 'You still haven't explained the Cornelia side of things, mind. Why should she go along with the scam? Let alone her father?'

'Because when it comes to the crunch Albus is a spineless weakling. Or maybe that's not quite a fair assessment, under the circumstances, given Cestius's character and position, but never mind, we'll let it stand. Once he and Publius have hatched their plan together Cestius goes round to Albus's house and threatens him with all sorts of consequences unless he confirms the story. Albus, in his own eyes, at least, has no choice: the guy's a real power in Carthage, and more important where his interests are concerned he's completely ruthless. Either he caves in, and takes his daughter with him, or Cestius, one way or another, will squash him like a beetle. Cornelia agrees to co-operate, but that finishes her where her father's concerned, and the two of them are like strangers for the rest of the guy's lifetime. What's the verdict? Still on track?'

'More or less.'

'Fine. I'll settle for that. Anyway, there isn't much more, not where you're concerned, at least. You've come out of it pretty well; after all, your own father's already disinherited you and thrown you out of the house, so if you stay in Carthage your future prospects – and your connections with it and with your family, barring your sister – are zilch in any case. What is there for you to lose? You take the money and bugger off here, changing your name in the process. End of story, happy ever after. Of course, there was a kid named Adon, that Cestius set up to take the rap you should've been facing and who died as a result, but what the hell? Unavoidable collateral damage. He wasn't even a citizen.'

He frowned. 'Yeah. That I did know about, at least well after it happened, and I'm sorry for it. Corvinus, I swear to you I'd absolutely nothing to do with that side of things. The original plan – the one I was told about and agreed to, anyway – was that the whole business of the stolen money would just be forgotten. Going ahead with a fake burglary angle must've been Cestius's own idea. Believe me, he was *not* a nice man.'

'Fair enough,' I said, and I meant it. Framing Medar's son Adon had been an act of pure, gratuitous brutality, and if it hadn't been my job to catch Cestius's killer, like Medar I'd've much preferred to shake the guy by the hand. 'The rest of it's true, though, isn't it?'

'Mostly, yes; like I said, you've got the gist, anyway. You were wrong about the key, though; Publius couldn't've got his father's original, the old man kept it on him all the time. But he knew where he kept the spare. That was the one he used.'

'Uh-huh. It wasn't hidden inside one of the book rolls, was it? Just out of interest.'

Virrius shrugged. 'I've no idea. It could've been, for all I know; that was Publius's concern, and I never saw it. Does it matter?'

'No.' I'd bet that it hadn't been – that part had been arranged purely for the purpose of incriminating Adon – but like I said the precise details of the scam weren't important. 'Was there anything else?'

'No, not really. You've done pretty well, all told, better than I've given you credit for.' His lips twisted. 'The bulk of the money's long gone, one way or another; setting things up here was expensive to begin with, and I'm not a very successful gambler myself. Still, I can't complain; I've always liked horses, I get by, more or less, on what I make out of the farm, and Utica's not a bad place to live. Plus' – he glanced at the closed bedroom door – 'there are other compensations. So what happens now?'

'Meaning, am I going to split on you?' I stood up. 'No, you're safe enough, from me at least. However, there is a very smart cookie back in Carthage by the name of Sextus Quirinius who might work things out off his own bat.'

He looked relieved. 'I'll take that risk,' he said. 'I've too much going for me here just to cut and run again, and I couldn't afford to do it in any case.' He held out his hand. 'Good luck with the investigation.'

I hesitated, then took it. Despite the verdict of the Great and Good in Carthage – specifically, Lautia and his father – Marcus Virrius wasn't a bad lad at heart, and maybe he'd settled down a bit these last two years.

'Thanks,' I said.

'You want to buy a horse, by the way? I can cut you a good deal.'

I grinned. 'Nah, I'll pass this time round.'

'Suit yourself.'

Well, that was that, then. Another box ticked. I collected my horse and rode back to Utica.

21.

We got back to Carthage six days later, to find Quirinius on the quayside with the complimentary carriage and mule-cart.

'Welcome home, Corvinus.' he said, when we'd disembarked. 'How was your trip? Successful, I hope.'

'Yeah, you could say that. Informative, certainly.'

'That's good.' He turned away and made a sign to the lads waiting to unload our luggage from ship to cart. 'You managed to talk with Marcus Virrius, then?'

'Who?'

'Come on! I'm not stupid!'

'I never thought you were, pal.' I hesitated. 'Do me a big favour?'

'Of course.'

'The trip never happened. Forget Utica, forget Virrius. He's past history, and trust me he isn't as bad as he's painted.'

That got me a straight look. Then he shrugged. 'Okay,' he said. 'I told you before you left; where this business is concerned, you're the boss, you don't have to explain anything you don't want to. Duly forgotten. I wouldn't mind knowing why, though. Just for my own satisfaction.'

'Maybe later. Before I leave for Rome. In fact, it might not be all that bad an idea for someone here to know the whole story.'

'Bargain.' He paused. 'Incidentally, there's been a development.'

'Yeah? And what's that?'

'Another death. Cluvius Scarus.'

'*What?*' I stared at him. Perilla, on the point of getting into the carriage, stopped and stared too. 'When was this?'

'Four days ago. The skivvy who cleans out the cubbies found him in his bunk. He must've died in the course of the night.'

Holy immortal gods! 'How did it happen?'

'The school's doctor in residence says poison. But you can talk to him yourself.'

Too right I would, first thing in the morning! Shit! 'That all you know?' I said.

He grinned. 'That's all I wanted to know. I've got enough to do already, and investigating suspicious deaths isn't my concern. Not when I've got someone else to do it for me. Besides, I thought if the man's death had any significance for you you'd want a clear field to ask your own questions. And because you'd said you wouldn't be away for all that long, I thought...well, frankly, I thought, bugger that, it can wait.'

'Very commendable.'

'Yes, I thought so.' He stepped aside to let me board the carriage after Perilla. 'Anything I can help with, of course, just let me know.'

'Will do. Thanks, Quirinius.'

We set off for home.

'You think it was Verania who killed him, Marcus?' Perilla said.

'Sure it was. Had to be.' I sat back against the cushions; I felt drained. 'Who else would have a motive? Let alone an opportunity. And poison...well, if you're a middle-aged woman and you want a professional swordfighter dead you're not going to risk trying to put a knife between his ribs, are you? Poison for Verania would be the sodding perfect weapon. Fuck! Double fuck!'

'Gently, dear.'

'The hell with that. This puts the mockers on everything. I might've been able to put pressure on Scarus re Appius Justus's murder in the hope that he'd crack, but I haven't a hope where Verania's concerned. Which, naturally, is why the bastard's dead. Damage limitation, make sure he doesn't talk by shutting his mouth permanently. With both Justus and Scarus gone, presuming Scarus was the perp there, which I am, there's absolutely no way of proving that Publius isn't Cestius's son. Which means he'll get his inheritance, his consular-family wife, the whole boiling, and there isn't a single thing I can do about it.'

'It'll all work out in the end. Just be patient.'

'Come on, lady! If that bitch and her elder son did plan Cestius's murder, which is looking likelier by the minute, then we've just lost our only real chance of nailing them. And there's no cosmic reason why things *should* work out. We can theorise from now until the Winter Festival, but the long and short of it is that we're screwed.'

'You're just tired after the journey. You'll feel better in the morning.'

'Yeah. Right.'

Maybe I would, but I had the sickening feeling, now, that for the rest of our time in Carthage we'd simply be going through the motions.

.   .   .

Mark you, whether it was the decent night's sleep that was responsible or sheer inherent bloody-mindedness on my part I woke up the next morning feeling a lot more cheerful. Oh, sure, I'd still no illusions about our chances of nailing Verania if she did happen to be our principal perp – I hadn't been kidding when I'd told Perilla that, under the present circumstances, we'd as much hope of that as a snowflake making it intact through hell – but I wasn't prepared to throw in the sponge yet awhile. There was just the possibility that, when I talked to the lads at the gladiatorial school, one of them had seen the lady sneaking out of the main gate at dead of night clutching a bottle labelled 'Poison'. Or, better still, she might have a sudden crisis of conscience and confess to everything in a fit of remorse.

Yeah, well, you can dream, can't you?

What *was* going to happen was that I was going to fill myself in on the details of Scarus's death and then have a very pointed heart-to-heart talk with young Quintus on the subject of telling porkies: dispiriting though Scarus's murder was – and for that Verania just had to be responsible, *nem. con.* – where Cestius's death was concerned she wasn't the only game in town. And when you got right down to it, officially his was the only case that I had a brief for.

So onwards and upwards, in this instance over to the gladiators' school.

This time, the trainer was in the exercise yard watching a matched pair – Thracian and net-man – going through their paces. I went on over, and he turned.

'Oh, it's you,' he said. 'The governor's aide told me you were away in Utica.'

'Yeah, I was,' I said. 'I just got back. Ah...Pettius, right?'

'That's me. Gaius Pettius.'

'Got a moment?'

He hesitated, his attention obviously divided between me and his two lads. 'Sure,' he said. 'If you must. I'm assuming it's about Scarus, yes?'

'Uh-huh. So what can you tell me?'

'Not a lot. It happened five days ago. He hadn't turned up for breakfast in the canteen that morning, but that was nothing unusual. And I wasn't too surprised when I didn't see him later at the training session, either. When he'd been out tomcatting the night before, which I assumed he had, he didn't generally roll in until about noon.'

'That, uh, standard behaviour for a professional sword-fighter here in Carthage?'

'No, it isn't. But Scarus was good, and it didn't spoil his game. Maybe even improved it, so I wasn't going to interfere. Excuse me.' He looked away briefly to bawl the Thracian out for a sloppy piece of shield-work before turning to me again. 'Anyway, I was willing to cut him a bit of extra slack.'

'So when did you know? That he was dead, I mean?'

'Not until half way through the morning, when the skivvy who cleaned his room went in and found him.' His eyes shifted back to the Thracian. 'Look, I'm sorry, but I'm working myself at the moment, okay? Best if you talk to the doctor; he knows more about it than I do.'

'Okay. And where would I find him?'

'Hospital rooms are over there, on the corner.' He nodded towards the other side of the yard. 'That's where he'll be.'

'Thanks a lot, pal.'

'Don't mention it.'

And that was all you got. Gods! So much for fame; Scarus had only been dead five days and already he was being shunted off to the sidelines. If the guy hadn't been such a five-star bastard I might even have felt sorry for him.

Mind you, on consideration maybe I was being a little harsh. Like I said before, professional sword-fighters are a callous lot – they have to be, in their job – and sudden, violent deaths, including presumably murders, are par for the course. And, like Pettius said, he'd his job to do, the same as everyone else.

As, indeed, had I. I went to see the school's tame doctor.

He turned out to be a little Alexandrian Greek who, it transpired when we introduced ourselves, rejoiced in the name of Hippocrates.

'No jokes, please,' he said. 'I've heard them all a hundred times and they're just not funny any more.'

'Let alone humorous.' I kept my face admirably straight.

'Including that one. Now. What can I do for you? As if I didn't know.'

'Right.' I perched on his surgery couch, after removing a tray of extremely unpleasant-looking implements. 'Cluvius Scarus. He was poisoned, yes?'

'If he wasn't then he gave a bloody convincing post mortem impression of it. Probably arsenic. You want the symptoms, as evinced by the state of the corpse and of the cubby in general? Severe and involuntary diarrhoea, ditto vomiting, extreme convulsions, in the course of which he bit off part of his own tongue–'

'Yeah. Okay. Got the idea,' I said hastily. Gods, I hate doctors! 'I'll take your word for it. Any idea how it was done?'

'There were some stuffed dates beside the bed. I'd imagine the poison came in those.'

'Fair enough. Pettius said he was found by one of the skivvies.'

'That's right. Glyptus.'

'Can I talk to him?'

'I don't see why not. Hang on here a tick and I'll get him for you.'

He went out, and I twiddled my thumbs for five minutes until he reappeared with an elderly slave clutching a broom as if it were some sort of protective talisman and looking worried as hell.

'This is Glyptus,' the doctor said. 'You mind if I leave you to it? I've got a patient to see. A live one.'

'No, we're fine.' I waited until he'd gone. 'So. Just–'

'I din't do it, sir! Gods be my witness, I only found the poor bugger when I came in to clean.'

'Relax, friend,' I said. 'No one's accusing you of–'

''S my job, you see.' He held out the broom as proof. 'I never killed no one, honest!'

'Understood. No hassle,' I said patiently. 'Just calm down and tell me what you know, okay?'

'Okay.' He took a deep breath. 'So. I come in at my usual time, din't I, 'bout the third hour, an' I find him lyin' stiff. Place a proper tip, too, the floor an' the bed covered in–'

'Yeah, we've already established that. The doctor said there were some stuffed dates beside him.'

He nodded. 'Word is, those're what done for him. Would that be right, now, sir?'

'Probably.'

'Thank the gods I never touched them, then. I might of done, seein' the fancy box they was in an' it bein' practic'ly full. But they was covered in puke as well, so I left them where they was.'

'You any idea where they might've come from, by any chance?'

'Nah. Some of the lads, the better-set-up ones like Scarus was, they're always gettin' little presents like that, from females, mostly, although we've a net-man who isn't too particular in that direction. Sometimes, if the ladies're shy about bringin' them in person, they're jus' left outside the gate with a note on. Maybe that was it. Or, o' course, he could of brung them in himself.'

Bugger. Well, I couldn't've hoped for anything else, could I?

'Mind you, sir, 'f you want my opinion, he got them from his fancy bint. His reg'lar, I mean. That'd make good sense, wouldn' it?'

My interest sharpened. 'Verania? You know about her?'

''Course.' He gave a sexagenarian leer. 'Common knowledge around here, an' he din't make no secret of it. Lucky bastard, 'least he was. She was a real looker, too, an' that's not somethin' you can say for all of them. There's some right hags come round, ugly as sin, paint an inch thick. Turn your stomach.'

'You've seen her?'

'Jus' the once.' The leer broadened. 'A lot more of her than her face, what's more. Lovely pair of–'

'When was this, exactly?'

'What?'

'When exactly did you see her?'

'I told you. Jus' the once. Must of been about two months back, in Scarus's cubby. I thought it was empty, see, 'cos it was on a morning before a fight day an' all the lads was supposed to be out in the yard.'

Jupiter! 'Tell me about it,' I said.

He shrugged. 'Not much to tell. Like I say, I was doin' my rounds as usual, an' I pushes open the door of Scarus's cubby, 'spectin' it to be empty. Only it wasn't. The two of them was in there hard at work, if you take my meanin'. They never saw me, bein' occupied like, an' I buggered off out of it before I got caught.'

Sweet immortal gods! So if we were talking about the same occasion, which seemed reasonable, then Scarus's alibi held up after all. Which in turn meant that whoever had killed Cestius it hadn't been him. Oh, sure, there were other candidates on the list, but if Verania was our grey eminence then Scarus had been my odds-on favourite by a mile.

I felt like weeping.

'Thanks, pal,' I said, taking a silver piece from my belt-pouch and handing it over. 'Very helpful.'

'You're welcome.' He slipped the coin under his belt. 'Scarus could be a right bastard at times, but he was no worse than most an' better than some. Good luck findin' whoever done it, sir.'

Well, that was more of an obituary than he'd got from Pettius, at least, and as an encomium it was probably on the right side of fair.

I went home to give Perilla the bad news. Not that I was looking forward to that side of things, mind, because the lady wasn't going to like the implications. She wasn't going to like them at all.

22.

She was in the upstairs study again, beavering away with her ordering of Albus's notes.

'I didn't expect you back so early,' she said. 'Problems?'

'You could say that.' I sat down on the reading couch. 'Or at least, if it's a simplification, which it also is, then it's one I'd much rather not have had. We can scratch Scarus from our suspect list for killing Cestius.'

'Oh? Why?'

'Bizarre as it may seem, it turns out there was a witness to his alibi.' I gave her the details. 'And of course that lets out Verania as the actual killer as well.'

'Did you ever seriously think she was?'

I shook my head. 'No. She didn't need to be, not with Scarus to do the dirty work for her. All the same, there was nothing wrong with the idea in theory.' Now we got to the tricky part; I took a deep breath. 'Which, ah, leaves us with the other main possibility.'

'Namely?'

'Quintus. Oh, fine, maybe in collaboration with Medar, like Verania would've been with Scarus, but even so.'

She laid the sheets of paper she was holding in her hand down on the desk and sat in the desk-chair. 'Marcus, you can*not* be serious!'

'Come on, lady! Just pull your head out of the sand, okay? I don't like it any more than you do; I've got a lot of time for young Quintus, and no, he doesn't strike me as the murdering type either. But the evidence is stacking up.'

'What evidence?'

'Fine. Wrong word. Choose one yourself. He's just beginning to look more and more likely, that's all.' I held up a hand and bent the fingers down one by one. 'Look. First: he's got motive. We know now that despite what he claimed his father definitely knew about his relationship with Cornelia. And from what we know of Cestius Senior and imply from the quarrel Eulalia mentioned he was in very, very serious schtook, maybe even on the verge of being disinherited. Second: he's got opportunity. He's family, so he'd know where his father was going that morning and where he was likely to rest up out of the sun. Also–'

'You're forgetting. Quintus has an alibi, confirmed by Cornelia. According to her they were together and miles away at the time.'

Jupiter, give me patience or strike me dead! 'Perilla, have a bit of sense, please! The girl is his fucking *fiancée*, for the gods' sake!' And, *a fortiori*, his probable accomplice, but I glossed over that bit; the lady was touchy enough already without adding to things. 'You think she's going to shop him for murder? Particularly if the murder was in her interests as well?'

At least she had the grace to look sheepish; to the extent that the lady ever can, at least. 'Don't swear, dear,' she said. 'All right, I'm sorry; fair point. Go on. Three.'

'Three. Also, if he's not your typical murdering type, which I admit, he's got a let-out. All he'd have to do, like I said when we talked about this, was ride over to Medar's camp, explain the situation, and have him do the killing. Medar's not going to jib, he has his own quarrel with Cestius, and since the only witnesses either to Quintus's presence in the camp or Medar's later absence are on their side the both of them are perfectly safe. Four. By killing his father, or having him killed, he's securing his long-term financial future as well. He means to stay in Carthage with Cornelia, not go back to Rome with the rest of the family. Even if by some miracle his father *didn't* put the mockers on the marriage he'd still be totally dependent on him for money. With Cestius dead he gets his probably quite considerable inheritance and can do what he likes without having to worry about keeping the old man sweet.' I lowered my hand. 'That enough for you?'

'What about Publius?'

'Pardon?'

'As the killer. What about his brother Publius? I would have thought that under the circumstances he'd have just as solid a motive for killing his father. Erstwhile father, at least. More of one, in fact, because if he were disinherited he'd lose everything at a stroke. And an alliance between him and his mother would make perfect sense, because if the truth about his birth came out she would probably go the same way. Also, correct me if I'm wrong, but he never *did* provide you with an alibi for the morning in question, did he?'

I sighed; perfectly true, mainly because on the one occasion we'd talked he was so far from being a suspect that I hadn't thought to ask for one. A situation which, I admitted, ought to be remedied now, asap. 'Look,' I said.

184

'No arguments, okay? Sure I could make an equally good case for him no problem, maybe a better one where character's concerned. But that doesn't alter the fact that your squeaky-clean Quintus is well in the frame and likely to stay that way.'

'He is *not* my squeaky-clean Quintus!'

Hell; there ain't no one more pig-obstinate than an intelligent woman with her maternal instincts aroused. 'Fine,' I said. 'Have it your own way. Even so, he has questions to answer, and the sooner he does it the better. Can you arrange another meeting through Cornelia?'

'I suppose I could, yes; in fact, we've arranged to meet this afternoon so I can tell her all about our trip. She's never been to Utica herself.' She must've caught the look on my face. 'And before you say anything, dear, no, I have not the slightest intention of mentioning Marcus Virrius. As far as she's concerned I persuaded you to take me there for a few days' sightseeing. As indeed I did.'

'Good. At least you're showing some common sense.'

'Thank you. In any case, if you're so eager to talk to Quintus why don't you just go over to the Cestius villa and check if he's at home?'

'Because the temptation to rattle Verania's cage while I'm there might be too strong, and I don't think that'd be such a good idea at this stage. Like you said, we've no actual evidence that she's stepped out of line in any way at all, including producing a fake son-and-heir. On the other hand, six gets you ten she knows I know that she has. Which is why Scarus has ended up safely dead. Best to let her sweat for the present.'

'So what now?'

'That talk with Quintus would be prime. Is Cornelia coming round here, or will you be meeting at her uncle and aunt's place?'

'Here, and quite soon. Around the seventh hour, she said.'

It was just after noon now, so in less than an hour's time. 'Okay,' I said. 'In that case I'll hang around and see if she knows where he'll be at present.' I stretched out on the couch full length. 'So. Change of subject. How's the editing going?'

'It's hardly that. I'm simply finding out what there is and putting it into some sort of logical order. It should make things a lot easier for Cornelia if she wants to take the matter further.' She hesitated. 'Mind you, I am beginning to feel increasingly guilty about doing it without her knowledge.

In fact, I was planning on telling her today, when she comes round, if that's fine with you.'

'Do what you like. I don't think it really matters all that much after all.'

'Then I will. Besides, it would be a shame to give it up now, because it really is fascinating stuff, and incredibly detailed in places. Albus must have been a complete obsessive where research was concerned. It seems he was even building up his own map of the old city, collating the known topographical facts and extrapolating from them.'

'Really? All of that?'

'Oh, Marcus! It's *interesting!*' I grinned. 'Particularly when the nature of the location is a puzzle in itself.' She picked up a pile of sheets from the desk, leafed through them and handed me one. 'Look at this, for example.'

On the sheet was a rough sketch with a curving line at the top, intersected three-quarters of the way along its length by what was obviously a road, with another, more minor, road leading off at right angles and following the curve. There were three places labelled: an area directly beneath the minor road marked 'Spice Market', a small square tucked into a depression in the curving line opposite it marked 'Shrine of the Two Brothers', and in the space between that and the road a cross and the words 'House of Jirced', heavily underlined.

'What's this House of Jirced when it's at home?' I said.

Perilla beamed. 'Exactly. I haven't the faintest idea. That's what I mean: fascinating.'

Yeah, well, whatever turns you on. I gave her it back. 'You don't think Cornelia might prefer just to file and forget?' I said.

She stared at me. 'Why should she want to do that?'

Total incomprehension; there spoke the card-carrying academic. 'She might. After all, it was her father's obsession, not hers. And I doubt that under the circumstances she feels she owes him any posthumous favours.'

'Perhaps not, but it would give her the option, at least. And even if she doesn't want to take things further then surely being a historian himself Quintus would.'

Assuming, of course, that events hadn't supervened and the guy had more pressing matters to attend to, such as facing a double murder charge. Still, as I say, there was a fair slice of selective blindness on the lady's part in operation here, and I wasn't going to risk having my head bitten off

186

again for quibbling. 'Okay,' I said. 'Just make sure you–' There was a knock at the door and Bathyllus came in. 'Yeah, what is it, sunshine?'

'A visitor, sir. Sextus Gratius.'

Odd. 'He say what he wanted?'

'No, sir.'

'Fine. I'll be right there.'

Perilla stood up. 'I'll come as well, dear. Since he and Albus were fellow historians I may as well pick his brains.'

We went down. Gratius had been perched on a stool in the atrium, but as we came in he jumped to his feet.

'Valerius Corvinus, sir,' he said. 'I'm glad you're at home. I thought perhaps you'd be out.'

Not exactly a scintillating start to a conversational visit, but the guy was obviously nervous for some reason, so I was ready to make allowances.

'Hi, pal.' I waved him back to his seat and sat down myself on the couch while Perilla did the same on the one across from me. 'What can I do for you?'

'Nothing, really. I just happened to be passing,' He cleared his throat. 'I thought I might call in and ask if I could be of any further help to you in your investigations. As it were.'

'Uh huh.' Jupiter! As an excuse 'thin' didn't even begin to describe it. The word 'emaciated' sprang to mind. Or maybe even 'skeletal'. And as an actor he wouldn't've made even spear-carrying level. 'You were just passing, right?'

'Indeed.'

'On your way from where to where?'

'I'm sorry, sir. I'm not with you.'

'Come on, Gratius! Your office is down by the harbour, on the other side of town, and you live above the shop. We're not on the route between there and the Cestius villa, either. So if you were just passing then where exactly are points A and B?'

'Ah...' He was turning an interesting shade of red. Not nerves after all; embarrassment.

I stretched out on the couch. 'Okay,' I said. 'Which one of them was it?'

'I beg your pardon?'

'Told you to call round and fish for information on what I was up to. Which particular member of the family, Verania, Publius or Quintus?'

He was definitely looking unhappy now. 'Master Publius,' he said.

Hmm. Interesting. 'He vouchsafe a reason for wanting to know?'

'No. He was just curious.'

Spoken without so much as a blink. Gods! *No one* could be that gullible! Unless it was loyalty, of course, which was equally possible, perhaps even more so since Gratius was a long way from being thick. Still, maybe I was being unfair: innocents like Gratius who were smart in other ways did exist, and if I'd developed a hyper-suspicious mind over the years then it was built into the job.

On the other hand, as a viable reason on Publius's part for sending the old family retainer round on a specious fishing trip idle curiosity didn't even rate a 'could do better'. Obviously, the guy was beginning to twitch, which was significant in itself.

'Is that so?' I said. 'He didn't think of coming round and asking me in person?'

'I'm afraid that's a question I can't answer, sir.'

There was more than a tinge of stubbornness in his tone, and I hadn't missed the elliptical wording, either. Nevertheless, I let it go. 'Fair enough,' I said. 'Tell him I'm getting there and I'll be round to talk to him and his mother very soon.' That should put the wind up the bugger good and proper. Verania too.

'I'll do that. Thank you.' Definite relief there; he stood up and made to go.

'Hang on a minute, Gratius,' I said. 'Maybe there is something you can help me with. It's not vital, in fact it's pretty trivial, but it'd be nice to know I haven't got hold of the wrong end of the stick.'

'Indeed, sir? And what would the stick in question be, exactly?' He'd turned cautious again.

'I know you said you'd only worked for your ex-master for eighteen years, but you also said you'd been with the Cestius family in general for a good while previously. That right?'

'Yes, of course. Ever since I was a boy. I belonged to the master's uncle. Publius Cestius.' He was frowning. 'I'm sorry, sir, but I don't see–'

'It's no big deal. I was just wondering if there was any contact between the two households at all. Enough for you to know what was going on the other side of the fence, as it were.'

'I'm not with you.' The caution was there now in spades; evidently the guy was moving towards full Old Retainer mode. 'They were certainly physically close, in fact the two properties were in adjacent streets on the Quirinal and there was inevitably a great deal of regular contact where both family and staff were concerned. But–'

'Fine. Before your old master died and you swapped over did you ever hear word of an Appius Justus? Seafaring man, based in Ostia?'

'Valerius Corvinus, I really do not think–'

'Come on, pal! It was over twenty years ago. Water under the bridge.' I kept my fingers crossed that word of Justus's death – or at least the guy's name – hadn't filtered through to Planet Gratius yet. Also, although I'd been deliberately vague as to precise dates and Justus's exact role, that although he'd know damn well what the latter must've been he hadn't immediately spotted the implications behind the question. 'Like I say, it's not vitally important, but you said you wanted to help. So help.'

'I admit the name's familiar, sir, now you come to mention it,' he said carefully. 'As is its context. But I was never one for gossip, even when I was younger. I very much doubt whether I can tell you anything more than you very possibly know already, nor would I have any wish to if I could.'

'So reading between the lines what you're saying, or rather what you're avoiding saying, is that this Justus was having an affair with Verania, yes?'

He hesitated. 'Presumably. Although not to my personal knowledge.' Glory and trumpets! I'd got that confirmed, at least! 'But it didn't last long. In fact' – Gratius cleared his throat again, and blushed slightly – 'I only knew of the man's existence because I was keeping company at the time with someone in the mistress's household. An under-cook by the name of Penelope, who was a terrible gossip. A persistent one, too, whether you wanted to hear what she had to say or not.' I found myself grinning: shades of Eulalia. Evidently a propensity for gossip was endemic to the culinary profession. She might even have been a relative. 'Why are you so interested, may I ask?'

So he wasn't totally devoid of prurient curiosity after all. Still, that was natural under the circumstances.

'No reason. Or not really,' I said easily. 'I told you; it's not vitally important.' I wasn't going to share the glad tidings of Publius's now-almost-certain illegitimacy with the family factor, no way, nohow, never. Mind you, judging by the look he was giving me he might be on the verge of putting two and two together for himself; whatever else he was, Gratius was no fool. 'Just one of these little avenues that open up now and again but usually end up leading nowhere.'

'Indeed, sir. If you say so.' *Definitely* more than a smidgeon of suspicion there. Even so, there was nothing I could do about that now, and I supposed that, cosmically speaking, it didn't matter all that much: suspicion was one thing, outright knowledge was another, and in Gratius's position even if he had sussed out what was going on the best thing he could do, career-wise, was keep schtoom and let things take their course. 'In that case, and if there's nothing else I can do for you, I'll be on my way.' He gave a short bow. 'Sir. Madam.'

He turned to go.

'Actually there is something, Gratius, if you will, and if you can spare the time.' Perilla had been sitting on her own couch quietly throughout. 'At least, I hope so.' She smiled. 'Nothing whatsoever to do with murders and mayhem, you'll be glad to know, or even in your professional capacity.'

He turned back. 'Of course,' he said. 'I'd be delighted. How can I help?'

'I understand from what Marcus told me that you were a friend of Cornelius Albus's, and that you're a historian in your own right, yes?'

'Indeed. Of a sort, at least where the historian part is concerned. Not nearly in his league, but I've always had an interest in that direction. Had you a specific reason for asking?'

'Oh, yes. Several, I'm afraid, mostly in the form of questions I'd like the answers to eventually. But if you could help me with just this one in the meantime I'd be really, really grateful.' She held out the small sketch she'd shown me earlier.

He took it from her and examined it.

'Where did you get this?' he said.

'Upstairs. In Cornelius Albus's study.' She had coloured slightly. 'It was, ah, part of a collection of notes I came on by accident in the drawer of his desk. Historical notes, to do with old Carthage.'

'Yes. Yes, I can see that.' He was frowning.

'Obviously a map of some kind. I wondered if he might be putting together some sort of plan of the city to go with a history he was intending to write.'

'Perhaps he was, yes.'

'You don't know for certain? That's a pity. I was rather hoping that you would.'

He looked up; the frown had disappeared. 'Not about his intentions in that direction, no,' he said. 'Or not in any detail, at least. As you've probably gleaned, Lucius was always very secretive where his work was concerned, and he kept things very much to himself. We were good friends, of course, and of very long standing, but we were never close enough for him to share confidences with me. No one was, apart from young Master Quintus. If you're really interested in that side of things then your best bet is to talk to him.'

'Very well. I'll do that.' She sounded disappointed, which I supposed was fair enough in the circumstances. 'You can't tell me anything about it at all, then? The plan, I mean.'

'Hardly anything, I'm afraid.' He handed the sheet back to her. 'It's of part of the city at the southern foot of the Byrsa, although so much will probably have been obvious to you already. The spice market and the Shrine of the Two Brothers are long gone, of course, but both are mentioned in surviving texts. Lucius must have worked out exactly where they were, how I don't know, but he was an extremely clever man.'

'And the...what was it...the House of Jirced?'

'There I have no idea whatsoever. "Jirced" is a Carthaginian name, certainly – a man's name – but who he was, and why Lucius should have been interested in locating his house, I don't know. Mind you, as I said, in comparison with Lucius my knowledge and abilities as a historian are very limited. The name may well appear somewhere, in fact for Lucius to have known it it most certainly does, and in an important context. But not one, I'm sorry to say, with which I'm familiar.'

'Oh.' There was real disappointment in the lady's voice now. 'Never mind. It was just a thought. Thank you in any case.'

He smiled. 'Under the circumstances there's hardly a need for thanks, madam. Now I must be going.' He nodded to me. 'Sir.'

He left.

'Damn,' Perilla said.

191

I was grinning. 'Don't take it so hard, lady. Into each fledgling historian's life a little rain must fall. I bet Titus Livius was constantly having his sources leaving him hanging and having to fudge things as a result.'

'Shut up, Marcus. Ooh, it is so *frustrating!*'

'You heard the man. If you're so interested then ask your squeaky-clean Quintus.'

'I told you. He is *not* my...!' She stopped. 'You're winding me up, aren't you?'

'Only slightly. But it wouldn't do any harm, would it? Tell you what; I have to talk to him again myself in any case. Why not come along? It might make the guy hesitate if he decides to clock me one, for a start.'

'Why on earth would he want to do that?'

'Yeah, well, hopefully he won't. But there again I am going to face him with the matter of the porkies, and even if he does have a reasonable explanation for why he told them he won't be too happy about it.'

'Cornelia may bring him with her when she comes round, as she did last time. In fact, she probably will: because we're in the secret, as it were, here is one of the few places they can meet without being noticed.'

'That's something I don't really understand,' I said. 'Okay, both their families would've disapproved of the relationship in the beginning, but the fathers are both dead, have been for months, and they were the ones who mattered. Why the hell shouldn't they just come out in the open about things?'

'I asked Cornelia that myself. It's quite simple: they don't want to cause trouble before everything's settled, at least Quintus doesn't. Particularly since when the break does come it's likely to be a total one on his family's side. If they wait, as they are doing, until his mother and brother are on the point of going back to Rome his part of the inheritance should be finalised and they'll avoid the embarrassment of a prolonged cheek-by-jowl separation.'

'That's sensible, I suppose.'

'They are sensible. The pair of them. Everything's been thought through and planned very carefully, down to the smallest detail.'

'Fair enough. Even so.'

'Even so what?'

'Jupiter, Perilla! They're not supposed to be sensible, they're hardly more than kids! And they're engaged, for the gods' sake. Where's the passion?'

'You're showing your age, dear. Besides, it's quite refreshing to meet with young people who actually *think* for a change.'

I grinned. 'Now you're showing yours, lady. And don't forget, you're eighteen months ahead of me.'

'Toad.'

Bathyllus oozed in. 'Cornelia Alba and Quintus Cestius, madam,' he said to Perilla.

Hey!

'Oh, good,' Perilla said. 'Tell them to come through, Bathyllus. We'll go out onto the terrace.' He oozed out again. 'And Marcus, do behave. They're here as guests this time, not as subjects for interrogation.'

'Good as gold.' I crossed my fingers. 'Promise.'

'Just remember, then.'

23

Bathyllus reappeared with the happy couple in tow. Quintus pulled up sharp when he saw me, and I caught the shadow of a frown before he covered it.

'Hello again, Valerius Corvinus,' he said. 'What a surprise.'

'Hardly that, pal. I do live here. Besides, I've a question or two that need answering.' I got up, ignoring the death-glare Perilla was giving me. Yeah, well, he'd started hostilities, after all, and I had a job to do; the lady could either like it or lump it. 'You want to sit out on the terrace?'

'Fine by me.' Stiff as hell. He and Cornelia exchanged glances, and I saw her give the faintest of shrugs. 'Anywhere you like.'

'Marvellous,' Perilla said, a little too brightly. 'Lovely to see you both. Bathyllus? Could you see to the drinks, please? Wine and fruit juice. And Marcus, we'll have a word or two later. On the subject of promises.'

Ouch. Still, it was probably the only chance I'd get, and much too important to pass over in favour of social chit-chat. We trooped outside in silence and sat round the table. There was a distinct Atmosphere.

Tough; I could live with that. It was definitely crunch time where squeaky-clean Quintus was concerned.

'Okay, Corvinus,' he said. 'You want to get the business part of things over with? What are these questions of yours?'

'I really don't think this is either the time or place to–' Perilla began.

'It's all right, Perilla.' Cornelia said quietly. 'We don't mind. Honestly.'

Frankly, I didn't give a toss whether they did or not. I ignored both her and Perilla, who was still looking daggers. 'First off,' I said to Quintus. 'You told me last time we spoke that neither your father nor Cornelia's knew anything about your relationship. Only it transpires that you had an almighty row with yours three or four days before he was killed, as a result of which he in turn comes round here, reason for visit unknown but presumably – by which I mean almost bloody certainly – to straighten things out with Cornelius Albus. Who conveniently, later that same morning, and subsequent to a visit by yourself which terminated at some time yet to be identified, trips over his own feet and dies as the result of a fall downstairs. You care to explain any or all of that?'

Silence. *Long* silence. He and Cornelia looked at each other.

'So you're accusing me of murder,' Quintus said. 'In fact, of two murders; my own father's and that of Cornelius Albus.'

'No. What I'm doing is stating the facts as far as I know them. But if the cap fits, then fine. Does it? If not, then I'm listening; you tell me.'

I waited. Even Perilla had gone quiet, and was staring at me in horror.

'All right.' Quintus was deathly pale. 'You're right about the quarrel; I'm sorry, I thought if I mentioned it it would complicate matters. It wasn't about me and Cornelia, though, at least not to begin with.'

'I never said it was,' I said. 'You'd just found out – from Cornelia, who'd finally decided to trust you with the secret – that the guy who interfered with her wasn't Marcus Virrius but your brother; that the whole thing was a cover-up that your father and hers had concocted between them. Or at least that he'd concocted and forced Albus to go along with. Also, that the collateral damage had included Medar's son Adon. And you felt that you ought to hand the lying bastard – your choice of adjective – his head.'

His jaw had dropped about five feet. 'How the *hell* did you discover all that?' he said.

'Because I'm smarter than I look. Believe it.' Bathyllus, always sensitive to Atmosphere, had sidled in with the drinks tray like one of Euripides's messengers bringing the news that the play's principal character was now a definite ex. I helped him unload and poured Quintus a belt from the wine flask, plus one for myself. Bathyllus set the rest of the drinks down and buggered off sharpish. 'I'm still listening. Keep going.'

'He asked me how I knew, of course, and it all came out. Naturally he was furious, but' – he shrugged – 'he said he'd give me time to think it over and change my mind before he did anything drastic. If anything needed to be done at all.'

'What did he mean by that?'

'I've no idea. But that's what he said. Anyway, that was where we left it, apart from me telling him to go to hell and slamming out. And then four days later he was dead.' His eyes came up. 'But not by my hand. I swear it.'

'I'm afraid swearing to it's not nearly enough, pal,' I said gently. 'Not at this stage of the game.'

'We told you!' Cornelia butted in. She was looking flushed, and angry. 'We were together that day, and miles from where Quintus's father was killed! Quintus couldn't possibly have done it, even if he'd wanted to!'

I turned to face her. 'Yeah, well,' I said. 'Like I say a bit of corroborative evidence would be really, really useful at this point. If you can't provide that then I'm sorry, but–'

'Nestor,' Quintus said suddenly.

I frowned. 'What? Who the fuck is Nestor?'

'*Marcus!*' Perilla snapped.

Quintus shook his head. 'That's not his proper name. It's only–'

'–what we call him.' Cornelia was practically bouncing with excitement. 'Or what I've always called him, at least. King of sandy Pylos. Of course! Nestor saw us!'

Gods, I was losing the plot here, and no mistake. I glanced at Perilla for elucidation.

'For goodness' sake, Marcus!' she said. 'Homer! Either the "Iliad" or the "Odyssey", he's in both. Take your pick.' She turned to Cornelia. 'Go ahead, dear. Explain.'

'He's an old man who lives on his own in a shack near the beach. In the cove we told you about, the one where we were. Like I said, I've been going there for years, and he's always around. He beach-combs.' She looked at Perilla. 'Is that the word? Phrase, rather.'

'It'll do.' Perilla was smiling.

'You're sure?' I said. 'That this guy definitely saw you?'

'Yes. We talked to him. And he would remember Quintus, I'm certain, because that was the first time he and I had gone there together.'

'Fair enough.' It was something I could check up on, at least. 'So where is this cove?'

'About a mile south of town,' Quintus said. 'You can see it from the road. A couple of long sand-spits ending in rocks and enclosing a lagoon.'

'Okay. I'll take a trip out there tomorrow morning, talk to this Nestor guy myself.'

'You want us to come with you?'

'No, I'll do that on my own, if you don't mind.'

He shrugged; we were back, it seemed, to the throw-aways. 'Suit yourself,' he said.

'Moving on. Cornelius Albus's accident.'

197

'That's all it was, as far as I know. An accident.'

'Maybe so, but it was pretty convenient as far as you were concerned, wasn't it?'

'Now you wait just one bloody minute!' he snapped. Cornelia put a hand on his arm and he subsided. 'All right. Sorry. Yes, I was there that morning, and up in Albus's study what's more. But I left a good hour before he died.'

'What did you talk about?'

'What do you think? I went to have it out with him about the filthy deal he'd made over the rape business, and tell him that whether he liked it or not Cornelia and I were engaged.'

'And did he? Like it, I mean?'

His lips twisted. 'Oh, he'd no objections. None at all. Apart from telling me straight that a marriage was completely impossible because my father would see us all in hell first and make damn sure we went there. He'd already called round – my father, I mean – to make that perfectly clear.'

'You know how Albus had reacted to that?'

'Naturally. He'd caved in straight off, like he always did.' He paused, frowning. 'Corvinus, don't get me wrong here: I had infinite respect for Cornelius Albus as a scholar and a historian, I even loved the guy as a second father, right up to the time when I found out what he'd done to Cornelia, but he was a total coward with as much backbone as a slug.' I glanced at Cornelia, but she sat impassive, her hand still resting on his arm. 'I didn't kill him, but by the gods in the course of that conversation I felt like doing it a dozen times over.'

'So you left?'

'I left. While I still had a hold of my temper.'

'Did anyone see you?'

He shook his head. 'Not that I know of. Chilo – that was the major-domo – wasn't around when I came down, so I let myself out. And that was that.'

'What did you do then?'

'I honestly can't remember. Not in any detail. Walked around for a while trying to calm down, ended up in some wineshop or other, don't ask me which because I don't know, and got totally plastered. Which is something, I should say, I don't make a habit of.' Probably true: he hadn't touched his wine, although neither had I, come to that, and I couldn't make that claim myself. 'So no alibi there, and not a hope of finding one.'

I sat back. 'Okay. Congratulations. Grilling over, for the moment at least.'

His relief was palpable, even through the hard shell look that was obviously his default image. 'You believe me?'

'Let's say the jury's out, at least where your father's death is concerned. Until I've had a word with this Nestor character.'

'And my father's death?' Cornelia said. 'What about that?'

'Yeah, well, that's a bit more problematical.' I was being tactful: it was, with bells on, because we had the *modus operandi* to consider, and that was a real bugger. Currently, in terms of that, as far as credible suspects went Quintus was the only game in town. 'Unless it was pure accident after all.'

'Of course it was!' Quintus said. 'Who'd want to kill Albus?' He gave a mirthless half-smile. 'Apart from me, that is.'

'True,' I said drily. 'You see my point.'

'Well, Marcus,' Perilla sniffed. 'If you've *quite* finished throwing accusations about for the present perhaps we can begin to enjoy our afternoon as planned. If, that is, Quintus and Cornelia still feel up to it.'

Quintus smiled properly this time. It made him look a lot younger.

'No harm done,' he said. 'At least, not much. And whatever else it's achieved the air's a bit clearer.'

'Fine by me too, lady.' I reached for my wine cup and took a decent swallow. 'Oh. You wanted to ask Quintus something as well. Wearing his historian's hat, I mean.'

'Ah, yes. The map. I left it on the atrium table. Wait a moment and I'll go and get it.'

She disappeared through the portico.

'What map's this?' Quintus said.

'Just something Perilla came across in the study when she was cataloguing Cornelius Albus's–' I stopped. Bugger! She hadn't told Cornelia what she was up to yet, had she? Or even asked her permission to look through the stuff in the first place.

'Cataloguing my father's what?' Cornelia said.

'Ah...' Damn! Now I knew what it felt like to be on the other side of a grilling, and it wasn't pleasant. 'Just some historical notes she found lying around.' In the closed drawer of his desk, true, but I wasn't going to bring out *that* little nugget unprompted. 'She was putting them in some sort of order. You'd have to ask her for the exact details.'

When in doubt, fudge like mad and squirm out from under. Having lived with the lady herself for twenty-odd years I was a card-carrying moral escapologist.

'Oh, *those*,' Cornelia said.

Perilla reappeared clutching the map. She was looking pink about the ears, and guilty as hell; obviously in the time taken to collect the thing the same thought had occurred to her as had to me.

'I found it upstairs, Cornelia,' she said. 'Along with a whole host of other historical jottings. I think your father must have been planning to put together some sort of history of the city.'

'Yes,' Cornelia said. 'He was.'

'Anyway.' Perilla cleared her throat. 'I'm afraid I let my interest run away with me a little and took to sorting them out. I'm sorry; I should have asked your permission before. You don't mind, do you?'

'Not at all.' Cornelia smiled. 'Anyway, that's Quintus's province now. I wouldn't touch any of my father's personal stuff without gloves on.'

Spoken quite calmly, which made the words all the more chilling. I'd forgotten that there was an oddness to the girl where talking about her father was concerned, and even now that I knew the reason for it it lifted the hairs on the back of my neck.

Quintus put out his hand. 'Can I see?' he said.

'Of course.' Perilla sat down again and passed the map over. 'I asked Sextus Gratius about it but he said you would know more than he did.'

'Then I'm afraid he was wrong.' Quintus was examining it. 'At least, if he meant that I'd know why Albus made the sketch in the first place. I don't. No idea whatsoever.'

'I thought it might be part of a sort of general map he was building up of the old city.'

'Maybe. But that would be a huge undertaking, even if it were possible, which I doubt, and if he had any such plan in mind he never mentioned it to me.' He grinned. 'Mind you, that'd be nothing new; he could be a secretive old devil when he liked. Which was most of the time. Did you find anything similar when you were rooting through his private papers?'

Perilla coloured, and I had to suppress a snigger. 'No. Actually, I didn't,' she said. 'I haven't so far, anyway.'

'There you are, then. It's probably a one-off.' He passed the sketch back. 'What the purpose of it was, though, as I say, I haven't a clue. He did get certain very odd bees in his bonnet from time to time, so it's probably one of these.'

Perilla took the map and laid it on the table. 'Gratius recognised the allusion to the spice market and the Shrine of the Two Brothers,' she said, 'but not this "House of Jirced". Any ideas about that?'

'No again. Jirced was a fairly common Carthaginian name, although not a popular one with the upper classes. So whoever he was I doubt that, if he does appear in any surviving text, it's with any prominence.' He shrugged. 'Which, I admit, makes it even more strange that Albus should single him out.'

'It's a mystery, then.'

'That it is. And, I'm afraid, liable to remain one.' He picked up his wine cup and turned to me. 'So, then. Cornelia tells me you've just got back from Utica. You have any other reason for going there, besides the sights?'

'Uh-uh,' I said blandly: the whereabouts of Marcus Virrius weren't my secret to tell. Quirinius might have guessed, of course, and I was pretty much sure that he had, but that was another matter. The last thing Marcus Virrius would want when he was in town dickering for fodder would be to bump into the girl he was supposed to have raped and the brother of the guy who'd actually done it. 'Perilla wanted to see the place while we were out here, and I thought I might just take a few days off to indulge her.'

'Worth the trip?'

'It had its points.' I reached over for the wine flask and topped up my cup.

'Oh, but, Marcus,' Perilla said, 'that's *quite* unfair! It was fascinating!'

Bugger. We talked temples. Or rather, Perilla did, and at length. You do not want to know.

'I think that went rather well in the end,' Perilla said when they'd gone.

'Yeah.' I emptied the remaining wine in the flask into my cup. 'Apart from your glowing and protracted encomium on the artistic and historical delights of downtown Utica, of course.'

'But what did you expect, dear? I told you, Cornelia dropped by expressly for the purpose of hearing about them. And considering that despite having promised to keep off the subject you used the occasion virtually to accuse Quintus of murder the fact that things *did* go well eventually is nothing short of a miracle.'

'Fair enough. So supposing when they do get hitched the happy couple decide to go there for the honeymoon, see the sights for themselves, meet a few of the locals, hmm?'

'I don't see why that should–' She stopped. 'Ah.'

'*Ah* is right. Mind you, from the glazed look on their faces when they left I don't think that's very likely. Well done, lady. Good job jobbed.'

She ducked her head and came up smiling. 'Marcus, you really are a complete toad. You know that, don't you?'

'Uh-huh.' I took a swallow of the wine.

'At least we know now that Quintus is innocent. I don't mind admitting that that's a huge relief.'

'What gave you that idea?'

The smile disappeared. 'Oh, *Marcus!*'

'Never mind the "Oh, Marcus". Even if this Nestor business does check out – and it probably will – that doesn't let him off the hook. Far from it.'

'Why ever not? As Cornelia said, he couldn't possibly have killed his father. He was miles away at the time.'

'True. But that doesn't affect the other part of the theory, does it? That it was a murder by proxy, with him putting his pal Medar up to it in advance. And if he knew the business was in train then going off for the day with Cornelia in completely the other direction would be a very smart move insurance-wise.'

'I thought you said he'd have to warn Medar that his father would be coming? Plus, if he did have a corroborated alibi pre-prepared then why didn't he tell you about Nestor in the first place?'

I shook my head. 'Warning Medar wouldn't be necessary, not if they'd agreed he'd kill Cestius the first chance he got. All Quintus needed to know – which he would've done – is that his father would be riding out that way that morning, because if so he'd be sure to check up on Medar's gang in any case. At which point he could go round to Cornelia's, or use whatever stratagem they had for getting in touch, and arrange the trip out to her cove. And as far as not telling me about Nestor to begin with goes, it'd be a lot more convincing an alibi if he only happened to remember it after he was accused. After all, it was true, or probably will turn out to be, so he'd have no worries on that score.'

'You make him sound very devious.'

'Yeah, well, I think there's at least a fair chance that he is. Like I say, I never did trust squeaky-clean, and underneath the love-struck innocent exterior that guy is razor-sharp and hard as nails. Besides, if we are thinking in terms of a linked double murder – Cestius's and Albus's – he's got far and away the best motive around. In fact, he's the only person who has a motive at all, apart from Cornelia, and the two of them are an item.'

'If Albus's death was murder. Don't you think, dear, that you're making a rather large assumption on that score?'

'Uh-uh, no way; the two deaths so close together are too much of a coincidence to swallow. And coming when they did, just as the shit re the Quintus/Cornelia liaison was about to hit the fan, makes the chances that one of them was an accident even more unlikely. Which brings us to opportunity. Quintus may have a clear alibi for the time of his own father's death, but he sure as hell doesn't for Albus's, quite the contrary. And if it wasn't him that did it, whoever it was would've had to get through a bolted front door, up to the study, commit the killing and get himself clear without anyone noticing. You tell me how he did all of that, plus provide a name and a valid reason, and I'll apologise to Quintus personally. Deal?'

'Hmm.' She was twisting her lock of hair. 'Very well, Marcus. I admit, I can't argue with any of that. But I still can't believe the boy is guilty.'

Boy. Right; that choice of word said it all. 'I'm not saying he is. But you can't ignore the facts, lady, and so far they're pretty much stacked that side of the balance.' I reached for the wine cup. 'Still, we'll see what tomorrow and this guy Nestor bring.'

24.

I was up and out just after dawn the next morning, headed for the road that led south-west to Tunes a bit further down the coast. I'd originally meant to pick up a horse at one of the hiring stables in town – to get to the Tunes road I'd have had to go through the centre in any case – but the day was cool and fresh, and in any case I always prefer walking to riding. Especially since I was likely to get stuck with some geriatric candidate for the local glue factory or, worse, an evil-minded brute that would do its best to throw me off first chance it got. Hiring a horse from a public stable is as much a lottery as putting up at a wayside inn: you may be lucky, sure, but it's far more likely that the hand of fate will land you a sucker-punch to the gonads. Especially since where provincial service-providers are concerned rooking know-nothing visitors from Rome is a matter of honour.

So on foot it was.

After I'd got beyond the town limits the road was pretty clear; certainly there wasn't much in the way of vehicle traffic. By the time what was obviously the cove came in sight – like Quintus had said, it was only a mile outside town, and a scant one, at that – I'd met no more than two or three other punters, and when I glanced behind me just to check that there was no upcoming threat from some speed-merchant with a fancy two-wheeler and matched greys I could only see one other bod travelling the way I was, and he was a good hundred yards off.

There was a path leading down the steep slope to the cove, and I took it. I could see what was presumably Cornelia's pal Nestor's shack now, tucked away under the shelter of a small cliff to my right, well away from the beach itself. There was a lone figure standing at the water's edge, pulling on what I assumed was a fishing line.

It was. As I came closer he drew the rest of it out, along with a respectable-sized mullet at the business end.

'Hi,' I said. 'You must be Nestor.'

He turned. Nestor was right – he must've been seventy, if he was a day – assuming that Homer's king of Pylos was into straggly beards and a tunic that, if he ever washed it, would probably come to bits in the process. Nothing wrong with his *sang-froid*, mind: he straightened up – he must've been a big guy in his time – and gave me a hard stare. Then he chuckled and shook his head.

'Friend of the young lady's, are you?' he said.

'Uh...yeah. Cornelia. Cornelia Alba.'

'That's the one. She took to calling me that, and it wasn't worth fixing. I never asked her why, or who the original bugger was, neither.' He unhooked the mullet and laid it down on the sand, where it kicked its way to gasping immobility. 'Titus Papinius, that's me by rights. But you can please yourself which name you use.'

'Valerius Corvinus.'

He reached out a hand, and we shook. I noticed that he kept a sling tied to his wrist, and he noticed me noticing.

'For hares,' he said. 'Or anything else that happens along. Practically the only thing I've kept from the old days, and I'm still a fair shot.' He patted the pouch of sling-stones at his belt. 'Fish are okay, but there's not a lot of eating on them. A bit of meat or some bird-flesh makes a welcome change.'

'You live here all the time?' I said.

He grinned, showing a perfect set of teeth. 'That what she told you? Nah, got a place up there, about a quarter of a mile off. A wife, too. Or wife of a sort, if you get my meaning.' He winked. 'But here's where I am most days, when the weather's good. I like my peace. 'Sides, we never really got on, the old woman and me, and it suits us both. You fancy a spot of wine?'

'Sure. If it's going.'

'It'll be nothing special, and nowhere near what you're used to, I don't doubt, but it's drinkable, at least. Still interested?'

'Sure.' To tell the truth, after a good mile-and-a-half's walk, even although with the sea breeze to help it hadn't got out all that hot, at that point I'd almost have settled for a mug of beer. Not quite, mark you, and definitely not, in the case of wine, the local date-sourced aberration. Which reminded me. 'Ah...just to check. When you say "wine" we are talking about the stuff made from grapes, right?'

He chuckled. 'You think I'd ruin my gut with that date-brewed horse-piss? No, you're safe enough there, sir. It may not be Falernian, but at least it's honest. Make yourself comfortable and I'll get my flask.'

I went over to one of the rocks at the sand's edge and sat down while he fetched the stoppered flask and a single earthenware cup, which he filled and handed to me. I took a cautious sip. Not bad at all; rough as hell, yes, but I'd been duly warned. Besides, I was prepared to make allowances. I drained the cup.

'You're an army man?' I said as I passed it back.

He refilled it, took a long drink, and wiped his mouth. 'Slinger unit, attached to the Seventh Lusitanians, twenty-five years' service. Got to be a decurion before I was demobbed and settled down here with my severance money.'

'You have a connection with the place?'

'Nah. My best mate was from Carthage – he died – and from what he'd told me about it over the years I just took a fancy to living there. Only not being much of a city man I wasn't too keen on being stuck in the town itself. Out here does me just fine.' He gave me a sharp, assessing look. 'So. That's my excuse. What's a toff like you doing out in the sticks, perched on a rock and swigging third-rate wine?'

I told him, plus what Quintus and Cornelia had told me about their whereabouts the day of the murder. 'So can you confirm that the two of them were here that morning?' I said. 'It's pretty important.'

'Yeah, I can see that.' He hesitated. 'Look, I can't swear to the exact day, mind; I've no use for a calendar, me. But the last time the young lass was out this way, far as I know, must've been about then, and she did have a lad by the name of Quintus with her. So if that much will satisfy you then fine, I'll back them. Fair enough?'

'Uh-huh.' Well, we'd got that box ticked, at least. For, as I'd told Perilla, what it was worth. I stood up. 'Thanks, pal. And for the wine,' I said. 'Now if you'll excuse me I'd best be getting back before the heat sets in.'

'No problem. Pleasure to meet you. Give the youngsters my regards.'

'I'll do that,' I said, and set off up the path.

The guy must've been waiting for me at the top, screened by the bushes. He came straight at me, and I just had time to see the knife in his hand before he lunged at my chest. I drove down hard on his wrist with my left arm and felt the point of the blade nick my thigh. We grappled, me with one hand at his throat and the other clamped round his right wrist, him

207

desperately trying to pull both of them free and have a proper go at me. I turned him so that his back was to the beach, meaning to use my weight to overbalance him and send us both rolling down the path...

Which was when there was a sharp *crack* and he froze, then went completely limp. I let go, and he collapsed like a rag doll.

What the hell? Not that I wasn't grateful, mind. I took a minute just to stand and breathe.

'You okay?'

I looked down the path towards the beach. The old guy was more than half way up, and coming towards me. 'Never better,' I said. Not wholly true; the cut on my thigh – luckily, from what I could see of it beneath my tunic it was hardly more than a scratch – stung like hell, but still. I waited until we were level. 'Thanks, pal. That was a pretty good shot.'

'Fair to middling,' he said smugly. 'So. What's the damage?'

I glanced at the man sprawled face down to my left. He lay absolutely still, and the back of his head was a pulpy mass of blood and bone fragments. What we had here was definitely an ex-mugger.

'Pretty much terminal, I'm afraid,' I said.

He grunted and shrugged. 'Bastard must've had a thin skull.' Not much concern there, but with twenty five years as an auxiliary behind you you can develop a fairly thick skin where sudden death is concerned. 'What happened, exactly?'

'He was waiting for me with a knife. Almost got me, too.'

Another grunt. 'Odd. You get the occasional robber out here in the sticks, sure, but not in broad daylight. Not one as determined as chummie here, either.' He reached down and turned the corpse over so that the face was showing. 'You don't happen to know him at all, do you?'

'No.' The guy was a total stranger. Except –

I frowned; there was something familiar about him, at that. Nothing I could put my finger on, just a niggle at the back of my mind.

'Fair enough. That makes it easy, then.' He bent down again and half-lifted the corpse by the shoulders. 'Give me a hand. We should be able to roll him down the slope onto the beach.'

'What?'

He let go and straightened. 'Don't want him cluttering up the road, do we? People would only ask questions, and I can do without that at my time of life. Don't you worry, sir, he'll tuck away nicely among the rocks out by the headland, and the crabs'll thank us for him.'

Jupiter! Callous wasn't the half of it! Besides, although I wasn't particularly superstitious I knew you could get into serious supernatural trouble feeding unburied bodies to the crabs.

'No, that's okay,' I said quickly. 'We'll just park him out of sight behind those bushes and when I get back to town I'll have the authorities send someone out to collect him.'

He looked dubious. 'You're sure?'

'No problem. And no hassle where you're concerned, I guarantee it.' There wouldn't be, I was certain, once I'd explained the situation to Quirinius. And at least, violent end or not, the murdering bastard couldn't complain that he'd been denied a funeral.

'Well, if you're certain...'

'Oh, I am. Absolutely.' Between us, we lugged the corpse out of sight of the road and stashed it in a handy patch of scrub. 'Thanks again. Not least for saving my life.'

'A pleasure. Don't mention it.'

He might be a callous killer, but at least he was a *polite* callous killer. I set off back towards town.

I was about half way there when I remembered where I'd seen the dead guy before. He'd been the blunt half of the wineshop scuffle I'd witnessed the day after we'd arrived.

What the hell was going on?

I called in at Quirinius's office to report the little contretemps and arrange for a no-questions-asked collection of the remains, then carried on to Cladus's wineshop in the Aesculapius district. I'd heard both sets of names at the time, the stroppy injured party's and the one belonging to my ex-mugger who'd been on the receiving edge of the complaint, but much as I cudgelled my brains I couldn't recall either one of them. With luck, though, the barman would know. Barmen, like major-domos, have an omniscient streak where their customers are concerned, and I'd bet that the guy who'd ended up with his head stove in, at least, was one of the regulars.

Fortunately I seemed to have hit a quiet patch, and the place was practically empty, with only a few punters sitting at the tables and the usual two or three dedicated bar-flies propping up the counter. I went across.

'Good afternoon, sir.' The barman put down the cup he was drying. 'Nice to see you again. What'll it be?'

'Same as last time, pal,' I said. 'The Carpian, was it?'

'Carpian it was and is.' He reached down a flask. 'Just the one cup?'

'For the present, yes.' I took the coins out of my belt-pouch and leaned on the counter while he poured. 'Plus a smidgeon of information, if you can give me it.'

'I'll do my best.'

'The last time I was in here there was a bit of trouble between two of your customers. Over the sale of some property. You remember that?'

'Of course.'

'You happen to know their names?'

'Not the name of the man who started it, no. I hadn't seen him before, and he hasn't been in since, not that he'd be welcome. The other gent, sure. Aponius Syrus.'

Syrus. Right; that I did remember now. 'You know where I can find him?' Currently under a bush a mile from town with no back to his head, true, but there was no point in complicating things.

'Sure. He's one of our biggest property dealers. He has an office just round the corner, in fact, in the courtyard with the public water fountain.'

Fair enough; an office meant that there was probably a clerk I could interview, at least. Mind you, it was the other man I really wanted to talk to. And I suspected that, under the circumstances, starting my enquiries from the other side of things mightn't be too hot an idea. I shelved the information for future reference. 'The first guy. The one who came in and caused the trouble. He gave Syrus his name at the time, that much I do remember. Still no bells?'

'I'm sorry, sir, I wasn't listening all that closely. And as I said, I'd never laid eyes on him before.'

Bugger. Well, it couldn't be helped; it would have to be the clerk after all, and at least that was a lot better than nothing. 'Never mind,' I said. 'No harm done. Thanks anyway.'

'You're welcome.'

I took a swallow of the wine. Okay, next stop chummie's office. At least it was just round the corner...

'Maenius. Titus Maenius.'

I turned sideways to find the nearest bar-fly looking at me.

'What?' I said.

'At least, that was the father's name. Used to have a bakery on the other side of the Byrsa that did a nice poppy-seed loaf. That's a good while ago now, mind.'

Hey! 'You know him, friend?' I said.

'Nah. Just the name, and where the shop was. The wife used to go over special, when she was alive.'

'So where was the shop? Exactly?' It might be closed down, sure, and the guy might've moved as a result – in fact, from what I knew of the circumstances from listening in to the frank exchange of views he almost certainly had – but at least it'd give me somewhere to start from. No doubt there'd still be neighbours in place.

'Other side of the Byrsa, like I said.' The bar-fly took a swallow of his wine. 'Close in, on the edge of Astarte near Potters' Market. It's gone now, these five years, at least, but that's where it was, right enough.'

'Great!' I drained my cup. 'What are you drinking, pal? On me.'

'That's good of you. Another cup of the Carpian would suit me fine.'

'Carpian it is.' I nodded to the barman, who unhitched the flask.

'Another for yourself, sir?' the barman said.

'No, that'll do me for the present.' I took the coins out of my belt-pouch and laid them on the counter. 'Near Potters' Market, right?' I said to the punter.

'As ever was. South side, the alleyway directly opposite the statue.'

'Got it. Thanks again, friend.'

Things were moving. Mark you, in what precise direction they were moving I hadn't the faintest idea.

25.

I found the alleyway – more or less at the foot of the Byrsa itself and directly opposite the statue of what was obviously one of the local worthies – and went down it.

The bakery, or what had been the bakery, was half way along, a two-storeyed property with a small yard to one side of the main building, between a cutler's shop and a shoemaker's. It was pretty much derelict; the brickwork was in poor repair, with serious gaps in the cement between courses, while judging by the rusted condition of their chain and padlock the shutters closing off the outside counter hadn't been opened for years. I glanced up at the first-floor windows. They were shuttered, too, and like the sales counter beneath they had that sad, closed-for-the-duration look that suggested the live-over flat hadn't been occupied for years, either.

Yeah, well. I hadn't really been expecting anything different, had I? On the other hand, the shop's main door had been replaced pretty recently by something that looked a lot stronger than its predecessor had probably been, and the gate to the yard was blocked by a mason's cart three quarters full of rubble and general detritus. Evidently, derelict as the place might be at present, Work was in Progress.

'Can I help you?'

I turned. A guy in a leather apron had come out of the shoemaker's shop next door and was watching me suspiciously.

'Yeah,' I said. 'Actually you can. I was looking for a Titus Maenius. Or maybe for his son, I don't know his given name. You happen to know where I can find either of them?'

He jerked his head back the way I'd come. 'Turn left at the end,' he said. 'Third street along to your right, about half way down. Flat above the haberdasher's.'

'Great. Thanks, pal.'

But he'd already gone back inside, and I was talking to myself. Obviously one of Carthage's friendlier locals. Never mind, onwards and upwards it was.

The property, when I found it, had an outside stair ending in a small landing with a door. I went up and knocked. Long pause, followed by shuffling internal footsteps.

'Yes?' An old man's voice from behind the panelling. 'Who is it?'

'My name's Valerius Corvinus,' I said. 'You're Titus Maenius?'

'I am. What do you want?'

'Just a word, if you can manage it.'

The door stayed closed. 'What about?'

The hard ones first. 'Uh...maybe we can just start from there and take things as they go?' I said. 'It's nothing bad, I promise you.'

There was the sound of a bolt being drawn back. The door opened.

'Fair enough. You'd best come in, then.'

Old was right; he must've been eighty, if he was a day. He waited until I'd gone past him then closed the door behind me.

'Now. Sit yourself down, sir,' he said. 'There's a stool over by the wall, if you can see it.'

That was tricky in itself, particularly since I was coming in from bright afternoon sunlight. There were windows, sure, but the flat was north facing and the light they let in was pretty sparse. As were the furnishings. I waited until my eyes had adjusted to the dimness, then found the stool and sat on it while he shuffled his way to a high-backed chair by one of the windows and eased himself into it. Which was when I noticed he was one hand short of the usual set.

'So,' he said. 'What can I do for you?'

I hesitated. 'To tell you the truth, I'm not quite sure. I understand you know a guy by the name of Aponius Syrus.'

'Yes, I do. He bought my bakery two or three months ago. Or what used to be my bakery.'

'You were, uh, happy with the deal?'

He was frowning now. 'Of course I was,' he said. 'How not?'

'It's just that, from what I saw of your son's encounter with Syrus in a wineshop half a month or so back, I had the impression that maybe you weren't. You know about that?'

'Yes. Titus told me. Now you can tell me, sir, why it should be any business of yours.'

That was reasonable. Not that I could give him a straight answer, mind, because I didn't have one.

When in doubt, tell the truth. Yeah, well, maybe not on every occasion, but my options were seriously limited here. 'Like I said, my name's

Marcus Valerius Corvinus. The emperor sent me out from Rome to look into the death of an ex-praetor. A man called Decimus Cestius.'

'And? I'm sorry, but I still don't see what this has to do with my sale of the bakery.'

'Believe me, neither do I. Thing is, for no apparent reason earlier today your Aponius Syrus followed me out the Tunes road and tried to put a knife through my guts.'

'He did *what?*' The old guy was staring at me in horror.

'Strange, right? And the only handle I have on him – the *only* handle – is that I saw him having a stand-up fight with your son in Cladus's wineshop. Hence my visit. So trust me, any light you can cast would be welcome.'

He shook his head numbly. 'I've no idea,' he said. 'None at all. It was a straightforward sale agreed by the both of us, all the paperwork duly witnessed and the price paid in full, cash on the nail.'

'Your son seemed to think you'd been swindled somehow.'

'Then he was wrong. *Is* wrong. I'd been trying to unload the place for years, ever since this happened.' He held up the stump of his right wrist. 'I'd've let it go for half what Syrus paid me and still reckon I'd come out ahead. But Titus is Titus; he doesn't listen, he never has.'

'Didn't he object at the time? Why wait until now?'

'He was in Tripolis, with his legion. He only got his discharge a month back.'

'Syrus approached you, right? About the sale?'

'He did. He was completely up-front about it, said he'd be demolishing the property, developing the site, then selling the result on at a whacking profit. That's the business he's in, how he generally works. I knew that from the start.'

'Was there anything unusual about the place at all? That you know of?'

'How do you mean?'

'Search me. Suspicious mind. But it's an obvious question. No walls where there shouldn't be? Signs of a hidden cellar beneath the floor?'

Maenius chuckled. 'Look, sir. My grandfather built it himself, about a hundred years back, mostly with his own hands, from the ground up. It's been in the family ever since, and we're just bakers. We always have been. So no secret rooms stuffed with treasure, I guarantee that. What you see is what you get.'

Bugger. Well, it had been worth a shot. Of course, the whole boiling might be complete coincidence and by all the signs probably was; after all, when they weren't trying to stick knives into interfering Roman busybodies even would-be assassins had to have a regular daytime job. And from what Maenius was telling me there wasn't the faintest whiff of bad fish about the transaction at all; quite the contrary.

Still...

'Paperwork,' I said. 'You said that everything had been done nice and legal, yes?'

'Of course.'

'You happen to have your copy of the deed of sale handy, then? Could I have a look at that, do you think?'

'It's in the strongbox next to you. And you're welcome to see it, certainly, provided you get it yourself. I'm not too mobile these days.'

'Strongbox' was a gross exaggeration: judging by the broken hinge on one side and the complete absence of a padlock the thing wouldn't have qualified as a safe in anyone's terms. Even the word 'box' was pushing things. I lifted the lid.

'It'll be at the top,' Maenius said. 'With the piece of red ribbon round it.'

I took the scrolled sheet out, carried it to the window, and unrolled it. Sure enough, it was a standard deed of sale and transfer of ownership, dated the Nones of July that year, with the names of buyer and seller written in. The only unusual thing about it was that Aponius Syrus was named only as the purchaser's agent. The property's new owner was Decimus Cestius.

Gods!

26.

Perilla was upstairs in the study when I got back, still methodically sorting through Albus's notes. Yeah, well, each to his own, and at least now she'd cleared it with Cornelia her editing jag – or whatever you like to call it – was legit.

'Oh, hello, Marcus,' she said. 'Did you manage to find–?' Her eyes went to the slit in the lower side of my tunic, where Syrus's knife had caught my left thigh. 'That's blood, isn't it?'

Hell. 'Uh...yeah,' I said. 'It is, as it happens. Nothing to–'

She wasn't listening. She got up from behind the desk, pushed past me through the open door and leaned over the banister.

'Bathyllus!'

I joined her. 'Look, lady,' I said. 'It's hardly more than a scratch, right? No problem whatsoever.'

She ignored me. Bathyllus had appeared at the base of the stairs and was looking up anxiously.

'Yes, madam?' he said.

'Hot water, vinegar, sponge and towel please. And a bandage. Now.'

Jupiter! Talk about overreaction! 'Come on, Perilla,' I said. 'I told you, it's just a small cut, right? I'd forgotten it was even there.'

'None the less.' She went back in, and I followed her. 'Now. What exactly happened?'

I told her. She frowned. 'But this man Syrus has had nothing to do with anything so far,' she said. 'Why would he suddenly want to kill you?'

'Yeah, well, I would've got round to explaining that side of it by now if you hadn't gone off on your female Aesculapius binge, wouldn't I? My bet – and it's a good one – is that it has a lot to do with a property deal he made on behalf of Decimus Cestius just before he died.' I gave her the rest of the story.

'Hmm.' She was twisting a lock of hair. 'So what you're saying is that this sale of a bakery is directly linked with Cestius's murder, yes?'

'That's the theory, sure. It has to be. How it works out in practice, mind, is something else again.'

'So where exactly is it? This bakery?'

217

'Not all that far from here, actually. In an alleyway this side of the Byrsa, pretty close in but not on the slope itself.' I grinned. 'You're wondering about a match with Albus's House of Jirced, right?'

'It would seem a reasonable possibility, yes. Even a probable one. And it would provide another definite link.'

'Forget it, lady. I covered that angle with Maenius. The old guy's grandfather built the place himself, and his family's lived there ever since. Up to last July, at least, when Syrus bought it. But according to Maenius it'd been on the market for years, with no takers.'

'You don't find that significant?'

'How do you mean?'

'Well, it's just that–' There was a knock at the door and Bathyllus came in with the lady's medical kit. 'Oh, thank you, Bathyllus. Just put everything down on the floor, please.' She got up and came round the desk. 'Let me have a look, dear.'

'Will that be all, madam?' Bathyllus said. I hadn't missed the look the little guy had given my damaged tunic, or the way his lips pursed. Our major-domo might be perfectly okay with wounds, but coming home with a stained and damaged tunic was another matter.

'Yeah, that's fine, Bathyllus,' I said. 'Hippocrates here has it covered. Back in ten minutes for the basin, right?'

A sniff. 'As you wish, sir.'

He left, I lifted the edge of the tunic, and Perilla began dabbing away with the wet sponge...

'*Ow!*'

She stopped. 'I'm only cleaning it, Marcus,' she said. 'I thought you said it didn't hurt.'

'It didn't.' Jupiter! Whatever the opposite of healing hands was, the lady had them in spades. 'Fine, never mind. Carry on. So what were you going to say about the bakery sale?'

'Hmm? Oh, yes. When did it happen, exactly?'

'The Nones of July this year, according to the deed.'

'Right. Six days before Cestius's murder, in fact. And four before Albus's accident. The property in question being, arguably if still subject to confirmation, on the site of a building marked as significant on a map drawn by Albus himself.'

'Yeah, well, if you like to put it that way–'

'I do. Grit your teeth. Vinegar.'

'What?'

Jupiterfucking Bestand Greatestand alltheotherfucking immortalgods!

'There. That should do you. No need for the bandage, I think. It was hardly more than a scratch after all.' She stood up and dried her hands on the towel while I limped over to the reading couch and laid my shattered body down. 'Actually, I came across something very interesting myself this morning that may fit in rather well.'

'Yeah? And what's that?'

She went back to her chair behind the desk and sat down. 'A page of notes referring to Carthage's last days. They are just that, of course, only random jottings, not a proper narrative, but the gist of them seems to be that before Aemilianus occupied the lower town and laid siege to the Byrsa Elissa – Hasdrubal's wife, if you remember, who organised the final defence – took a large part of the family's gold reserve from the treasury in the Temple of Baal and hid it elsewhere.'

'Uh-huh. And you think she stashed it in this House of Jirced, yes?'

'More or less. Why not? It would explain Albus's singling it out in the first place. And if the site *is* identical with that of your bakery it would clear up a lot of awkward problems at a stroke.'

'Such as what, lady? Look, it's a good enough theory, no arguments; for all I know it may even be right. But at present there are holes in it you could drive a cart through.'

'Namely?'

'One. I said: the bakery building has only been there for about a century, and it was built on virgin ground. If–'

'No.'

'No what?'

'Marcus, there *is* no such thing here as virgin ground! Not within the confines of the original city, at least, and certainly nowhere near the Byrsa. When Aemilianus destroyed Carthage on the senate's orders he did just that. The whole city was flattened. *Literally* flattened; what few buildings were still standing after the final conflagration, before the Byrsa fell, were pulled down and covered over, and the new surface rammed flat. Modern Carthage, all of it, was built on top. Even if Maenius's grandfather dug decent foundations, which presumably he did, they wouldn't go deeper than the first layer of rubble. And if the Barcas' gold *was* hidden in the

219

house occupying the site originally the chances are that it lies much, much deeper than that.'

'Okay,' I said stubbornly. 'Scratch that objection. Two–'

'One.'

'Whatever. You said yourself that up to now Aponius Syrus hasn't figured in the investigation at all. So how and where does he fit into the scheme of things? And how the hell did he know where I'd be this morning to begin with?'

'I can't answer the second question, dear, except to say that he did. The first...well, you know the answer to that yourself, from the deed of sale. He was acting as Cestius's agent. What that implies, and to what degree he was conscious of what was going on, I don't know, but the link is there.'

'Gods, Perilla, Decimus Cestius has been dead for months! He's the fucking *victim!*'

'Don't swear.'

'Okay. But all I'm saying is that the only tie-in we have for Syrus is Cestius himself. If he's been acting off his own bat since the murder, which seems unlikely, then you need to explain how he's got to know everything about this business that he'd need to know before he could get anywhere. And how he's managed to get anywhere at all in the first place.'

'Very lucidly put, dear.'

'Come on, lady, don't fudge! You know what I mean well enough. The guy may have been involved up to the eyeballs from the very beginning in whatever is going on, but there isn't a chance in hell that he's our principal perp.'

'Agreed. I never said he was.'

'Well, then.'

Impasse, and a long silence. Finally, Perilla sighed.

'Look,' she said. 'We're getting tied up in knots here. Maybe we should just lay out everything we already have or think we have, facts and possibilities, and see where that takes us.'

'Fair enough, go ahead. You start.'

'Very well. Whoever our principal is, their target is to recover the Barca family's gold, which Cornelius Albus, in the course of his historical research, has discovered was moved for safe keeping by Elissa to somewhere called the House of Jirced. Yes? Reasonable assumption?'

'Fine by me. Carry on.'

'Albus then sets about finding where exactly that was, in terms of the modern city. He–'

'Hang on. Point of order. Albus may have had his faults, but I'd bet he was no crook. Not even a potential one. Our perp self-evidently is.'

'True. So?'

'So maybe, in the light of what happened later, that was the point when chummie becomes involved. After all, if you are a crook, or a potential one, at least, and some egghead historian tells you he's discovered the existence of a local treasure trove you'll damn well want to know where it is. Yes?'

'I suppose so, dear. In any case, Albus matches the site to a patch of ground now occupied by the Maenius bakery. At which point our perpetrator–'

'Call him X. It's simpler, and it's traditional.'

'All right. X, then, takes matters into his own hands. He–' She stopped. 'This next part makes no sense at all.'

'Just lay it out. We'll work on the sense later.'

'X arranges through an agent, Aponius Syrus, to buy the property in due legal form. Then, immediately afterwards, to ensure that the secret of the gold goes no further, he kills Albus and disguises the murder as an accident.' She shook her head. 'Marcus, that cannot *possibly* be right! It would mean our X was Cestius, which would be stupid!'

'True. Leave it and move on.'

'I can't. It just gets worse, because Cestius himself is murdered two days later. Unless–' She stopped again. 'Oh.'

'Right. Unless, despite what the bill of sale says, the purchaser – and so our X – was someone else. If Syrus was the front guy who actually negotiated the deal and paid over the money then he could put down whatever name he liked.'

'But surely eventually–' I could see the penny drop. 'Ah. Only of course there wouldn't be an "eventually", would there? Two days later, Cestius would be dead as well.'

'Correct.' I was watching her closely. The next stage was going to prove sticky, and Perilla was much too smart not to make the logical jump.

'Except,' she said slowly, 'the death of the legal owner, the *stated* legal owner, wouldn't make much difference, would it? The property would simply go to his heir.' There she went. I didn't comment, just waited.

221

'Which would be Publius. But Publius had no connection at all with Cornelius Albus, so he couldn't possibly have known about the gold, or where it had been hidden; plus if he *were* intending to recover it then he wouldn't be so eager to go back to Rome. In which case the only other possibility for X is–' She was staring at me. 'Oh, Marcus! *No!* He couldn't! He wouldn't!'

'You have the ball, lady,' I said gently. 'So you have to run with it. I'm sorry, but these are the rules.'

She's a tough proposition, Perilla, far tougher than me when the chips are down, but I could see this was costing her. She cleared her throat.

'Very well,' she said. 'Congratulations, dear. Our villain was Quintus after all.'

Bleak as hell. 'I'm sorry,' I said again. I was, too; bitterly, on my own account as well as hers. He'd been okay, young Quintus, within his limits. Still, it wouldn't be the first time that I'd had more sympathy with the perp than I had for the victim, and in those circumstances you just have to grit your teeth and get on with things. 'But he ticks all the boxes, the only person who does. He was Albus's closest confidant, a historian in his own right. He was the only person we can be absolutely certain was with the old guy on the morning he died, and we only have his word for it that he left before it happened. He had valid reasons, independent of the gold, for engineering the two deaths. He was the only one of the family to be staying behind when they moved back to Rome, and I doubt if he'd've had any difficulties in getting Publius to include the Maenius place in his inheritance package. And, finally, he was the only person, barring Cornelia, who knew I'd be heading down the Tunes road this morning bound for open country. Because he'd sent me there himself.'

'Yes, I know all that, and I agree. He has to be guilty, no arguments, none at all. All the same–'

There was a knock at the door, and Bathyllus came in with a tray.

'The basin, sir, if you've finished with it,' he said. 'And I've brought you up some wine and a juice for the mistress.'

'Thanks, sunshine,' I said. 'Things are a bit fraught at present. Just leave the tray on the desk and we'll help ourselves.'

'Of course.'

I turned back to Perilla. 'Okay,' I said. 'You still have the ball, and I'm listening. All the same what?'

222

She took a deep breath. 'All the same, Marcus, I can *not* believe that he could commit a murder. Certainly not if it entailed coldly and deliberately pushing an old man down a flight of steps. I'm sorry, but it is just totally incredible.'

The gods save me from stubborn women who can't put logic and common sense before their knee-jerk maternal instincts! 'Jupiter, lady!' I said. 'Give me a break here! We've been through this a dozen times!'

'Don't exaggerate.'

'Okay. Fine. So it wasn't him; he'd already left the house like he claimed. But if you can explain to me how someone else could've sneaked in from outside and got up here without anyone noticing, done the job, and sneaked out again ditto, then–'

'By means of the back stairs, sir,' Bathyllus said.

I stopped. 'What?'

'He could have used the other set of stairs, sir. The servants' ones.'

Holy gods! 'Bathyllus,' I said slowly, 'just let me get this straight, pal. You are telling me that there's another way up here? Another staircase?'

'Of course.'

'Then where the fuck is it?'

'*Marcus!*'

'At the other end of the corridor.'

Bloody hell!

'Show me,' I said. Then, when he dithered: 'Just put the bloody basin down and do it!'

We followed him outside and turned left. I'd never been this way before, because there'd been no need: the main staircase was immediately next to the study, our bedroom was directly opposite, and although there were other doors beyond they were, presumably, bedrooms in their own right, Cornelia's for one. And as far as I could see the corridor itself finished in a dead end.

Only it didn't. Look to your left when you reached the far wall and there was another set of stairs, much narrower and steeper than the front ones.

'Lead on, little guy,' I said.

I made my way down after him, with Perilla close behind me. The stairs ended in an open door giving out onto a back courtyard, evidently used for storing rubbish destined for the local dump and adjacent to the kitchen and servants' quarters.

'This door always kept open, sunshine?' I said.

'Only during the day, sir. It's always locked at night, as are the others.'

I went over to the gate in the courtyard wall. That was open, too, the difference being that it showed every sign of staying that way. No bolt, and the hinges didn't look like they'd put up with too much extended use. Mind you, if the communicating doors to the house were all locked after dark there wouldn't be much to attract a would-be thief in any case. Old wine jars and vegetable peelings have a pretty low resale value.

Gods alive! Granted that they knew the layout of the house once they were inside, and did their visiting during the hours of daylight, anyone could've slipped up to Albus's study the day he died. Anyone at all.

Provided, as I say, they knew where they were going in the first place. And that they knew enough about the daily routine and the master's habits to be confident that they wouldn't be seen, either on the inward or the outward trip...

So, *pace* all the evidence to the contrary and going exclusively on Perilla's gut feeling and, I had to admit, my own, if Albus's killer, our X, *hadn't* been squeaky-clean young Quintus, then who was left? Who, in other words, ticked the necessary boxes? Or ticked the most important ones, at least, including above all the ones to do with Albus and the location of the gold?

Put that way, the answer was obvious, if not, on the surface, instantly credible, because there was only one name on the list...

Shit, no; there had to be something wrong with the logic. As a candidate for our X the guy was even less likely, if that were possible, than Quintus. And in any case, the day Albus had died he hadn't been near the place...

Or so he'd said. But then now we knew about this other way in the basic mechanics would've been easy-peasy; the rest was just minor detail and fudging. And where going back to Italy was concerned, with all of the Barca gold to draw on he could easily jump ship, disappear into the bushes, buy himself a new name and identity, and live very comfortably, not to say in filthy luxury, for the rest of what remained of his days.

'Sextus Gratius,' I said.

Perilla looked at me wide-eyed. 'What?'

'Our perp. X. It's the factor, Sextus Gratius.'

'You're sure?'

'Certain of it. Unless it's Quintus, who'd be far the better bet.'

'It isn't.'

'There you are, then. The trouble is, we're stuck with the usual problem. No proof. Zero. Zilch. If his sidekick Syrus had still been a viable commodity we'd at least have had him to lean on, maybe cut a deal with, but as it is he can afford just to look hurt and shocked by the accusation and swear complete innocence. Being the mild, inoffensive citizen in good standing that he is he'd probably get away with it, too. At least, as long as he needs to before he does his disappearing act. Fuck!'

'Marcus, dear...'

'Yeah. Yeah, I know. Just bad luck. Or rather, good planning on his part. If only he hadn't been so careful about covering his tracks when he–' I stopped. 'Holy fuck!'

'*Marcus!*'

Got the bastard! I waved her to silence. 'Okay,' I said. 'Forget Quintus altogether. X is definitely Gratius, and we can prove it.'

'How?'

I told her. 'All I need is another word with Albus's ex-major-domo.'

That was, of course, assuming that the old guy's memory was up to scratch. But I'd worry about that side of things if and when I had to.

27.

There was no need to worry: Cornelius Chilo's memory, when I went over to his wife's pastry shop by the racetrack the following morning and talked to him, didn't let either him or me down. Proof positive.

So that was that. I called in at Quirinius's to bring him fully up to date and borrow a couple of Galba's lictors. I doubted if Gratius would be capable of any serious resistance, let alone anything to justify muscle on that scale, but we had to conform to the formalities; although I had my imperial procurator status once I'd fingered Gratius my job was over, and the ball was completely in the local authorities' court.

Not that I was looking forward to doing it, mind. Oh, sure, the guy was a killer, no question, although I'd risk a heavy bet that it had been his pal Syrus who had knifed Cestius. Even so, he was definitely not my idea of an out-and-out villain. If I'd had my way out of the suspects who were still around our end-user perp would've been Publius, or better still his mother: Verania I hadn't forgotten about – I was hundred-per-cent certain she'd been directly responsible for Scarus's death, to begin with, and the motive force behind Appius Justus's – but if I was going to nail her in some way it would require careful thought.

So down I went to Gratius's office near the port, with my two hefty insurance policies padding along behind.

He was in, and sitting behind his desk discussing something with his copy-slave. When he saw the two axemen squeezing their respective bulks through the doorway his expression froze.

'Valerius Corvinus,' he said. 'And how can I help you this morning, sir?'

I ignored him and turned to the other man. 'Uh...Quadrus, isn't it?' I said.

'Yes, sir. That's right.' The guy was looking puzzled.

'I'm sorry to keep throwing you out, pal, but do you think you could leave us alone? This is rather delicate.'

The copy-slave glanced at the axemen, then at Gratius, who nodded. He swallowed and made for the door with as little speed as he could manage, closing it behind him.

227

There was no point in drawing things out. We might as well get this over and done with as fast as possible.

'You killed Cornelius Albus,' I said to Gratius. 'And either you or your friend Aponius Syrus murdered Decimus Cestius.'

Gratius didn't move. Then he said, very quietly: 'I'm sorry, sir. That is complete nonsense.'

'I'm afraid it isn't. Unfortunately. But there we are.'

'But this is–' He shook his head. 'Look, sir. Forgive me for saying this, but do show a bit of common sense. Please. Cestius was my ex-master, and Lucius was my closest friend. Why on earth would I want to hurt either of them? Even if I were capable of it, which believe me I am not.'

'Because of the Barca treasure buried under the old Maenius bakery near Potters' Market. Bought through Syrus shortly before the two of them died, and which you hold the deeds for.'

'I do no such thing. They're in–' He stopped, then carried on slowly and deliberately. 'They are in the master's name, not mine. Decimus Cestius's. I told you when we first talked: the master was in the habit of buying up land as and when it became available, and only informing me later. Which was the case here. Naturally I was aware – *am* aware – of the purchase, since I am the family factor. The treasure part of things, well, I'm afraid I know absolutely nothing about that. If it even exists, which I very much doubt.'

'Oh, it exists all right. According to the notes my wife Perilla found in Albus's study, at least. And there's a difference between buying up stretches of agricultural land outside the city boundaries – which was what we were talking about – and property within the city itself.'

'Forgive me again, sir, but you're splitting hairs. I made no mention of the master's property dealings in town because they weren't relevant. As you well know. In actual fact, he acquired a considerable number of urban properties over the years. If you'd care to look through my records I can provide you with a full list.'

'Uh-uh. That won't be necessary.'

'Then that is something, at any rate.' He was getting angry, and holding it in well: we'd got to the icily-polite stage. Behind me, I could hear the two lictors shift their positions. 'As for my killing Lucius, that is total rubbish, even assuming his death was *not* an accident, which of course it was. I was a frequent visitor to the house, yes, but not on the morning in

228

question. I hadn't been there for days. And if you don't believe me his major-domo Chilo will confirm it.'

'He'll confirm you didn't visit through the front door as normal, sure. But you didn't come that way, did you? You came through the yard at the back and up the servant's stair. And after you'd decoyed the old man to the top of the main staircase and pushed him down it you left the same way.'

'This is simply insane!'

I shook my head. 'Uh-uh. It's the plain truth. Unfortunately, like I say, because I don't think you're a killer by nature—'

'Thank you!'

'— but you were there that morning right enough, and I can prove it.'

'How?'

'Because you left your freedman's cap behind. Or rather, Cornelia's pet monkey snatched it off you while you were in the study talking to Albus. She told me she'd given one back to you at the funeral. And I've just checked with Chilo. When you left after your visit two days previously, the only time, according to both of you, that you'd been there before the accident, you were properly kitted out. No missing cap. So if you hadn't been back to the house between times then when exactly did you lose it?'

Complete silence. Eventually:

'Very well,' he said quietly. 'What happens now?'

All the anger, fabricated or not, had gone; the guy just looked old, and tired, and grey. Gods! I hated this part, particularly since, like I say, I could've wished for a better end to the case, and a different perp.

I made my decision.

'That might be up to you, friend,' I said carefully, very conscious of the governorial task force at my back. 'You mind setting me straight as to a few details in the meantime?'

'Not at all, sir.' He gave me a weak smile. 'I'll be glad to help in any way I can.'

'Fair enough.' There was a stool to one side. I pulled it over so that we were sitting facing each other either side of the desk. It made things less confrontational that way, and we'd moved far beyond the confrontational stage now. 'The gold. How did you know it existed in the first place? Did Albus mention it to you?'

He shook his head. 'No. You know how he was, through hearsay if not personal knowledge. Something like that – well, he'd treat it as an academic curiosity, a piece of historical fact like any other, of neither greater nor lesser importance than the rest. And he liked to have all his facts neatly bundled together into a complete package before he shared them with anyone. That was his way. So no, sir, he didn't tell me about it; he never would have.'

'How, then?'

'I told you when we talked that first time. I wasn't born here, and I wasn't born a slave, either. My father had a small farm in Italy, just outside Crustumerium. We'd lived there – the family, I mean – for generations. At the time of the third war with Carthage one of us, a youngest son, was pressed into the army.' He shrugged. 'It happened, and it was no bad thing, particularly when there were too many sons for the land to support, and for all I know he might have been a willing recruit to begin with. Anyway, he was sent over here with the rest of his legion. I don't know any of the details – this was two centuries ago, you understand, and parts of the story have got lost over time – but he got into trouble, bad trouble, so bad that he decided to desert. He went over to the Carthaginians and signed up with them.'

'Uh-huh.' Perilla had mentioned a group of deserters from the Roman army involved in the final stand on the Byrsa. Things were becoming clearer. 'He survived, right?'

'How, again, I don't know, but yes. It took him a long time, years, but finally he made it back home. And he brought the story of the gold. It's been part of our family's lore ever since, one of the only stories I can remember my father telling me. So when my first master died and Master Cestius brought me over here as his factor' – he shrugged again – 'well, you can understand. It was like going back, in time as well as space. For the first time in almost two hundred years one of us had a chance to follow the story up. To see if there had been any truth in it.'

'And you got Albus to do a bit of digging.'

Another weak smile. 'Metaphorically speaking, sir, yes. Lucius was a good historian, one of the best. And of course despite being Roman he had local connections of his own, brought up in a different tradition.'

'His wife's family. Medar.'

'Exactly. He learned a lot from them that isn't in any of the official histories, that's been passed down the generations by word of mouth. The result was that, eventually, he was able to confirm that the story was true and to take it further. He worked out where the treasure must have been hidden – buried beneath the floor of a cellar in the lower town, in a house belonging to an old servant of Hasdrubal's wife, where no one would have thought of looking – and where that was in terms of the present city. That last really took time, but he was certain by the end that he'd got it right. He was very excited when he told me, of course – we'd worked together on the problem from the start, naturally, so he'd no qualms about sharing the information with me – but as I said for him it had simply been an academic puzzle to be solved. He would have been – he *was* – quite content to leave things there. Lucius had no interest whatsoever in anything as common as treasure.'

'And you did?' But I said it gently.

He gave me a sharp look. 'Of course I did! You've never been poor, sir, and you haven't lived most of your life as someone else's property. Besides, although I knew then, as I know now, that I had no right to it if it was recovered, after all this time no one else had either. And the family connection at least gave me a claim. Of a sort.'

'Big enough a claim to kill a friend for?'

I could've bitten my tongue off as soon as I'd said it, because he winced. 'Perhaps not,' he said. 'Believe me, I'm not proud of that, quite the reverse. But Lucius would never have understood. And he would have made the secret public, eventually, in which case, realities being what they are, I'd never have seen a copper coin of the money. I told you, sir; you've never been poor, or a slave. You don't understand either, and I wouldn't expect you to, any more than I would've expected understanding from him.'

'Fair enough. So what about your ex-master? Did he have to die too?'

'He was going to take me back to Italy before the end of this year's sailing season. This was only two months ago, remember. I would've had four months at the very most, probably much less, with no chance of coming back. I needed more time than that.'

'You couldn't just have stayed behind?'

He just looked at me. Right. Someone like Quintus could have done that – *was* doing that – but Quintus wasn't an ex-slave with an ex-slave's ties, and even without his father's blessing and financial support he was one of the local Great and Good. He wouldn't've starved, by any means. That was something his kind – my kind – never has to worry about. For people like

Gratius things are different. Besides, from what I'd heard of Cestius and the dangers of crossing him telling him to find another factor would not have been a safe option.

Finally, Gratius shook his head. 'Killing the master was Syrus's idea,' he said. 'Although I couldn't fault his logic. And before you ask, no, I don't feel much remorse in that direction. I've hated that man all my life for what he was; a complete monster.'

'How did the pair of you manage that, by the way?' I said. 'Killing Cestius?'

'It was easy enough. I simply told the master that I had my doubts about whether Medar's folk were doing a good job with the harvesting, and advised him to ride over and check. When he stopped on the way back for lunch at the grove, as I knew he would, Syrus was there waiting for him.'

'Uh-huh.' So. That was that one solved. 'Syrus. How did you fall in with him?'

'I'd used him before as an agent when the master expressed an interest in adding to his city property portfolio. He was honest enough, by his lights, but his honesty didn't go all that far. Especially considering what I offered him.'

'Which was?'

'Equal shares in the treasure. And I meant it. There's no point in being greedy when each of you is likely to net over fifty million in gold.'

I blinked. 'It was that much?'

'It was – *is* – that much. You're not tempted yourself, by the way?'

'No. I'll pass.'

Another weak smile. 'I didn't expect so. Never mind. It was just a thought.'

'So how did you plan to take things from here? If you'd got away with it, I mean.'

'You've seen the site? The bakery?'

'Yes.'

'You'll have noticed the mason's cart, then. The building itself is only a shell, left intact to hide what we're doing. Syrus has men working at the excavation, removing the old rubble, taking it away and dumping it, shoring up the sides of the pit as they go. It's taken time, obviously, particularly since we can't be too blatant, and it'll take a lot more, but they're down now as far as the first floor of the original house. And as I

232

said, the gold is buried beneath the original cellar. The plan, once we'd uncovered it, was to transport it in stages somewhere safe outside the city. Legally, the property belongs to young Master Publius now, and with the gold gone he would have been welcome to it. When the family go back to Rome next year at the start of the sailing season I would simply have surrendered the deeds, along with all the other property documents, and told them that I'd decided to stay on here after all.' His lips twisted. 'Young Master Publius isn't like his father, sir. Considering my age, he'd give me up without a murmur and congratulate himself on not having to support me when I was no longer able to perform my duties. And I doubt that his mother would raise any objections either. Once they'd gone' – he shrugged – 'well, I said: I'm not greedy, and I'm far from stupid. There would be far too much gold for my needs. I would probably have left most of it where it was, safely hidden, and bought a small estate a long way from Carthage where I could have spent my remaining years in comfort. That was the plan, at least. All changed now, of course.'

There wasn't anything I could say to that; we knew, both of us, that he'd no years left to spend. And after I handed him over to the authorities what little time he did have wouldn't be spent in anything like comfort. Still...

'One last question,' I said. 'Before we finish. How did Syrus know where to find me?'

'I beg your pardon, sir?' He looked blank. 'When exactly are we talking about?'

Oh, bugger! He didn't know anything about my trip to the beach! Or, by extension, that Syrus was dead. I wondered whether, if he had done and realised that with his partner gone he was the only game in town where extracting a confession was concerned, he might've tried brazening things out a bit longer. He might have succeeded, too: Gratius, if nothing else, was a sharp cookie.

'Yesterday morning,' I said. 'He followed me out the Tunes road and tried to kill me.'

'He's dead himself now?'

'Obviously, if I'm still walking.'

He was quiet for a long time. Then he said: 'I'm sorry, sir. Truly sorry. If killing you was his intention then it had nothing to do with me, and I knew nothing of it beforehand. As you said, I'm not a killer by nature. Syrus, rest him, was. I'm glad he didn't succeed.'

'So am I, pal. Very. So you don't have an answer?'

'No. But he certainly knew who you were, what you looked like, and what you were doing in Carthage, because I was careful to tell him about you after our first talk. Syrus being Syrus, he would probably have been watching out for you ever since then, looking for an opportunity. Yesterday morning, you say, and the Tunes road?'

'Yeah.'

'Then if you were starting from Lucius's house you'd have passed through a fair bit of the town to get there. I can only assume it was a complete accident, that he happened to see you and took the chance he'd been waiting for when it was offered.' He half-smiled. 'Perhaps there's such a thing as divine justice after all.'

He could be right, at that: if it hadn't been for Syrus, and my overhearing of that argument in Cladus's wineshop, I'd never have known about Maenius's bakery. Or, indeed, made the connection with Gratius himself. If divine justice was taking a hand here then the lady was working her immortal socks off.

Or there again it might have been pure coincidence. You pays your money and you takes your choice.

'It doesn't matter,' I said. 'Water under the bridge.'

'Indeed, sir. Now. If that's all the help I can give you?'

'Yeah. That about wraps it up.'

'In that case I was wondering if, before you and your friends here take me back, I could fetch a few things from upstairs. Some small personal items I'd be sorry to leave behind.'

'Sure, pal,' I said gently. 'Off you go. Take all the time you want.'

'Thank you, sir.' Behind me, my two heavies stirred. One of them cleared his throat. I turned.

'It's okay, lads,' I said. 'After all, we're down here and there's only one way up or down. Right?' I said to Gratius.

'Quite correct, sir. And I won't try to escape through the window. You have my word for that.'

'Fair enough. Go ahead.'

The stair was in the far corner of the room. He climbed it, and I could hear him moving about on the upper floor. Then there was a sudden thump, and the sounds stopped.

I waited. When I'd given him a good ten minutes with no signs of a reappearance I stood up myself.

'Okay, lads,' I said. 'Stay where you are for now. I'll shout if I need you.

I went upstairs. Gratius had been considerate to the end, and there was no blood involved. I picked up the stool he'd stood on to fasten the rope to one of the rafters, took the knife that he'd carefully left for the purpose, cut him down and laid him out neatly on the bed. Then I came back down.

Case closed. All done and dusted.

28

'So that's that,' I said when I got back the next day from my promised talk with Quirinius re the Marcus Virrius side of things. 'Holiday over, passage hopefully arranged within the next few days, depending on the winds. If that's okay with you.'

'Perfectly, dear.' Perilla was sitting outside on the terrace with a cup of fruit juice. 'In fact, I'll be glad to get back. I thought we might go over to Castrimoenium to spend some time with Clarus and Marilla, before the summer goes completely.'

'Fair enough.' I put the wine cup I'd picked up from Bathyllus on the table and sat down. 'How's the editing job going? You don't need more time for that?'

'No, quite finished. I'll leave everything in order for Quintus and Cornelia. She may not want to have anything to do with her father's historical projects at present, but I'm sure she'll come round eventually. Particularly with Quintus being so keen.' She took a sip of the fruit juice. 'Oh. Apropos that. They dropped by while you were in town to ask whether you'd confirmed his alibi, and I brought them up to date with events. They were very relieved, naturally, but Quintus is rather sceptical about this treasure of yours.'

'Is he, indeed? And why's that, now?'

'Not about it existing. Or rather, not too sceptical on that account. But according to him when Albus had a bee in his bonnet about something he did tend to be rather uncritical where his sources were concerned. Particularly where solid confirmation of the underlying theory went.'

'You mind putting that into plain Latin?'

She grinned and ducked her head. 'Just that he may have been too optimistic in identifying the site so precisely.'

'He doesn't think the treasure is hidden under the bakery at all?'

'No, for all he knows it may well be. But equally it might be under any of half a dozen other properties in the area. History may not be an exact science, but historical topography is even less so.'

Me, I'd be sorry to see him proved right. Not because of the gold per se, but because it would mean that Gratius had died a murderer for nothing. 'So he's not going to carry on with the digging?' I said. 'Assuming, that is, that given he's staying on he manages to wangle the property deed as part of his inheritance.'

'Oh, yes, he'll be very careful to do that, just in case. And to make sure that neither his brother nor his mother realise its significance. I told you: Quintus isn't the *ingénu* you seem to take him for, dear; he has his head very firmly screwed on, and coming from the family he does it would be very surprising if he hadn't inherited some of its more dubious traits. Personally I think that if he does find the gold and they get to know about it, which they will, inevitably, it will serve them right.'

'Yeah.' I frowned. 'I've been wondering about that aspect of things. She may not fit into my original remit, but Verania is as much a murderer as Gratius was, twice over, and I hate to see the bitch getting away with it.'

'She won't. Trust me.'

'She will. We've no proof that she poisoned Scarus, as far as the authorities are concerned Appius Justus was mugged for his purse, perp unknown, and with his real killer Scarus dead the only thing linking him with her is the word of a kitchen skivvy. Oh, I'll put my suspicions into the report I give Claudius, sure, no problems there. But at the end of the day it'd be an unsupported charge against the wealthy and respected widow of an ex-praetor who's also a friend of his wife's mother's, while the victims are a no-account slave-trader and a provincial sword-fighter. Even if he did trust my judgment, which he probably would, the chances that he'd take the matter further are in the flying pigs bracket.'

'True. But I wasn't thinking of Claudius.'

'Who, then?'

'Domitia Lepida.'

'What the hell good would that do? She's not–'

'Marcus, you really don't understand how incredibly important upper-class society conventions are, do you? Particularly the female variety. I distinctly remember you making the point yourself, when you first mooted the theory of Publius not being Cestius's son: to have a temporary fling with a good-looking young slave-trader is one thing, no one cares about that; but to have a son by him whom you then pass off as your husband's and finally try to marry into one of the leading families is quite another. That is class betrayal, and completely unforgivable. Believe me, once I've had a quiet word with Lepida when she goes back to Rome Verania will find herself exiled just as effectively as if she had been tried and sentenced by a court, Vettius Rufus – or his wife, rather – will have broken off the engagement before her ship has even docked, and Publius will have as much chance of a political career as a three-legged cat. The pair of them will still be very wealthy indeed – I can't do anything about that side of things – but for people like that, who've always taken it for granted, money alone isn't important. Social position and power are, they will have neither, ever again, and it will hurt. I absolutely guarantee it.' She smiled sweetly. 'So. Will that do you, dear?'

Jupiter! 'Uh...remind me never to try crossing you, lady,' I said.

'Don't worry. I won't make a habit of it.'

'Fine.' I took a swallow of the wine.

Not the most satisfactory end to a case, I had to admit – I still felt bitterly sorry about Sextus Gratius – but I reckoned that this time around we'd at least won on points. And, like Perilla, I was beginning to twitch.

Holidays abroad are all very well, but I'd be glad to get back.

———————

Printed in Great Britain
by Amazon